I0723394

COME BACK TO YOU

Destiny Falls

ALEXA RIVERS

Copyright © 2022 by Alexa Rivers

Come Back to You.

All rights reserved.

No part of this book may be reproduced in any form or by any electronic or mechanical means, including information storage and retrieval systems, without written permission from the author, except for the use of brief quotations in a book review.

This book is a work of fiction. All people, places, events and organizations within it are fictional or have been used fictitiously. Any resemblance to real people, places, events and organizations is entirely coincidental.

Editing and proofreading by Paper Poppy Editorial and Hot Tree Editing.

Cover photography by Lindee Robinson.

Cover design by Shanoff Designs.

To my parents
For your love and support.

Chapter One

KENNEDY

Hi Liam,

Yet another email I'll never send you.

I was offered an acting job yesterday by one of Malcolm's old clients. It's just a minor part. A fill-in, really, but it pays well. We're not hurting for money, but only a year after Malcolm and Mom died, I've already gone through a scary amount of what should be saved for the kids' college funds. Maybe I should start working to make sure I don't inadvertently limit their options. But then, is it better for them to have that money in the future, or for them to have me around 24/7 now?

I've got no idea. You'd know better than I would. Your family has always been so strong. I feel like I screw up every day, and I worry I won't give them what they need. I wish I could talk to you about it.

I miss you.

Love,

K xx

. . .

I DROVE INTO DESTINY FALLS AS DUSK WAS SETTLING OVER
the township. The last rays of sunlight gilded the colonial
style shopfronts of Centennial Street in gold. To the right,
an older lady wrapped in a fluffy purple jersey and a
matching knit hat brought in the Open sign outside
Destiny Fibers. I smiled. Desdemona Smith. It was nice to
know some things hadn't changed.

The street was mostly empty of people, with a few
gathered outside Drunken Destiny, which looked to have
been repainted during the eleven years I'd been gone, and
several others clustered around a cafe a couple of buildings
down from Desdemona's shop. That was new. I glanced at
signwriting on the window. Taste of Destiny. My lips
curved into a smile. I'd always loved the way the locals
played up to the town's name.

For a brief moment, I considered pulling over for a
coffee. I'd flown from Los Angeles to New Zealand the day
before yesterday, and then I'd been driving all day
yesterday as well as today. Prior to leaving, I'd been rushing
through a tourist Visa application. Now, I was exhausted
and not in the mood to deal with the possibility of tourists
at the cafe recognizing me. Being a successful actress had
its perks—I never needed to worry about money again—
but it had downsides too.

A shiver ran through me. *Serious* downsides.

Like the stalker who'd been hassling me with anony-
mous social media messages, disturbing videos, and had
escalated to infiltrating my house. I still didn't know who
the person was, but that shouldn't matter, since they'd
surely never follow me halfway around the world—
assuming they'd be able to locate me in the first place.

Not that the stalker was the reason I'd decided to
return to Destiny Falls. They—and my friend, Gray—had
just prompted me to look at my life, and I hadn't liked

what I'd seen. Beneath the glitz and glam, I wasn't happy. Hadn't been in a long time. Blair, Mina, Joel, and Jamie had all moved out, so for once, I'd been able to put myself first and come back to the place my heart had yearned for since the accident that changed everything.

Back to the *man* I'd never stopped loving.

I didn't know anything about Liam's life now. He could be married with kids. He might have moved away, although I highly doubted it. He'd always been so determined to stay in Destiny Falls. Even if he was single and still in town, he probably wouldn't want anything to do with me. But I was no stranger to adversity. I'd raised my half-siblings when I wasn't much more than a child myself. I wasn't afraid of working hard for forgiveness and a second chance.

I pulled onto a side road and followed it for a couple of blocks until I arrived at the cottage I used to rent from Grace Smith, a woman a couple of years older than me. I scanned the outside. The weathered boards were the same shade of white they used to be, with no sign of wear and tear. Perhaps they'd been repainted over the years, or maybe Grace had simply maintained them in pristine condition. The door was a muted green with a metal flap for letters to be pushed through and an old-fashioned brass ringer. The tiled roof had the same cozy appeal that had once drawn me to it. In short, it looked like I'd never left.

Pocketing the keys, I got out of the car and headed for the main house. As far as I could tell, Grace still ran the operation here. I'd made my booking through an automated online system under a different name—partly because I was worried she'd cancel it if she knew who I really was and partly because it was just good sense to do that as a celebrity. Hopefully Grace wouldn't be too angry about the deception. I paused for a moment to gather my courage, then pressed the doorbell. I could hear it ring through the house, and I gnawed on my lower lip, preparing for a hostile welcome.

The door swung inward, and there she was, as beautiful as I remembered. Her face had more maturity, but nothing else seemed to have changed. I fought the urge to hug her, knowing she probably wouldn't return the affection.

Her smile faltered, and she stopped abruptly, crossing her arms over her chest. "Let me guess. Katy?"

I winced. "I'm sorry."

She shook her head. "I never thought I'd see you again. Not after all this time."

I shifted from one foot to the other, unable to read her. She clearly wasn't pleased, but she didn't seem furious either. More… cautious.

"Things changed," I said, knowing the weak excuse couldn't possibly sum up the many ways in which my life had been tipped upside down over the past decade. I'd need hours to explain the whole painful story. "I can leave if you don't want me here."

Grace pursed her lips and was quiet for a long moment with her hand on the door, effectively barring me from entering the house. She searched my eyes. I didn't know what she hoped to find, but I held her gaze.

Eventually, she spoke. "If you're expecting to be welcomed back with open arms, you're going to be disappointed."

I released a bitter laugh. "I know. Believe me."

"People are going to be upset," she continued, her tone level despite her words. "They won't be happy if I open my doors to you."

I nodded. She was probably right.

"Why the subterfuge?" she asked. "I'm sure you have

plenty enough money to buy your own place and not feel a pinch in the pocket. Why rent mine?"

Honestly, I'd wondered the same thing.

"Nostalgia, I guess." It was the closest thing to the truth I could offer her. "I have a lot of good memories here." I'd been happy in the cottage with its pink curtains and cute kitchen.

Grace's hand dropped from the door. "You can stay," she finally said, though she didn't invite me in. "I always thought there was more to the story than what you told Liam." She reached out to touch my shoulder, and I felt like crying just from that small gesture of acceptance. "You were smitten with him, and you never seemed homesick while you were here. I figured you must have your reasons for ending things with him and staying away, but others aren't so open-minded. They'll take a while to come around. Assuming you're not just here for a visit?" She arched a brow.

"I'm here to stay." No amount of frostiness would deter me.

"Good." She withdrew her hand. "Don't make me regret my decision."

"I won't. I promise."

Grace passed me a key from the pocket of her jeans. "Here. Let me know if you need anything."

A fraction of the tension that had gripped me eased. "Thanks. Is there anywhere new I can buy dinner?"

"No." She looked sympathetic. "The cafe will be closing at any moment. Other than that, it's just the pub, unless you want to drive to the resort. Tabitha extended their coffee shop into a full restaurant a few years ago."

Damn. No avoiding confrontation then.

"Okay." I could do this. I needed to woman up and bite the bullet. There would be no driving to the resort, where I knew I'd get a warmer reception, just to avoid an uncomfortable situation that would have to happen sooner or later. It wouldn't be easy, but if it was a choice between temporary ease and long-term disappointment, there was no contest. "Thanks, Grace."

Next stop: Drunken Destiny.

Chapter Two

LIAM

Is it possible to love and hate someone at the same time? - Unsent text message from Liam to Kennedy

The pub was relatively quiet. But then, it was a Monday night, and most of the locals were at home, so that was no surprise. I sat at a table near the bar, cradling a pint of beer and listening to Toby brag about the hot tourist from the resort he'd been hooking up with. Apparently she was Swiss, blonde, and adventurous as hell, although I tuned out most of his colorful description. The state of my own sex life was nonexistent, and I didn't need a reminder of how great his was. It would only make me feel pathetic.

I drank more beer. Thirty should be too young to feel this old. Toby was only five years my junior, and he was out there, playing the field. Why couldn't I bring myself to do the same anymore?

I reached for a chip and popped it into my mouth, scanning the other occupants of the pub while Toby rhapsodized about his hookup's killer body. Dad was behind the bar because it was Bailey's night off. Mum and a couple of her friends sat on stools, chatting to each other and bringing him into their conversation every now and then. A group of weather-beaten men clustered in the back, alternating between drinking and playing darts. They were doing surprisingly well considering how much beer they'd drunk. But then, these craggy old guys could put booze away like no one's business.

"…you, Liam?"

"Huh?" I snapped around. Toby and Asher, my best friend, were looking at me, both wearing wry smiles.

"I asked if you've been seeing anyone lately," Toby said, apparently unconcerned that I'd zoned out.

I huffed. "No."

"That makes…."—Toby pretended to do math in his head—"a fucking long time without any action, am I right?"

Asher gave him a light shove. "Don't be an asshole. We can't all be as girl crazy as you. Some of us actually have to work around here."

Toby launched into a protest about how being a ski instructor counted as a real job, even if he was technically only employed for half the year. I sent Asher a smile, grateful for the distraction. He knew I hated anyone prying into my affairs. Especially when there wasn't anything to talk about.

I tuned back in to the conversation, and that was when the pub fell eerily silent. I looked around, expecting to see that someone had broken a plate or a chair, but nobody cursed or shouted an apology. Instead, all attention was focused on the door, where a woman stood silhouetted against the rapidly descending darkness.

Fuck. It couldn't be.

I stared, taking in the long blonde hair that was darker at the roots, the cute upturned nose, and the unique eyes I thought I'd never gaze into again for as long as I lived.

Kennedy.

She was back in Destiny Falls. In the pub. Only a handful of yards away.

Why was she here?

Someone coughed, breaking the hush. Eyes burned into me as our audience waited to see how I'd react so they could follow my lead. The community had been a great source of support when she first made a name for herself in Hollywood. They'd rallied around me, boycotting everything Kennedy Carter. The store had refused to sell any tabloids with her picture on the front. The movie theater had never played the films she starred in. And if anyone ever happened to learn anything about her, they sure never mentioned it to my face. A few had gone further and helped shield me from reporters who'd come to town, trying to dig up dirt about Kennedy's time in Destiny Falls. Now, she was here. Inexplicably.

I had no doubt someone here would toss her out if I gave any indication that was what I wanted. Hell, either Asher or Toby would gladly volunteer for the job. I just needed to force myself to move.

"Liam." Someone jostled my elbow. Firm fingers gripped it. "Let's go, man."

It was Asher, trying to get me to leave. But I couldn't look away from the woman who'd crushed my heart and stolen my future.

"What the fuck is she doing here?" he muttered. "Come on."

I stood up.

"Help me, Tobes," Asher urged.

Before my brother could move, Kennedy lifted her chin

and crossed the room. I caught a waft of her scent as she stopped in front of me. Slightly sweet but unfamiliar. My throat threatened to close over. I didn't even know what she smelled like anymore. Somehow, that made me want to kick shit down.

I could still read her face though. She was nervous. Rightfully so.

Asher tugged my arm again. "Liam has nothing to say to you," he snapped at her.

It wasn't true. I'd had plenty to say to her over the years. Questions, angry rants, random observations I knew she'd have appreciated. But she hadn't been around to share them with. Because she hadn't wanted me enough to stay—or rather, to come back.

"Can we talk?" Her voice was deeper than it used to be. Smoother. That tiny discrepancy jolted me into action.

"I wanted to talk eleven years ago," I bit out, "but you weren't interested. So no, we can't talk." I brushed past her, heading for the exit with Toby and Asher flanking me. As soon as the door swung shut behind me, I released a shaky exhale. "Did that just happen?"

"Yeah, mate." Asher clapped me on the back. "Come on. We're going back to your place."

"She's in Destiny Falls." I could scarcely believe it. Kennedy had become something of an urban legend in these parts. The Hollywood It Girl who'd broken the hometown boy's heart—discussed in whispers behind my back but never, ever to my face. "Why the fuck is she here?"

"Who cares?" Asher guided me to my Ute. "I'm driving. Toby, you get beer and meet us there. We're going to need lots of it."

Toby saluted. "Aye aye, captain."

I climbed numbly into the passenger seat, registering that it felt odd not to be driving my own vehicle, but my whirring thoughts kept me from dwelling on it as Asher started the engine. Kennedy Carter—or Cox, whatever stage name she was calling herself these days—had a lot of nerve showing up in my father's pub.

"She won't stay," I murmured to myself. I needed to remember that, and hold onto my anger at her for leaving without even giving me the chance to consider going with her. Many years had passed, but no matter what had brought her back here, I couldn't afford to let her into my life. Kennedy was a chapter of my past that needed to remain closed.

Chapter Three

KENNEDY

Hi Liam,

Someone asked me on a date this morning. It was the first time that's happened since we broke up. I was at a coffee shop, enjoying some downtime for once. I hardly get any of that these days.

Even though it's been months, and even if I thought I'd have the time to date, I couldn't say yes. It felt wrong. The only man I've ever wanted a future with was you.

Love,

K xx

Well, that had been a dismal failure.

I let myself into the cottage and locked the door behind me. Then I set my takeout meal on the kitchen counter and flopped onto the couch, drawing my knees to my chest and resting my forehead on them. I'd wanted to go after Liam, but when I'd gotten outside, he and Asher had already been climbing into Liam's Ute—the same one he used to drive—and then I'd been accosted by two teenage girls who'd apparently seen me go into the pub from their car and came to check if I really was who they thought I was.

After I'd dealt with them as politely as I could, I'd returned inside to order dinner. Eugene Braddock had served me but suggested it would be best if I didn't return. His iciness had been difficult to stomach. He'd always been such a warm, open person. But I hadn't expected anything less. At least he'd spoken to me. Heather had just glared with open hostility.

My stomach growled. I'd better eat. I went back to the kitchen and opened the paper-wrapped bundle of fries and chicken, serving a portion onto a dinner plate. My personal trainer would have a conniption if she could see me, but I'd already decided I was saying goodbye to Hollywood Kennedy. No more calorie counting and insane workouts. I'd keep in shape, but I'd do it how I wanted. Still, it wouldn't hurt to stock the pantry tomorrow so I could cook something healthier. For now, I'd enjoy the treat.

I bit into a fry. It crunched satisfyingly. I ate in silence, then cleaned the dishes.

The quiet unnerved me after years of sharing a house with my siblings. When Jamie and Joel had moved into their frat house a few months ago, I'd kept expecting to hear them banging doors or talking too loudly. The solitude had felt strange. Unsettling.

I washed my hands, unzipped my suitcase, and pulled out the faded scrapbook tucked inside the lid. I carried it to the bed, sat cross-legged, and flipped through, perusing the photographs I'd long ago glued into place.

Liam in front of the lookout.

Me with the entire Braddock clan at Eugene's birthday party.

Me and Summer, arms around each other.

Liam and me at the waterfall.

I paused on that one, my heart aching as I remembered how hopeful I'd been, excited for a future that had never happened.

With a sigh, I set the scrapbook aside and opened the email account on my phone, thumbing through my draft box until I found the one that had been sitting there for ten years. Once I'd finally managed to pull the broken pieces of myself together after my parents' deaths, I'd wanted to explain everything and let him know how much I'd cared. I'd only ended our relationship because I thought I'd been protecting him. My life had turned upside down, and I'd suddenly found myself unable to come back to him as I'd promised to. By breaking up with him, I'd been trying to prevent him from coming after me and being miserable. He'd always insisted he could never be happy away from Destiny Falls, and I'd no longer been in a position to leave L.A.

But even once the mental fuzziness caused by my grief had cleared, I'd never sent the email. I didn't think I could have handled it if he'd lashed out, or worse, never replied. At least this way, I'd been able to wonder what might have happened if I'd been braver.

I exited the draft and composed a message to Gray, who I'd visited briefly when I'd first landed in New Zealand. He was a former costar and one of the few genuine friends I'd made in Hollywood. He'd had a rough time in the past but seemed to be coming out the other side better off. He was healing. I suspected his new girlfriend had a lot to do with that.

Kennedy: *Safe in my cottage in Destiny Falls. Had my first encounter with Liam. Didn't go well, but they didn't run me out of town with flaming pitchforks, so I guess it could have been worse.*

Gray: *Glad to hear you're safe. Be careful out there. Don't forget that you deserve to be treated well.*

My heart melted. Gray wasn't generally a warm person, so his reminder meant a lot. I shot him a quick reply, thanking him, and switched over to my latest text conversation with Blair, my brother and only full sibling.

Kennedy: *In Destiny Falls. Still alive. The locals haven't discovered how to kill with their eyes yet, but it didn't stop them from trying.*

The reply was instantaneous.

Blair: *Not funny. Don't joke about shit like that. Glad to hear you're okay.*

I sighed. While Blair was younger than I, he'd appointed himself my personal protector since I'd risen to fame. His attitude was sweet but a little frustrating. He liked to say that I'd given up my twenties to raise him and our other siblings, so I deserved to have someone watching out for me, but I didn't necessarily see it that way. Yes, I'd sacrificed a lot when I decided to stay in Los Angeles, but I'd do it again in a heartbeat. My brothers and sister were the most important people in the world to me. I loved them, and I'd never regretted choosing to stay and care for them, even when it hurt. But if it made Blair feel better, I didn't mind checking in with him. Especially not when I was closer to him than pretty much anyone else on the planet.

Kennedy: *Sorry. Bad taste. Booked any gigs lately?*

Blair was lead guitarist in a band that fit somewhere between the realms of pop and folk music. They played at bars and clubs most weeks but hadn't had a big break yet. He could easily have used his connection to me or Malcolm to shortcut the process, but he was determined to make it on his own, and I respected that.

Blair: *Nothing major. Does the place where you're staying lock?*

Kennedy: *Yes.*

Blair: *Does it have security cameras?*

Kennedy: *Not that I've seen. But I'm in the middle of nowhere, and no one knows I'm here. I'm safe.*

Blair: *You'd better be.*

I felt a pang of guilt. Part of his protectiveness stemmed from the fact we'd lost our father as kids and then our mother and stepfather as teens. He didn't want to lose anyone else. He probably thought he was well on his way to losing me simply because I'd left L.A.

Kennedy: *Cross my heart. Love you, B.*

Blair: *Yeah, yeah. Enough of the mushy stuff. Go get your beauty sleep, it must be night there.*

Kennedy: *Talk soon?*

Blair: *Count on it.*

Before I put my phone on to charge, I decided to do a quick check of my social media accounts. I had an assistant who used to run those for me, but I'd let her go before moving here—although I'd made sure she was set up with another actress I knew would treat her well first. Now, I was on my own.

I scanned anything I was tagged in. Unsurprisingly, my absence from an annual party held by a wealthy socialite had been noted. Sources close to me apparently claimed we were on the outs. I smirked. Total bullshit. But that was what you got. Most of the so-called news about me was fake these days.

I'd been mentioned in a review of a film I'd starred in that had recently premiered. According to the review, my performance had been the only thing holding a lackluster plot together. My lips twitched. I'd have to pass that comment on to Gray, since he'd written the screenplay and it would no doubt amuse him.

I opened my private messages and scrolled through. It looked to be mostly notes from fans. I replied to a couple, but I decided to leave the rest until later. I needed a good sleep or my head was going to explode.

But then something caught my eye. A message from a user with a generic name followed by a bunch of numbers. There was a video attached. Dread formed a hard pit in my stomach as I clicked onto it. The clip was only a few seconds long, but that was all it took to make me gag as a stranger jerked off over a photograph of me. The photo looked to have been taken at the airport, shortly before I'd boarded a flight to come here.

I dropped the phone and ran to the bathroom, emptying the contents of my gut into the toilet. I wretched again, then wiped my mouth, slammed the lid down, and flushed. I rinsed my mouth at the vanity, then sank against the wall and buried my face in my palms.

It was *him*.

That photograph hadn't been in any tabloids. As far as I was aware, nobody other than my trusted friends, family, and former employees even knew I'd left the country, which meant he'd been following me. Watching me.

A shudder ran through me, and my stomach threatened another purge. I rose onto shaky legs and went to the kitchen for a glass of water.

It wasn't the first time he'd sent a video like this, but it was the first one I'd seen. My assistant had found the others and flagged them with security before I'd known they even existed. If he'd held true to form, it would be the kind of recording that self-deleted as soon as it had been viewed once.

Regardless, I finished my water and went back to my phone to let the company who managed my security know. They replied that they'd see if they could trace it, but I doubted they'd find anything. They never did.

Chapter Four

LIAM

I saw you in a magazine today, and it sucked. Please stop putting your face where I can see it. - Unsent text message from Liam to Kennedy

"Please tell me you're not thinking about Kennedy."

I glanced up from where I was ensconced in one of the armchairs at the Fire Station to find Asher standing over me. "Of course not."

He sighed and sank onto another chair. "Liar."

I gave a half-hearted shrug. "I can't help it. I want to know what it means that she's back in town. It must mean something."

I'd spent years trying to get over her, and it felt like they might as well not have happened. The wound she'd caused by leaving felt as raw as it had when we were young. Although, perhaps it had festered a little.

We'd had something real. Something that mattered.

Or so I'd thought.

I'd never been able to work out what had been true and what must have been in my imagination because, if we'd loved each other the way I'd thought we had, she'd never have cut me off so abruptly.

"It means she's selfish," Asher said without an ounce of doubt in his voice. "If she gave a crap about you, she wouldn't be here, stirring up old feelings."

I frowned because I got where he was coming from, but I also didn't understand why she'd be here if she'd moved on without looking back as I'd once believed.

"Stop thinking so hard," he chided. "It shouldn't matter why she's here. You need to steer clear of her so she can't get her claws into you again."

"I know." I grabbed my water bottle and drank just so I'd have something to do with my hands. "But I never connected with anyone like I did with her."

"And you never had your heart broken that badly either," he reminded me.

It was true. Maybe if she'd simply vanished from the face of the earth, I'd have eventually gotten over it—although I doubted that—but when I'd unexpectedly seen her in a film a couple of years later, while I'd been visiting a friend in Christchurch, all of those old hurts had resurfaced. I'd wanted to walk out as soon as I realized who was on the screen, but I hadn't been able to make myself move, so I'd sat there and watched her pretend to fall in love with another man. I'd known it was fake, but I'd seethed, and when they'd kissed, something inside me had broken. Perhaps they'd been acting, but she'd still kissed him for half the world to see.

When I'd left the cinema, my world had been fractured. Ever since then, no matter how well the township tried to shield me, evidence of her existence slipped through the cracks. It had been utter hell.

Now, she was back. And I wished she'd stayed gone.

"Fuck."

"Mm," Asher agreed. "Amen to that."

My phone buzzed, and I checked it. The moniker "The Sheriff" filled the screen. That was our nickname for my older brother Nate who was now in charge of the local police force.

"Hey," I answered.

"Grace is a goddamn traitor," he growled. "Do you know where That Woman is staying?" He didn't give me a chance to answer. "In her cottage, that's where. The same damn cottage she rented back then. It's like she thinks this is some kind of fucking fairytale reunion."

"Kennedy is staying with Grace?" Talk about nerve.

"Yeah, I just found out. Gracie should have kicked her to the curb the moment she showed up, but you know what a soft touch she is." He made a sound of disapproval, even though I knew he loved Grace's big heart, just not at times like this. "I told Grace to pack her things for her and make sure she got the message she should leave. Do you know what Gracie said?"

I had a feeling I was about to find out. Usually, Grace could do no wrong in Nate's book, but they'd clearly discovered how far his faith in his friend extended.

"She said they had a contract. I said to tear it up, and she said not to tell her how to manage her business." He seemed to be running out of steam. "The woman is too fucking generous."

"Kennedy is at Grace's," I repeated, because that was all I'd been able to process. I didn't like the fact that Grace had rented her a place, but it wasn't her fault Kennedy had returned, and I didn't hold it against her. She was a businesswoman, and she'd never been one to cast judgment like Nate did.

"That's what I said." Nate sounded impatient. "Talk to her, Liam. Make her see reason."

I rubbed my temples. I didn't need this. Not today. "She's running a business. Neither of us like it, but that's the way it is."

Nate scoffed. "Nope. I'm not going to accept that, and neither should you." There was a buzz in the background of the call. Perhaps his police radio. "Shit, gotta go. There's been a traffic accident on the highway."

At that moment, an alarm blared through the fire station. I shot up and Asher did the same.

"We've got the call too," I told Nate. "See you there."

I'd have to mull over Kennedy's reappearance later. For now, there were people who needed my help.

Chapter Five

KENNEDY

Hi Liam,

It's been a year today since Mom and Malcolm died. We went to the cemetery and left flowers. The kids took turns talking to them, except for Blair, who has a lot of anger toward Mom for abandoning us. I don't know how to help him. Especially when I'm so busy with the younger ones. I've tried to get him to talk to a therapist, but he's not interested. He's great with the others. A godsend, in a lot of ways. But I worry.

You were a teenage boy once. What would you do?

I wish I had the courage to send one of these emails, but I know they'll gather virtual dust in my inbox until I finally delete them.

Love,

K xx

IN THE MORNING, I DONNED A SUMMER DRESS AND TIED MY hair back before I covered it with a floppy hat. I applied sunscreen and walked to the coffee shop I'd seen yesterday,

Taste of Destiny. A queue stretched across the room, and I stood in the back and pretended to look at something on my phone, surreptitiously scanning my surroundings. I saw a few familiar faces but no one from the Braddock clan. Probably just as well, after last night.

When it was my turn to be served, the girl at the counter's eyes widened comically. "Oh my God. You're—"

I held a finger to my lips and gave her a meaningful look.

She glanced around, not subtle at all, then leaned forward. "You're Kennedy Cox."

I sighed, sensing the man behind me glance at his watch impatiently. At least the girl had been quiet enough that no one had heard the announcement. "Yes, I am."

"People around here like to say they knew you before you were famous, but I thought they were full of it." She shook her head in wonder. "But here you are, in little old Destiny Falls."

My jaw tightened. She was sweet, but the last thing I needed was more attention. Redeeming myself would be difficult enough without anyone making a fuss about my presence. "Here I am."

"But why?" she mused, as the man behind me cleared his throat.

"I missed it." May as well be truthful. "And I missed Liam."

"Ooh." She winced. "You've got your work cut out for you there. People have been calling him the broken-hearted Braddock for as long as I can remember."

"Yikes." Being stuck with a moniker like that wouldn't sit well with him, even if nobody said it to his face. "Thanks for the tip." I forced a smile. "Want me to sign something for you?" She thrust a napkin toward me, and I took a pen from the counter and autographed it. "What's your name?"

"Eden."

I added a small personal note and passed it to her. "Here you go."

She clutched it to her chest. "Thanks. Now, what can I get you?"

Finally. "A trim latte please."

"Sure, no problem. To take away?"

I glanced around, noting several people watching us. "Yes, please."

"That'll be five dollars."

I paid, left her a tip, and then stood aside so the guy behind me could be served. A few minutes later, with my coffee in hand, I made my way along Centennial Street, the thriving hub of Destiny Falls. I passed several historic buildings, including one that housed the museum. Across on the other side of the street stood the Information Center. I knew better than to pop in and have a look around, since Heather Braddock used to be in charge and might still be. Instead, I continued past the commercial district, reaching an intersection. If I turned left, I'd come across the fire station, or at least, where it used to be. I hesitated for a moment, then detoured in that direction. Not to see Liam. Just because I wanted to know if the station was still there.

It was. And Asher Heaton sat on a foldout chair near the open garage doors. He shot to his feet as I approached and stalked toward me with a dark scowl.

"No." He waved his hands as though ushering me backward. "You can fuck right off."

"I wasn't coming to see Liam."

His glare was full of disbelief—and okay, maybe I'd been hoping to run into Liam. I'd imagined seeing his face so many times, and I hadn't had the chance to catalog all the differences yesterday.

"You need to go before he realizes you're here."

"But—"

"No buts." His hands landed on his hips, and fury flashed in his eyes. "I encouraged him to give you a chance back then. Did you know that?" He didn't let me respond. "I told him he should put himself out there, and that you were different from his ex. I've regretted that every single day since you broke his heart over a goddamned phone call." His expression twisted in disgust. "You didn't even have the decency to see him face-to-face. It fucking broke him."

Shame and guilt, my familiar friends, tangled in my chest. I didn't argue because I deserved his censure. I'd promised Liam I'd come back, and I'd let him down. I have to live with that.

Asher stepped closer. "If you really care about Liam, you'll leave town and never bother him again."

"I can't do that," I said softly.

His eyes narrowed. "No one wants you here. Least of all Liam."

With that, he turned on his heel and strode back to the fire station. I bit my lip almost hard enough to break the skin, and tears prickled in my eyes. The pain in my chest burned hotter. The words Asher had fired at me felt like bullets. I couldn't blame either of them for being angry with me. All I could do was prove with my actions that this time I was here to stay.

As I started walking back the way I'd come, my phone pinged with an email from my security company. I read it quickly. They wanted me to return to L.A. or to hire someone local to play bodyguard. I couldn't do that. Besides the fact there was no need because hardly anyone knew where I was, it wouldn't make a good impression on the locals if I had hired muscle following me around. I typed a quick reply, vetoing the idea, and sent it. I was safe here in Destiny Falls.

Chapter Six

LIAM

Miss yu Kenmedt. Why'd you have to rune evertng? - Unsent text message from Liam to Kennedy, after having had too many drinks

By Wednesday, I'd managed to go nearly two whole days in the same town as Kennedy Carter—Cox, or whatever she called herself—without seeing her again. Considering the size of Destiny Falls and the fact that she wasn't making any attempt to keep to herself, that was a damn good effort on my part. Unfortunately, my streak came to an end when I walked out of the fire station at the end of a shift and found her standing outside, a cardboard box clutched in her hands.

"Hi."

She hurried over to me, looking as drop-dead gorgeous as ever. Now that the shock of seeing her again had worn off, I noticed the regrowth of her brown hair beneath the bottle blonde she'd sported since becoming famous. I hated those dark roots. They reminded me of the girl I'd known. When she was perfectly styled and camera-ready, I could almost pretend she wasn't the person I'd once loved with all my heart. Now, the past and present were coalescing in my mind, and it was ugly.

I ignored her greeting and moved toward my Ute. She trotted beside me. I glanced down at her feet and noticed she was wearing open-toed sandals with a sensible sole. Perhaps she'd suspected she might need to chase me.

"I have brownies," she said.

I spun to face her. "Brownies?"

As if that could possibly make up for what she'd put me through.

She smiled, the expression so full of hope, it was painful to see. "They're homemade."

"I'm not interested in your bribery brownies."

Since when did she bake? She never used to, and I couldn't imagine Hollywood encouraging actresses to make junk food. She opened the container so I could see them. They smelled amazing, and my mouth watered.

"You don't have to say anything," she replied. "Just listen for two minutes, and if you want me to leave after that, I will. You can have the brownies either way."

Could I really be bought by brownies?

Tempting, but no. Not when they came from a heart-breaking she-devil. I unlocked my car and got in, pretending not to see the hurt in her eyes. I wished I could take some form of petty satisfaction from her pain, but I didn't, because even though she'd screwed me over, I'd never wished anything bad on her. Perhaps it would have been easier if I did feel that way.

I pulled away from the curb, making a concerted effort not to look in the rearview mirror, and breathed a sigh of relief as I rounded the corner. The relief was short-lived when I arrived home and noticed Summer's Ute—emblazoned with the logo for Destiny Falls Veterinary Clinic—parked in front of my house. No doubt she was here about Kennedy. She'd been calling over the past two days, and I'd been dodging her. Summer liked to overanalyze. I preferred avoidance.

I got out of the vehicle. When I reached her Ute, she wound the window down.

"You haven't called me back." Her tone was deceptively casual. If not for the slight narrowing of her eyes, I might not realize she was annoyed with me. "What if it had been an emergency?"

"Then you'd have called emergency services."

She scowled. "What's the point in having a firefighter, a doctor, and a cop in the family if I don't get to take advantage of that sometimes?"

I didn't reply because we both knew that wasn't what she'd come to discuss.

She studied me curiously. "Asher said he'd seen you and Kennedy together. He was worried about you."

"So he messaged you?"

She grinned and got out of the car. "I'm the peacemaker. Everyone knows that."

I rolled my eyes. "Max is the peacemaker. You're just the one we love best, so you get away with anything."

She shrugged. "Perhaps. Being the only girl has its perks." She rounded the hood and leaned on the passenger door. "So, what did you and Kennedy talk about?"

"Nothing. She offered me brownies, and I turned her down."

Summer looked disappointed. "That's it?"

"Yeah. She wanted to chat, but I wasn't interested."

She made a thoughtful sound I didn't like.

"What?"

"Nothing." She waved a hand dismissively. "I always

thought there was something strange about the way she ended things. She obviously cared about you. Everyone could see it."

I stuffed my hands into my pockets. "You never did the sisterly stalking-my-ex thing to find out what else might have been going on?"

She hesitated, then shook her head. "I was tempted. So tempted. But you didn't want to know, so out of respect for you, I kept my nose out of her business."

I huffed a laugh. "That'd be the first time."

She rolled her eyes. "Whatever. All I'm saying is, maybe you should listen to her."

"Yeah, sure. I'll just sit down and give my ex the chance to tell me all the reasons why I wasn't enough for her to leave her home and family behind. That sounds like a really good time."

Summer sent me a look of almost maternal disapproval. Damn, Mum had taught her well. "Would you prefer never to get closure?"

"I'd prefer to never discuss this with you again."

She sighed. "You never got over it properly. Maybe if you hear her out, you'll be able to move on with your life. Date someone else and actually give them a fair chance."

Discomfort wormed up my spine. "It's not your problem."

"You're my brother." She sounded exasperated. "I care about you. That makes it my problem."

"Do you think you could care a little less?"

She pushed off from the car and stalked back around to the driver's seat. "Think about it. If you don't change something, you're going to end up sad and alone."

She pulled away dramatically, no doubt pleased to have had the last word. I was just relieved she'd let it drop for now.

Chapter Seven

KENNEDY

Hi Liam,

You're not going to believe this, but I'm actually learning how to cook. Nothing fancy, just things from some of Mom's recipe books, because the kids deserve better than takeout every night. The other day, Joel was begging for Mom's macaroni and cheese, so I had to go digging through the cupboards until I found the recipe. I didn't do a great job of it, but at least it was edible. Tonight, it's pizza with a homemade crust. It wasn't half bad.

Maybe I can do this thing after all.

Love,

K xx

After Liam's Ute vanished around the corner, I took a deep breath, squared my shoulders, and marched into the fire station. Thankfully, luck was on my side and Asher wasn't there. I didn't think I could handle arguing with him after my encounter with Liam.

Igor and Zane were playing cards at the table with a kid who must have been around twenty. I felt a pang. With his floppy blond hair and infectious grin, the younger firefighter reminded me of Liam when we'd first met.

"Holy shit." The kid's eyes landed on me. They were mossy green and full of surprise. He glanced at the others. "You guys were serious? Liam actually used to date a celebrity?" He tripped over his feet on his way to greet me, but stabilized himself with a goofy grin. He stuck out a hand. "I'm Darcy."

I shook his hand. He had a firmer grip than I expected, and he pumped it enthusiastically. "Hi, Darcy. Nice to meet you."

"Darce," Igor warned, his French accent less pronounced than it once was.

"Hi, Igor." I released Darcy's hand and waved. "Zane."

Igor opened his mouth—probably to tell me to leave— so I saved him the trouble.

"I'm not staying. I just wanted to drop these off." I passed Darcy the box of brownies. "Liam didn't want them, so I thought you guys might. If you'd prefer to throw them in the trash while I'm not looking, that's okay too."

Darcy opened the box and beamed. "These look amazing!" He turned to show the others, who didn't respond. "Did you make them?"

"Yeah." I crossed my arms, not quite sure what to do with my hands now that they were free.

"Wow." He shot me a cheeky grin and winked. "You're barking up the wrong tree with Liam, but if you decide you'd prefer the newer model, I'm here most days."

That brought a smile to my face. I knew he was being silly, but I appreciated it. His expression softened for a moment, almost as if my smile was what he'd been hoping for.

"Don't give up," he whispered.

"Thanks." I jerked my head toward the door. "I'd better leave before anyone calls the cops."

Darcy winced. "Oh, yeah. About that. Has anyone told you?"

"Told me what?"

"That Nate Braddock is the local sergeant these days. So you *really* don't want anyone to call the cops."

My eyebrows shot up. When I'd left Destiny Falls, Liam's brother Nate had still been waiting to find out where he'd be placed for his years on the beat, but he'd obviously ended up back here one way or the other.

"Thanks for the heads-up." I said a quick goodbye and left.

At the cottage, it was time to prepare dinner. I hadn't made anything before I'd left in case my conversation with Liam went well and we'd decided to eat together. I'd known it was a long shot but couldn't help hoping for the best. I checked the refrigerator, which was newly stocked, and considered my options. I didn't feel like much, but I needed food. Lunch had been too long ago.

While I thought, I sent an update to Gray, letting him know I still hadn't had any luck, and another status update to Blair so he'd know I was alive and well. I'd just set my phone aside and decided on a stir fry when there was a knock at the door. I frowned, unable to think of anyone who'd willingly seek me out.

Grace was on the doorstep. She smiled hesitantly. "Hey. Have you eaten?"

"Not yet. I was just about to put something together."

She touched the side of her neck, a gesture I recalled her doing when she was nervous. "Would you like to eat with me? I've made fish kofta and couscous with vegetables."

My stomach grumbled. That sounded far better than what I had planned. But why the invitation? She'd seemed perfectly content to let me do my own thing since I'd arrived. I supposed there was only one way to find that out.

"That would be lovely, thanks."

I grabbed my phone and a sweater in case I needed it and followed her down the path. A sprawling vegetable garden separated the main house from the two rental cottages positioned side by side at the end of the property. The other cottage appeared to be empty at the moment. I hadn't seen anyone coming or going.

As we entered Grace's home, a delicious aroma greeted us. A combination of spices with a hint of fish. Grace led me to the dining room where the long, formal table she used to serve guests was laden with food, plates, wine, and cutlery.

"This looks good," I told her, sitting in one of the chairs.

She claimed another seat at a ninety-degree angle to me so we could speak without having to raise our voices. "Thanks. Hopefully it will taste nice too. It's one of Desdemona's recipes."

I'd never known what the deal was with Grace's parents. They didn't live locally. Or at least, they hadn't eleven years ago. She was closer to her Aunt Desdemona, who ran Destiny Fibers and was a wonderfully quirky soul, than to any other family.

I took a taste. "Delicious. Thanks so much for inviting me."

"You're welcome." She consumed a mouthful of her own meal, then reached for the bottle of wine in the center of the table and poured herself some. "For you?"

"Please."

"The invitation wasn't totally selfless," she said, placing her glass on the table. "I'd like to know what you've been up to for the past few years and hear how things are with your family. I was always a little jealous of all your siblings."

I laughed. "They're each crazy in their own way, but I love them." I tried to think of what I could tell her without giving away everything. "My family situation changed a long time ago. I took on a different kind of role within it. But the kids are happy and healthy—although 'kids' might not be the right word anymore."

"They must be in their early twenties?" she prompted.

"Blair is twenty-six. He's a musician. Mina is at college. Technically, Joel and Jamie are at college too, but they're only there to play hockey and live the frat lifestyle. Hopefully they'll be picked up by the NHL." Failing that, Jamie had declared his backup plan was to become a male stripper, and I didn't think he was joking. Joel liked to think of himself as coach material, but he had a lot of maturing to do before that point.

Grace nodded. "Sounds like they're doing well. Are they all in Los Angeles?"

"Yeah." I knew I sounded wistful, but there were moments when I missed having them around. The twins in particular felt as much like my children as my brothers at times.

"And has there been anyone special for you?"

My mouth dropped open. "Grace Smith, are you asking about my love life?"

She pinned me with a look. "You can't blame me. It's all anyone is talking about now that you're back in town, and I never read about you in the tabloids or online because it felt like such an invasion of privacy."

Yeah, I'd assumed the gossip would be running wild. "I appreciate that, but no, there's been nobody special."

Her expression turned skeptical. "So, what? You've been pining away for Liam all these years while starring opposite some of the sexiest men alive in films?"

Kinda.

But when she put it like that, I knew it sounded unbelievable.

"That… situation… I mentioned. It changed my policy on dating."

She was quiet for a few seconds as she ate. "You're being awfully cagey."

I swigged more wine than was wise and wiped the back of my mouth on my hand. "Look, Grace." I waited until I had her full attention. "I know a lot of my life is out there for anyone to read about, but I took a stage name for a reason, and that was to keep as much distance as possible between my personal and public lives. There are certain parts of my private life that I like to keep under wraps, and despite everything, I've managed to be reasonably successful at that. If you don't know everything already, then I'd rather it stay that way until Liam hears the details—presuming he hasn't already." I'd like to think he'd at least speak to me if he knew about my parents' deaths. "So if I'm being cagey, it's because of that."

"Okay." Her intense eyes seemed to see into my soul. Sometimes, I could swear she had a little of Desdemona's psychic gift. "I respect that."

"Thank you."

We finished our meal with polite chitchat about where I'd been and who I'd seen since I arrived. Neither of us seemed to want to delve into deeper topics. When we finished, I carried our dishes to the kitchen despite Grace's protests.

"Don't be ridiculous. You cooked, so the least I can do is clean," I told her.

"You're my guest," she said, as though that explained everything.

"Exactly. You gave me a place to stay, and don't think I don't know how poorly that must have gone down with the

Braddocks." It meant a lot that she'd gone out on a limb for me, whatever the reason.

I filled the kitchen sink with hot, soapy water and frowned, realizing something I hadn't noticed until now. I hadn't seen any sign of a man around, and Grace hadn't mentioned anyone.

I turned to her. "Is there a man in your life?"

Her eyes crinkled with humor. "The only men in my life are fictional or Braddocks."

"You and Nate never became an item?" I asked as casually as I could.

"We're just friends." Her words didn't ring true, just like they hadn't eleven years ago.

Elsewhere in the house, I heard the snick of a door opening and the tread of heavy feet on the wooden floor. Panic flared across Grace's face.

"Stay here," she ordered, hurrying away.

My heart leaped as I heard her voice and then another, very male. I should have tuned out their conversation, but I was intrigued by what had gotten her off-kilter when she was usually calm. A moment later, I discovered the reason. Nate Braddock charged into the kitchen, all rugged handsomeness, with the grace of a lumbering bull.

He came up short when he saw me and dragged a hand over buzzed blond hair. "*You.*"

"Me," I said weakly, wondering if it was too late to climb through the window. Of all the Braddocks, he'd always had the hottest temper. "How are you, Nate?"

He stomped toward me, his nostrils flaring. "I'd be better if you'd stayed where you belong. What the hell do you think you're up to, coming here and stirring up all this old crap? Do you have any idea what it's doing to Liam?"

"I have no intention of hurting him again," I said, but it didn't diminish Nate's anger.

"You're hurting him just by being here," he snarled. "I

speak for our whole family when I say we want nothing to do with you."

"Nate." Grace stepped between us, her hand on his chest. "Kennedy is a guest in my house and I won't let you yell at her."

"Y-you," he sputtered, turning red in the face. He didn't move a muscle though. For all his temper, Nate wasn't the type to be physically violent. Especially not around Grace. "How could you—"

Grace's spine was infused with steel. "I'm afraid if you can't be polite, I'll have to ask you to leave."

Nate gave her a look of disbelief and stomped out of the kitchen, the sound of his footfalls echoing through the house as he made his way to the exit.

"I'm sorry," Grace said. "You shouldn't have had to deal with that." Her face creased with concern. "Are you okay?"

My lower lip wobbled, but I managed to nod. "I'm fine. Don't worry about it. I deserve to hear whatever he has to say."

After that, I made an excuse and retreated to the cottage. When my phone pinged with a notification, I began to dismiss it, but then froze. Heart in my throat, I clicked on the tab. A photo popped up of me standing outside the firehouse with a box in my hands. The image had been taken from a sideview angle and showed Liam opposite me, scowling. My hands trembled. The photograph had been uploaded to social media by a popular tabloid and was accompanied by a headline speculating on what I might be doing in a ski-resort township with a hunky local man.

I stared at it in horror. How did they know I was here? And how had they gotten that photograph? I hadn't noticed anybody taking it, and I was usually pretty good at spotting paparazzi. Clearly, someone had slipped beneath my radar. But had a local or a tourist taken it and simply sold it to the tabloid, or had one of their photographers actually followed me to Destiny Falls?

I shivered, feeling suddenly cold. In L.A., something like this would barely cause a raised eyebrow, but here it sent off all kinds of warning sirens. Or was I just overreacting because I was feeling raw after my run-ins with Liam and Nate? I gritted my teeth. At least they didn't have Liam's name.

I crawled into bed and curled into a ball, trying to get myself under control. After all, I hadn't cried when Nate confronted me or when Grace showed me kindness. But unfortunately, the dam had broken, and the tears began to flow.

Chapter Eight

LIAM

A Lorde song came on the radio today and I started singing, expecting you to chime in, but you didn't. That's when I remembered you were gone. - Unsent text message from Liam to Kennedy

On Thursday, I arrived at work to discover my traitorous coworkers had eaten Kennedy's brownies. That put me in a foul mood, but it was nothing compared to leaving the station at the end of the shift to find her waiting, once again, with a box of baked goods. Donuts, this time.

On Friday, she brought a packet of the expensive coffee beans I liked.

On Saturday, she was standing in line at Taste of Destiny when I went in with Asher for breakfast. We ducked out as soon as we spotted her, but the damage was done, and she was all I could think of for the rest of the day.

Sunday brought blessed peace. I went up the trails with Connor, well and truly out of range of anywhere Kennedy might pin me down. My brother worked as a park ranger and needed to empty some traps and clear fallen logs from the trail, so I loaned an extra set of hands. I fell into bed that night exhausted but satisfied.

On Monday, I was almost disappointed when I completed my shift and there was no sign of her. But then, as soon as I returned home, I found her standing beside my letterbox.

"Get lost," I said, brushing past her.

"Just take this." She thrust an envelope at me.

Dread curdled in my stomach. "What is it?"

She gnawed her lip. "It explains everything. If you don't want to talk, maybe you'll at least read the highlights, then you can decide if you still want nothing to do with me."

I snatched the envelope from her hand and took it inside, leaving her on the path without so much as a backward glance. As soon as the door shut, I tore the letter in two and shoved it into the garbage bin. I didn't know what she hoped to accomplish with this strange crusade of hers, but I didn't trust her. Not even a bit.

On Tuesday, there were no unexpected gifts, but I received a voicemail from Grace, suggesting I hear Kennedy out. Teeth gritted, I deleted the recording.

On Wednesday, Summer sent me a similar suggestion. Except my sister was a lot more direct than Grace. That was what came from being raised in a household of predominantly men. She also messaged and called several times, and I dodged them all, knowing it would only be a matter of time until she cornered me.

On Thursday, I was well and truly fed up. When

Kennedy appeared outside the fire station with a basket of goodies, I didn't think twice. I marched out, took it from her, and emptied every delicious morsel onto the ground. I felt like a complete asshole as soon as I did it, but she didn't look frightened or upset. More like resigned. She turned and walked away. For some reason, that made me sad.

I didn't want to run the risk of seeing her on Friday, so as soon as I clocked out, I took the rear exit and went to my Ute, which I'd parked a couple of blocks over. Then I bought a carton of beers from the pub and carried them to Destiny Falls's iconic waterfall. I hadn't been there often since Kennedy broke up with me. The memory of asking her to move in was too strong, and being there killed me on the inside. But right now, I needed that. I needed to remember why I couldn't give in and listen to whatever she had to say. That door was shut and needed to stay that way.

I perched on a rock near the edge of the falls, cracked open a beer, and let myself remember every moment of the conversation we'd had here and then the raw devastation that had followed our breakup. Tourists came and went, although fewer than there would have been earlier in the day. By the time I packed the empty cans back into the carton and sauntered home, I was beyond tipsy and way too maudlin.

Shit, I needed to get myself together.

Chapter Nine

KENNEDY

Hi Liam,

It's winter here, and the lack of snow feels wrong. I know I only spent one winter in Destiny Falls, and I didn't exactly love the cold, but somehow having a chill in the air felt like the way things ought to be. Now, the warmth is just another thing reminding me that I don't have the life I wanted so badly. That I'm not with you.

Wherever you are, whatever you're doing, I hope you're well.

Love,

K xx

The drive to the Destiny Peak Ski Resort seemed much different under the December sun than it had been that fateful day I'd rolled my car off the road and been rescued by a gorgeous firefighter. Tussock plains stretched around the mountainside, gradually changing to forest nearer town. I didn't encounter much traffic, but that was to be expected, since the only people currently at the resort would be guests, customers using the spa, and those intending to eat at the restaurant Grace had mentioned. Ski season had ended months ago.

As I pulled into the parking lot, I experienced a pang of nostalgia. Liam wasn't the only person I'd missed while I'd been gone, although he'd left a gaping hole in my heart. I'd also missed Tabitha, my old boss, who'd been kind and had faith in me. We'd kept in touch over the years, but not as much as I'd have liked. I'd simply gotten too busy with my family, my career, and all of the trappings that accompanied being an actress. I regretted that.

Getting out of the car, I looked up at the sky, enjoying the heat of the sun on my skin. I was wearing a T-shirt and jeans, but I'd brought a jacket in case there was a cool wind. It seemed I wouldn't need it. I didn't bother wearing a hat or sunglasses to hide my face because I knew Tabitha would tell me to take them off as soon as I was inside. I made my way up the stairs and into the main building of the resort. The woman behind the reception desk didn't seem surprised to see me or taken aback by having a celebrity here, but then I'd hardly be the first famous person to enjoy the luxuries of the resort.

"Good morning," she said with a professional smile. "How can I help you?"

"Hi." I leaned against the desk. "Is Tabitha around?"

"She's in her office. Would you like me to get her for you?"

I hesitated. If she was busy, I didn't want to interrupt, but it would be so good to see a friendly face. "Can you just check and see if she's free?"

"Of course." She stood, smoothed her impeccable black dress, and glided away.

When she returned a couple of minutes later, I was pleased to see Tabitha was beside her. My former boss had aged well. She must be in her late fifties or early sixties, but she still had soft brown hair, a slender figure, and a welcoming smile.

"Kennedy," she exclaimed. "It's so good to see you. I always knew you'd come back."

She did? Well, then she'd known more than I had.

"I missed you, Tabby." I enveloped her in a hug, breathing in the twin scents of a perfume and fresh mountain air. Tabitha had always given the impression of being both classy and practical, and I'd loved that about her.

She let me hold her for a moment, then pulled back and scolded me. "What have I told you about calling me that?"

My lips twitched. "That you're a person, not a cat."

"Exactly." She winked. "When I heard you were in Destiny Falls, I'd hoped I'd see you sooner or later. Come on." She gestured toward a hall that led down to a wing of accommodation rooms and the coffee shop where I'd once worked. "Let's get a hot drink and chat, shall we?"

I smiled. "I'd like that."

We walked down the corridor together. Not much seemed to have changed. The resort had a sense of timelessness. But when we turned a corner and entered a well-lit restaurant with floor-to-ceiling windows overlooking the hillside, my breath hitched.

"Wow."

"Beautiful, isn't it?" Tabitha sounded proud. "We had enough guests requesting more than basic cafe facilities that it seemed a worthwhile investment. It's become more successful than I ever could have dreamed. We have a first-class chef and foodies travel here to eat at the restaurant even if they don't want to stay overnight."

"What kind of meals do you serve?" I asked, curious what approach she'd decided to take.

"Simple gourmet classics and locally grown produce." She guided me to a seat near the window and nodded to one of the waiters. "A long black for me, thanks." She turned to me. "What will you have?"

"A skinny latte, please."

He nodded. As with the receptionist, if he recognized me, he did a good job of hiding it. "We'll be out with those shortly."

"Thank you." As he left, I shot Tabitha a conspiratorial smile. "Your staff are well trained."

"They're wonderful." She relaxed into her chair. "I've been very lucky."

I snorted. "Luck has nothing to do with it, and you know it."

She shrugged. "Luck plays a part, but so do hard work and sheer bloody-mindedness, as I'm sure you know."

"You've got me there." Hollywood was much the same, although I'd lucked into a certain amount of success, so I hadn't had as much of a difficult time as some of my costars had. "Tell me what else is new with you."

We chatted for an hour or so, and when I left, it was with the promise of returning to share a meal with her soon.

I was making my way back to my car when I heard someone call my name. I flinched, looking around on instinct in case it was the person who'd photographed me the other day. My gaze fell on a man with an expensive haircut who was wearing designer jeans and jogging down the steps toward me. He had a classically handsome face: symmetrical, with a strong chin, cool brown eyes, and a hint of a flirtatious smile. He was vaguely familiar, but I couldn't put my finger on where I might have seen him before.

"I thought that was you." His accent was similar to mine. A dimple appeared in his cheek. "It's great to run into you again."

Uh-oh. Clearly, I was supposed to remember this guy,

but my mind was coming up blank. Given the recent issues with my unidentified stalker, that sent alarm bells pinging. I fell back a step, putting more space between us.

"You don't remember me?" He deflated, looking like a kicked puppy.

"I'm sorry," I said out of politeness more than anything else. "Have we met?"

"At the premiere of *Hung Up On You,*" he said. "We chatted for a while at the after-party."

"Oh, right." That sounded familiar. I tried to recall his face, but I met so many people that I really couldn't summon a clear memory.

"Aiden Waldron," he added, visibly disappointed that his prompt hadn't helped.

"Nice to see you again, Aiden. Are you staying at the resort?" *And is your being here a coincidence?*

"Yes." He flashed a set of teeth that must have cost a fortune based on how white and straight they were. "My friends and I are considering investing in a property nearby and establishing an exclusive lodge for wealthy international travelers. We're scoping out the area and the competition."

I frowned. "Does Tabitha know?"

He nodded. "We've discussed it with her. She obviously doesn't love the idea of competition, but she knows that having more businesses like what we've got in mind would bring more money into the area. But I didn't come over here to talk work." He grinned. "How are you? And what on earth are you doing here?"

"I'm good." Although a little unnerved. The presence of a group of men from L.A., at least one of whom I'd previously met, in Destiny Falls made me nervous. I'd have to get my security company to look into them, just to make sure there was nothing red-flag-worthy going on.

"My plans are still up in the air." I didn't intend to tell

this practical stranger that I wanted to move to the area permanently.

"In that case, you should join us," he offered, oblivious to the anxiety rocketing through me. "We're driving to Queenstown today to do more reconnaissance. We'll stay for a few nights and have plenty of fun—bungee jumping and hitting the clubs. We've got room for one more."

"Uh." The fact he'd just invited me—someone he'd met once—to a multi-day event with his friends had tendrils of unease unfurling within me. Perhaps he thought it was okay to extend the invitation because I was famous and he wanted to party with me for social standing. What-ever the case, I didn't see why any woman would take off with a guy they barely knew. That was how people ended up in trouble. "Thanks, but I've already got plans."

He cocked his head. "Are they as exciting as bungee jumping with some seriously cool guys?" He moved closer. "I'll make it worth your while."

And nope. I was out.

"I'm afraid I really can't." I backed off again. "Have a good time."

"We will."

I grabbed my keys and started toward the car.

"I'll see you around," he called after me.

I cringed. Not if I could help it.

I started the engine and drove away. When I was safely back at my cottage, the first thing I did was contact my security company and ask them to do a background check on Aiden Waldron.

Chapter Ten

LIAM

EVERY TIME I SEE YOU ON TV, I CAN'T HELP BUT WONDER IF you've become one of those phony people who look down on others and throw their money around to get what they want. - Unsent text message from Liam to Kennedy

I DIDN'T SEE KENNEDY ALL WEEKEND. IT WAS A GODDAMN miracle. On Monday, I got to the fire station ten minutes early and made semi-decent coffee for my workmates. If I'd let Asher or Zane have the honors, we'd be drinking instant crap diluted to the point of being flavored water. Igor had reasonable taste, but he was notorious for being late, so I couldn't count on him to keep us supplied with the good stuff at the beginning of a shift. I farewelled the night-shift guys as they packed up and headed out with red eyes and sleepy faces.

"You're the best person I know," Asher announced as he strode into the staff room and breathed in the scent of dark blend. "One day, I'm gonna name my firstborn son after you."

"Yeah, yeah." I grinned. "Drink up, Heaton. You'll need it, or I'll kick your ass in the weight room."

He flipped me off and poured himself a mug.

"Braddock."

I snapped to attention at the sound of Parks' voice. My boss was standing in the doorway, a keep cup from Taste of Destiny in one hand. "Yes, sir?"

"My office."

Asher whistled under his breath as Parks disappeared down the hall. "What did you do?"

"No idea." I followed Parks into his personal office, a small shabby room with a wooden desk that was probably as old as me and a stack of paperwork that made me feel dizzy just looking at it. I loved my job and had no ambition to rise to his rank. I'd much rather be out in the field and hanging with the guys than sitting behind a desk, navigating this mountain of bureaucracy.

"Have a seat, Braddock."

I did as he asked. "Is something wrong, sir?"

He pursed his lips, studying me with an intensity that made me edgy. Something bad was about to happen—I knew it. "You have a ride-along today."

"Oh." My shoulders relaxed. That wasn't so bad. I'd done a few of those, and they were usually fine. "Is it a kid who wants to be a firefighter?"

"Not quite."

My hackles rose. I didn't like his tone. "Then who?"

Parks sighed and steepled his hands on the desk. "We've received a very generous donation from Kennedy Carter, but it's contingent on her spending the day shadowing you. She says she wants to see how her money is going to be spent."

White hot fury tore through me.

I stood up, planting my feet wide, my hands clenched at my sides. "She can't do that!"

Parks shrugged. "It's her money. She can do what she likes with it."

"But she's trying to buy time with me!" My chest burned with anger. I leaned over the desk toward Parks. "Come on, boss. You know that's what she's doing."

"Sit down, Braddock." His tone was icy cold. I sat. "You need to put your personal feelings aside. If Kennedy wants to pay for the privilege of your company, that's fine by me. She's donating enough for us to upgrade our gear and systems. Think how many more people we'll be able to help if we're better equipped."

My nostrils flared and the muscle in my jaw ticked as I fought the urge to argue. He was right. He'd been trying to get funding to improve our facilities for years now, with no luck. If I refused to cooperate and the station lost out on that money because I didn't want to share space with my ex, that would be pretty damn petty of me.

But I didn't like it.

She was trying to manipulate me and get her way by throwing money around. The girl I remembered wouldn't have done that. The Hollywood life in her beloved City of Angels had warped her.

"Why can't she shadow one of the others?" I asked.

"Because she requested you specifically." Parks sighed and rubbed his temples. Suddenly, he looked weary. "Liam, I won't order you to do this. That's not the kind of boss I am. We need to be able to trust each other in high stress situations, and you won't be able to do that if I force you into anything. But please consider how much good we could do if you agree."

My stomach sank. Damn, he was talented at making people see things his way.

"Fine," I grumbled. "Just for one day."

"Thank you." He didn't smile, but I could sense his relief. "She'll be here at nine."

Oh well. Better get it over with quickly. "She moves fast." "Try not to be an ass," Parks said. "You're dismissed."

I stood up and left the office. The morning had started well, with coffee and promise, but it had taken a turn for the worse.

"What did he want?" Asher asked as I reentered the staff room.

"To tell me I have a ride-along today."

He passed me my coffee. It wasn't as warm as it had been ten minutes ago, but I drank it anyway.

"Who?"

"Kennedy."

His jaw nearly hit the floor. "What the fuck?"

"Apparently she's made a big donation to the fire station. You know how Parks has been after funding for ages."

"So, he's pimping you out?" His anger made me feel better, even though I was no longer furious with Parks myself. I was still angry at the situation, and at Kennedy for not taking a hint and hitting the road.

"Don't blame him. It's her that's the problem."

Asher gripped my shoulder. "Damn, man. That's rough. I'm sorry."

"Yeah, not great for my mood."

"Well, we haven't had any callouts, and Parks hasn't assigned us any tasks yet today, so what do you say we hit the weight room and work out some of that frustration?"

"Sounds good."

Unfortunately, by the time Kennedy arrived at nine sharp, I was a whole lot sweatier and no less frustrated.

"Good morning," she said, her smile a little too large.

She was carrying a tray of coffees. "It's a lovely day, isn't it?"

"I wouldn't know."

Her smile didn't waver. She tried to pass me a cup, but I didn't accept it. I wasn't drinking her bribery coffee. She shrugged and offered it to Asher, who stood behind me. He glared and crossed his arms over his chest.

She sighed. "Okay, it's like that. Will you at least show me the way in?"

We backtracked to the staff room, where she set the tray of coffees on the table and took one for herself. Igor, the traitor, grabbed one as well. When I narrowed my eyes at him, he shrugged apologetically. Coffee snob. Of course he couldn't say no to a barista-made cup of power fuel.

Kennedy perched on the sofa, smiling at all of us as though she was thrilled to be here. No one smiled back, but it didn't seem to deter her.

"So, what's the plan for today?" she asked.

"No plan," Igor said, the coffee apparently having softened his mood. "We wait until we're needed."

"Okay." She rested against the sofa, ignoring all the "go away" vibes everyone was sending to her. "I'll make myself comfortable, then."

We all shuffled our feet, none of us quite sure what to do. The others seemed to be looking to me for guidance, but damned if I knew what to say.

A siren cut through the tense silence. Thank God. I hoped no one was seriously injured, but the interruption couldn't have come at a better time.

Parks appeared in the doorway. "Let's go, boys."

"You're with me," I told Kennedy, thrusting a high-vis vest at her. "Wear this and don't leave the engine unless one of us tells you to. It's your main job to stay out of the way."

"Got it." She nodded and slipped the vest on.

Chapter Eleven

KENNEDY

Hi Liam,

I've been cast in a new romantic comedy as the hero's foul-mouthed firefighting best friend. I was really excited about the role to begin with because it reminded me of you and also gives me the opportunity to represent a strong woman who takes no shit. Unfortunately, every time I'm told to do something on set, all I can think is that it's not how you'd do it in real life. I know enough from spending time with you to pick up on when something is wrong, but I'm not earning any friends among the production team when I point out their mistakes. I'm only trying to help, but they don't seem as interested in accuracy as I'd hoped.

If you ever see this film, it's going to make you so angry.
Love,
K xx

THE ENGINE'S CAB WAS CLAUSTROPHOBIC WITH firefighters packed inside. This wasn't what I'd imagined when I made my request of Parks. I'd forgotten firefighters always moved as a unit. I'd gotten caught up in a romantic vision of Liam and I cruising the local roads in a fire engine and talking through our past.

Crazy, I know.

Still, I had to make the best of this. I listened to the men talking to each other. It sounded like we were heading to a traffic accident on the road out of Destiny Falls. Car versus truck.

My stomach clenched. Ever since Mom and Malcolm had been killed in a traffic accident, I'd had a hard time dealing with the emotions that arose whenever I encountered one. If I ever had to detour because of an accident, I'd feel sick, and be compelled to check the news later that day to see if anyone had been seriously hurt. They seemed like such needless causes of death and destruction. A single mistake, a two-second hesitation, could mean the difference between living and not.

Overhead, the siren wailed. A police car was parked across the road, forming a barrier, its lights flashing. The churning in my stomach intensified, and I tasted bile in the back of my throat. Great. Not only an accident, but one with Nate Braddock present. I got the feeling he and Asher were co-presidents of the Kennedy Carter Anti-Fan Club.

The engine stopped, and the firefighters piled out.

"Stay here," Liam reminded me.

I nodded, too wound up to speak. From here, I had a perfect view of the carnage. It appeared that a sleek rental sedan had been trying to pass a rusted Ford and had a head-on collision with a food-transportation truck traveling in the opposite direction. The sedan's front end was crushed, and Liam headed straight to it. I could see someone in the driver's seat, but they weren't moving. The truck had fared better, although the trailer had swung around, spilling apples across the road. The third vehicle, the Ford, seemed to have been clipped along the driver's side. Perhaps by the rental car as they tried to avoid the truck.

A woman sat on the side of the road, hovering over a man wearing a blood-soaked shirt. He didn't seem to be conscious. The woman screamed, and Asher hurried to check for a pulse. He and another paramedic, whom I hadn't been introduced to, began CPR. The woman started to cry.

My throat constricted. Black spots appeared in my vision. The horror show before me could have come from my worst nightmares.

I forced myself to draw a breath even though it hurt my aching throat. Then another. The spots cleared, although my mind was still spinning.

Asher and the paramedic continued CPR. The man didn't seem to be responding. The woman let out a blood-curdling shriek and tried to grab the other paramedic and pull him aside so she could get to her husband. The paramedic pushed her away, but she threw herself over the man. Before I knew what I was doing, I was out of the car and running to her side. I grabbed her arm and gently pulled her back.

"You need to let them work," I said when she swung to face me with wild eyes. All I could think was that this woman might be about to lose a family member or friend if she didn't let the paramedics do their thing. I couldn't let that happen to someone else the way it had to me.

"Come over here." I guided her a few feet away and put an arm around her shoulders. She was shivering violently even though the temperature was mild.

The paramedic who wasn't Asher shot me a grateful look.

"What's your name?" I asked the distraught woman.

"Jackie." She was breathing raggedly, unable to take

her eyes off her husband. "Why isn't he moving? They're doing it wrong."

"Jackie," I said, firm enough that she glanced at me. "They're doing everything they can."

At that moment, there was a beep and Asher touched the defibrillator to the man's chest. He jerked, and they resumed CPR. A few seconds later, Asher yelled out. "He's breathing, and we have a pulse."

"Oh, thank God." Jackie collapsed against my chest, crying, as the paramedics shifted her husband onto a stretcher and carried him to the ambulance.

"Come on," I said, since she seemed unable to move. "You want to go with him, right?"

That jolted her into motion. I helped her over to the ambulance. Asher directed her into the front seat, then climbed into the back himself. The other paramedic rounded the vehicle, telling someone through a radio that a second ambulance was on its way.

I stumbled off the road. Now that nobody needed my help, the full horror of the situation sunk its claws into me again. I surveyed the wrecked vehicles and twisted metal. The driver of the rental car had been dragged onto the side of the road. From the look of him, I suspected he'd died on impact.

A husky guy who might be the truck driver stood talking to Zane. He seemed shaken but unharmed. My gaze dragged back to the body. So lifeless. Mom and Malcolm had once been like that. Had they lain ruined on the side of the road while emergency staff struggled to save the people who caused the crash?

I fell to my knees and vomited.

"Hey, whoa!" A hand landed on my back. "I told you to stay in the engine for a reason, Kenz. Are you okay?"

I wretched again, then looked up into Liam's deep blue eyes. In them, I saw frustration, but there was a hint of concern as well. To my complete and utter embarrassment, I burst into tears.

He backed off, hands in the air as if I'd threatened him with a gun or knife. "Oh, shit."

Then, with a sigh, he pulled me off my knees and into his embrace. I buried my face in his chest and sobbed. God, I wished I'd had someone to hold me like this eleven years ago. I'd needed comforting so badly. That thought only makes the tears come harder.

"I'm sorry," I sniffed. "I'll be better in a minute."

He cradled the back of my head and murmured gentle nothings. I shut my eyes. Despite the circumstances, it felt good to be close to him. But I couldn't stay in his arms, so I pulled back and swiped at my cheeks. "I'm okay now."

He gave me a dubious look. "Go sit in the cab. Wait for us there."

I started toward the fire engine, but then caught sight of a man kneeling beside a car parked behind it. He was holding a camera, aimed at me. A flash went off. I blinked, startled. Then I saw red. This was surely the same asshole who'd photographed me outside the fire station. He must have followed us to the accident, and now he was snapping pictures while my insides felt like they were getting torn out and an injured man was fighting for his life.

Every morsel of training I'd had advised me to leave the paparazzi alone. To ignore them and maintain my dignity. But any self-control I had was long gone. I ran toward him, yelling words that didn't even make sense. His eyes widened, and he leapt into his car and jerked it into motion, swinging it around just as I reached him. I kicked the back bumper as he screeched away.

Damn. I muttered under my breath as I stalked back to the engine. How had he found me here? What did he want? And what on earth was he going to do with those photographs?

I pulled myself up into the cab, sank onto a seat, and belted myself in. Then I closed my eyes, embarrassed that Liam and his team had witnessed my breakdown. Liam probably thought my reaction had been a result of how disturbing the scene was. He didn't know about how I'd lost Mom and Malcolm.

I needed to get out of here. To retreat to the safety of my cottage and talk to someone who understood.

I needed Blair.

The wait seemed to take forever. The guys were downcast when they returned and stayed quiet during the drive back to the fire station. Liam asked me about the photographer, but I blew his questions off with a wave of my hand and a comment about the fact I must have been careless and left either my Bluetooth or location tracker app on my phone switched on, so he'd been able to find me. I knew I hadn't made that mistake, but didn't want Liam to know how much the encounter had rattled me.

When we got back to the station, I took Parks aside to speak to him. "I'm going home."

He frowned. "You have a whole day ahead. We agreed you could sit through the entire shift."

I shook my head. "It's been a bit much. Don't worry—you'll still get your money."

He looked a little uncomfortable, but he nodded. "Thanks, Kennedy. We appreciate it. I hope you get whatever it is you need."

I couldn't manage to smile, so I just left, glad that the others were too busy to notice my exit. What I needed was a cleansing conversation with my brother, a call with Jeff from my security team, and maybe a glass or two of wine.

Chapter Twelve

LIAM

You did me a favor by leaving. I used to hold myself back at work because I wanted to come home safe to you at the end of the day. Now, I'm fully committed to the job because there's no one waiting for me. - Unsent text message from Liam to Kennedy

After someone broke your heart, shouldn't your capacity to worry about them disappear? Yet here I was, concerned to discover that after going through a traumatic incident, Kennedy seemed to have done a runner.

"Braddock," Parks barked from the doorway. He motioned toward his office, and I joined him. "What did you say or do to upset Kennedy? She was supposed to stay for the whole day but left as fast as her legs could carry her as soon as we got back."

I frowned, annoyed by the accusation. "I didn't do anything."

He gave me a look.

"I didn't." I shrugged helplessly. "I was too busy with the accident for any petty stuff."

"Hmm." He crossed his arms and sat back in his chair.

I leaned against the doorframe. "Perhaps it was a bit much for her. We lost a man, and it's probably the first time she's seen anything like that. Or it could be about that guy who was taking pictures. She seemed pretty upset about that."

He nodded. "Could be." He dragged a hand down his face. "Fuck. The last thing we need is to upset one of Hollywood's golden girls. If she had a mind to complain, we could be in deep shit."

"But she was the one who wanted to come with us," I protested.

"And I'm in charge for the safety—physical, mental, and emotional—of anyone within the station's care." His expression said there was no point arguing with him. "I'll call to check in with her later and let her know we have a therapist if she needs to talk to someone about what she saw."

"Good idea." The knots in my stomach loosened now that I wasn't in the firing line. But to my irritation, I couldn't shake a niggle of worry about Kennedy. Sure, she'd tried to manipulate me with her money, but the girl I remembered had a sensitive soul and would have taken a scene like the one today hard. "Let me know how it goes?"

"I can't share anything private."

"I wouldn't expect you to."

He waved at the exit. "Get yourself a glass of water and decompress with the guys. The day is only just starting."

Dismissed, I returned to the others.

Unfortunately, the underlying concern for Kennedy stayed with me all day. When the shift finished and my coworkers headed home, I found myself driving to Grace's place instead. I parked on the side of the road and stared into space, trying to persuade myself to turn around and drive home. Kennedy's well-being was none of my concern. But I couldn't seem to help myself. If I didn't check on her, I'd spend the night worrying and probably wouldn't sleep well. Better to just get it over and done with.

"Damn," I muttered as I went up the path to the cottages. I recalled Nate saying she was staying in the same one she'd used back then, so I knocked on the door. For a moment, no one answered, and I thought I was off the hook, but then the door swung inward. My stomach sank. From all appearances, Kennedy was far from all right. Her eyes were red-rimmed and puffy. She'd clearly been crying, and she looked nothing like the stylish, aloof woman I imagined she was in Los Angeles.

"Hi." Even with that one word, she managed to sound confused. "What are you doing here?" She had one hand on the door frame and the other on the door itself, blocking the entrance. For someone who'd been trying to talk to me for days, she was giving off some serious nonverbal cues to leave her alone.

"I wanted to make sure you're okay. The crash earlier must have been difficult for you to process, since you're not used to seeing things like that." My voice was strained. Foreign to my own ears.

Kennedy raised her chin. "You'll be glad to hear I'm fine. You can leave with a clear conscience."

Yeah, no. Not buying it. Not even a little.

I sighed. She obviously didn't intend to make this easy, and I couldn't go without getting a better read on her state of mind. "Can I come in?"

She hesitated, visibly reluctant.

"Please." God, I couldn't believe I was actually asking. Not only that, but wanting her to say yes.

Her shoulders slumped and her hands fell away from the door. "Fine. But I don't have the energy to fight, so can we declare a temporary truce? I won't try to talk about the past, and you don't mention it either?"

"Okay," I agreed. Better that than give her the chance to unleash whatever it was she'd been waiting for a chance to say. Although I did have to wonder, if she was giving up the perfect opportunity to force me to listen, just how upset was she?

"I'm making a grilled cheese," she said, moving away from the door so I could enter. "You want one?"

"Sure." I hadn't eaten yet, so I may as well. "Thanks."

I leaned against the kitchen counter while she put together ingredients for a second grilled cheese and started cooking. It was strange to watch her do something so mundane. It wasn't like I thought she'd be traveling with a massive entourage, but I guess I'd overlooked the basic details of what living in Destiny Falls would be like for her. I was sure she had "people" who took care of things like cooking for her back home.

"How was the rest of the shift?" she asked, not meeting my eyes as she filled the kettle and set it to boil. "Tea?"

"No, thanks." I looked around the room to avoid letting my gaze linger on her graceful fingers as they prepared a brew. I wondered if it was chamomile, which she used to drink in the evenings, but I didn't ask. It was better not to know things like whether she still enjoyed chamomile tea. Easier to keep my distance. "The shift was fine. We had a minor kitchen fire that had already been put out by the time we arrived. Then had to warn some kids at the campground about the fire ban. They'd lit a bonfire, and someone called in a complaint. Oh, and Desdemona's cat Claude got stuck up a tree again."

"Again?" she asked, interest in her voice.

"It happens every few weeks. The cat is too chunky to

be chasing birds, but he doesn't seem to realize it until he's ten feet above the ground and can't figure out a way back down."

She laughed, the sound throaty and over too soon, but I counted it as a win. "Are you ever tempted to leave him there? I'm sure he'd get down eventually."

"Nah." I felt myself relax, and I frowned. I wasn't supposed to be letting my guard down around her. That way lay trouble. "The first time he did it, Desdemona waited overnight, figuring he'd come down when he got hungry, but the next morning he was still there, yowling to the whole neighborhood about how miserable he was. Now we just send a ladder up and help the poor thing."

"I bet the tourists love that. Hot firefighters rescuing a stranded kitty."

My lips twitched. I pressed them into a firm line. I couldn't afford to find anything about her charming. "You have no idea."

I was just grateful nobody seemed to have shown her the charity calendar we'd posed for a few years ago. Mum had been raising funds to support the repainting of a bunch of buildings on Centennial Street and had emotionally blackmailed us into taking our shirts off and posing with dogs for a calendar to support the efforts. She'd conned all of the Braddock men—including Dad, because apparently women love silver foxes—and most of the guys at the fire station into participating. I was just glad I'd been further along in the calendar. Asher had been on the cover, and Toby was Mr. January. Of course, my player of a baby brother had lapped up the attention.

A timer pinged, and Kennedy served the grilled cheeses onto a pair of plates. We moved to the sofa to eat, with a TV show on in the background. We made occasional small talk, but true to her word, kept everything surface level.

By the time I left, I wasn't convinced she'd completely recovered from the day, but the puffiness around her eyes had reduced, and she'd smiled once or twice. I felt all right about leaving. Even if everything else felt upside down.

I'd had a nice time with her, and that was dangerous.

Chapter Thirteen

KENNEDY

Hi Liam,

You know what the weirdest thing is about being an actress? People recognize me when I'm out on the street. They talk to me as if they know me. They mean well, and most of the time I'm happy to meet fans, but every now and then, I can't help feeling a bit violated. Like I have no right to privacy, and every part of my life can be used to entertain the public.

It's times like that when I wish I had you to confide in.

I miss you every day.

Love,

K xx

THE NEXT MORNING, I WAS LESS OF A MESS THAN I'D expected to be, thanks to Liam's evening visit. Even though we'd been tense, both afraid to put a foot wrong, we'd had a civil conversation, and it felt like progress. It had been kind of him to check on me when we weren't on speaking terms, so I wanted to thank him.

I walked to Taste of Destiny a little before the change of shift happened at the station. I'd asked how the roster worked when I'd discussed a donation with Parks, and it was useful information to have. My intention was to bring him a coffee to start his shift. I made my way inside the cute cafe and joined a line of locals looking for their caffeine fix before work.

"Kennedy, hey."

I jolted in surprise, my hand flying to my throat. Aiden Waldron stood behind me. Discomfort curled in my gut. My security team had cleared him of having any prior convictions or allegations of stalking or abuse, and they confirmed that he had a valid reason to be in the area, but my gut told me not to trust the guy.

"Aren't you supposed to be in Queenstown?" I asked, unnerved.

His eyebrows drew together. "We stayed there Saturday and Sunday nights, then came back late last night. Hey, are you okay after what happened yesterday?"

I felt a chill. "What do you mean?"

He opened his mouth, but before he could speak, the barista interrupted, calling my name.

I turned and gave Eden a tight smile.

"What can I get for you?" she asked.

"One trim latte and one cappuccino with cinnamon, please. Both large."

She jotted down the order. "Coming right up."

I paid, and she took Aiden's order, still surreptitiously sneaking glances at me. The girl could never have a career in acting. She was too obvious.

"So, who's the other coffee for?" Aiden asked me as we stood to the side to wait for our drinks.

"An old friend of mine." I didn't like the way he asked as if he had a right to know.

"Just a friend, or…?"

I left the question hanging. No way was I going to answer that. "What did you mean before, about what happened yesterday?"

He frowned. "You were at the scene of a fatal accident."

My fists tightened reflexively. "How do you know that?"

He cocked his head. "You haven't seen?"

"Seen what?"

He took his phone from his pocket and swiped the screen a few times, then passed it over. The browser was open to an online celebrity magazine that showed a photograph of me comforting the woman from the traffic accident yesterday while the paramedics performed CPR on her companion. It must be the photo the paparazzo from the accident scene had taken. I scanned the text. Fortunately, there was nothing concrete, although it included plenty of speculations about why I might have been there, such as research for a film and reconnecting with an old friend—a theory the article's author considered to be supported by the earlier photograph of Liam and me outside the fire station.

My heart sank. Why couldn't they leave me alone?

"I didn't realize," I said dully.

"Hey." He touched my hand as he took the phone back. "Seriously, you okay? That would be a hard thing for anyone to see, and to have had the paps there like vultures is sickening."

I flinched away from him, feeling a pang of guilt at the hurt that crossed his face. He was only trying to be nice. "I'll be fine."

He gave me a searching look, then nodded. "You know where to find me if you ever want to talk."

"Yeah." I tried to think of something to say, but my mind was blank.

"I'm heading up to the falls soon," he said.

I pressed my lips together. "They're lovely. It's a really beautiful spot."

"You've been there?" He sounded surprised.

"Just once."

Eden passed us our coffees, and I thanked her and headed for the exit. Aiden walked alongside, falling into step with me as we left the building. The discomfort in my gut grew. Did he intend to follow me all the way to the fire station?

"If you want to get your mind off what happened yesterday, you should come with me," he suggested. "I'd love to have company."

"Uh." I thought fast. While I hadn't consciously made the decision to wait, it didn't feel right going back to the falls until I'd cleared up the past with Liam. "Thanks for the offer, but I have things I need to do."

Things I need to do? Jeez, could I be any more vague?

I turned a corner and the fire station came into view. Relief flowed through me, followed quickly by dread as Aiden rounded the corner too.

"I can wait," he said easily. "I've got the day off today. My friends hit the clubs in Queenstown a little harder than I did, and they need to rest."

This guy really couldn't take a hint. Was he just that bad at reading body language, or did he not care that I didn't want to spend time with him?

I picked up the pace, eager to get inside the fire station. "Thanks for the offer, but I really will be busy all day."

The twin garage doors were open, the ambulance and

fire engine visible. A pair of men stood near the station, talking. Liam and Zane.

Liam glanced up and caught my eye, then his gaze settled onto the man beside me and narrowed.

"Hi, Liam," I called. "I brought you coffee."

Scowling, he folded his arms over his chest and sauntered toward us. "Morning, Kennedy." He tipped his head to me, then glared at Aiden. "Who's this?"

Aiden stuck out his hand. "Aiden Waldron. I'm a friend of Kennedy's. We ran into each other at the coffee shop."

I widened my eyes in a silent attempt to convey to Liam that he was not, in fact, my friend. He must have sensed my distress because he put a hand on my shoulder. The warmth of his touch soaked through me, feeling like a sip of water after days in the desert.

"Come in." It was as much an order as a request.

"Nice seeing you," I said to Aiden. "But I'd better go."

He glanced from me to Liam and pursed his lips. "Let me know if you change your mind about coming up to the waterfall." He passed me a business card. "Here's my number."

I tucked it into my pocket. "If I do, you'll be the first to know."

Liam cocked an eyebrow.

"Okay, I guess I'll see you around." He raised a hand in a casual wave and strolled away. I relaxed, glad to see the back of him.

"Who was that?" Liam asked as soon as he was out of earshot.

"Some guy I apparently met once at a premiere and then again the other day at the resort.

He snorted. "It seemed like he thought there was more to it than that."

I shivered, a bitter taste in my mouth. "Yeah, lots of people think that these days. Here." I passed him the cup.

"This is just to say thanks for coming to check on me." His steady blue gaze didn't waver from my face, and I squirmed. He saw more than I wanted him to. "You didn't have to do that, and I appreciate it."

"No problem." He sipped the coffee and smiled his enjoyment. "Just how I like it."

"Glad to know some things don't change."

He stiffened. "Kennedy."

I held up a hand. "No talk of the past. I know."

He hesitated. "Do you want to come in?"

"I'd better not." He'd just started to open up to me, and I didn't want to push my luck. "See you around?"

"You got it."

Chapter Fourteen

LIAM

Do you love being famous? Do you have everything you've ever wanted? Some days I hope so. Others, I hope you're as lonely as me. I wonder, did I ever really know you? - Unsent text message from Liam to Kennedy

I FELT A TWINGE OF SOMETHING LIKE DISAPPOINTMENT AS Kennedy walked away. I should be pleased she was leaving without a fuss and seemed to have genuinely dropped by only to give me a coffee and nothing else, but deep down, I wanted her to keep trying to talk to me. After all, if she'd really missed me and wanted to make things right, shouldn't it take more for her to give up than just a week of being ignored and a bad day on the job?

Yeah, I'd admit it to myself if to no one else. I was disappointed she hadn't fought harder for me.

I forced myself away from thoughts of our relationship as I reentered the fire station, my mind instead traveling to the guy who'd been with her this morning. From what she'd said, they were barely acquaintances, but he'd clearly been interested in her. Who wouldn't be? She was stunning, rich, and successful. But I'd definitely got the feeling she didn't want anything to do with him, and that rubbed me the wrong way. Did she feel obligated to be polite to him because of that deep-seated need she'd always had not to cause a fuss? I'd assumed she'd gotten over that during her years in the limelight, but maybe she never had.

The entire encounter unsettled me.

"Hey, man." Asher clapped my shoulder as I flopped onto the sofa beside him, coffee still in hand. "What was that about?"

I cringed. He was going to make a big deal of this. "I visited Kennedy last night. I wanted to make sure she was okay, since she hightailed it out of here so fast yesterday. This is a thank-you coffee."

Asher opened his mouth, the intention of delivering a lecture stamped all over his face.

"Ash," I interrupted as he prepared to launch into it. "Just don't, okay?"

He closed his mouth and fell silent for a moment. "I don't want you hurt again," he said quietly. "Today, it's coffee, but tomorrow it could be something else. Just promise you'll be careful."

I nodded, knowing he was right. It was a slippery slope, and he was looking out for me. "I will."

"Good."

We sat together without talking for a while. Zane was playing solitaire at the table, and even though he glanced our way, he opted not to weigh in. Zane and I had become friendly over the years, but we were work friends, not close friends. He didn't pry into my personal life, and I stayed out of his, for the most part.

Igor flounced into the room, ten minutes late. "Do I smell coffee?"

"Not for you," Asher told him with a smirk. He'd been the one to make the shared brew today, so Igor wouldn't be missing out on much. "Coffee is only for people who respect punctuality."

Igor rolled his eyes. "It's nearly Christmas. Where's your festive spirit?"

I groaned. "Damn, I still haven't done my shopping yet."

Asher made a face. "Me neither. Want to do it together? Safety in numbers."

"It's not that bad," I scoffed.

"Says a guy who doesn't have to shop for three women."

"I'll give you that." While my family consisted of five brothers and a single sister, Asher had two sisters and was the lone boy. He never seemed to know what to get for his sisters—a fact that wasn't helped by the fact they were both older than him and living very different lives from his. One was happily married in the city, and the other was engaged, pregnant, and enjoying life in a cutesy home with a literal white picket fence.

"What does your family have planned?" he asked.

"A roast lunch at my parent's place, same as always."

"Nice. Anyone bringing a plus-one?"

"Not that I know of." We'd had a few girlfriends and boyfriends come along over the years—and for a while, Nate's ex-wife would reliably attend every family event, but we were either all single at the moment or being tight-lipped about dating. Any day now, I expected to hear that Max, Nate's twin and the only doctor in town, would be shacking up with a sweet-faced woman who liked to bake and would give him two-point-five kids. I could tell he longed for a family, but he seemed to have run into the same problem finding someone locally as I had.

I doubted Nate would ever be willing to open his life to a woman. He already had his daughter, Tess, his best friend, Grace, and his ex-wife, Maddy, to contend with. Connor, the next brother after me, was a loner and seemed to prefer it that way. Toby was a player, and I doubted he had any intention of settling down. As for Summer….

Well, she had five overprotective older brothers getting in the way. Plus Asher, who seemed to take an instant dislike to any man she brought home. That didn't stop her from trying though. Sometimes I wondered if she enjoyed riling us. A couple of the guys she'd introduced us to were such duds, I was sure she must have been screwing with us.

"Good," Asher said. When I raised a brow, he flushed. "You know what I mean."

"How about you?" I asked. "What's the plan in the Heaton household?"

"A champagne breakfast at Mum and Dad's, then a light dinner at Frannie's." Frannie was the pregnant sister who lived not far from me. "Is Grace joining you?"

I shrugged. "Perhaps later in the day."

Thinking of her brought Kennedy back to the forefront of my mind. I wondered what she'd be doing on Christmas Day. Would she be alone?

Not your business, Liam.

Chapter Fifteen

KENNEDY

Hi Liam,

How are Grace and Desdemona? I've been thinking about them lately, and Tabitha, and everyone else who made me feel as though I could call Destiny Falls home. I miss them like a part of me has been cut out.

I miss you like my heart has been carved from my chest. A little melodramatic, perhaps, but that doesn't make it untrue.

Love,

K xx

I SPREAD CREAM CHEESE ON A BAGEL, THEN DOLLOPED raspberry jam on top. I lifted it to my mouth and took a bite.

Mm. Delicious.

Grace's soft laugh rang out across the table. "I didn't think you Hollywood types ate anything with carbs or fat."

"Oh, Hollywood types don't," I assured her. "But I'm

not one of those anymore. I'm an unemployed former actress who's allowed to gain a few pounds if I want to." And I had. It was a relief, actually. I didn't mind a little extra padding on my hips and breasts if it meant I no longer had to feel constantly hungry.

Grace shook her head. "I don't know how you did it."

I shrugged, a little self-conscious. "Honestly, when you're surrounded by the constant pressure of everyone saying you need to look a certain way, it doesn't feel that difficult. It's just how it is." I offered up a small smile. "I'm glad for the change though."

"Me too. It's nice to see you smile. You haven't done much of that since you've been back."

The observation disquieted me. I'd forgotten how perceptive Grace could be.

"I guess I haven't felt like I had much to smile about." It was nice to be here, but it was obvious most of the locals didn't want me around. It seemed like the past couple of days had made a difference though.

"That might be changing. I saw Liam out at your cottage the day before last."

I smiled softly. "We have a long way to go, but at least he doesn't shut down at the sight of me anymore."

"That's good, Kenz." Grace sliced a strawberry into quarters and dropped it into a small bowl of yogurt. "What are your plans for Christmas?"

There was a pinch in my chest. This would be my first Christmas away from my family in eleven years. My throat clogged. We wouldn't even be celebrating on the same day. By the time Christmas was over here, it would only be starting for my siblings.

"I'm having a quiet one," I managed to say, feeling her eyes on me but refusing to expand on the matter.

Her hand landed on mine. I glanced up. Her expression was kind.

"Why don't you have breakfast with us?" she asked. "Here at the house."

"Really?" I bit my tongue, repressing a surge of emotion. "Are you sure?"

"I wouldn't ask if I wasn't." She diced another strawberry and wiped her fingers on a napkin. "It'll just be Desdemona and me. We're going to have pastries. You'd be more than welcome."

"Okay, thanks. That sounds lovely." A thought occurred to me, and I added, "Nate won't be here?"

"No." She scooped a mouthful of yogurt and berries. I reached for a berry myself, figuring I probably should have something at least halfway healthy. "I'll be visiting the Braddocks later. In the morning, it's just us."

"Then I'd love to. Thank you so much for the invitation."

When breakfast ended, I returned to the cottage and was assembling the photography equipment I'd ordered online when my phone rang. I glanced at the Caller ID, which said "Blair", and picked up. "Hi, Blair."

"Hey." He sounded cautious. "How is everything?"

"Pretty good, actually."

"Is it really?" He hesitated. "I just read an article online reporting on the traffic accident you told me about. You never said the paparazzi were there."

I winced. I'd intentionally held back that detail because I'd known it would make him anxious. "It was just one guy."

He grumbled something unintelligible. "Why was he even there? Was he from a Kiwi news outlet?"

"I don't think so." I'd done some investigating on the matter after seeing the article. "Since the story originated from *HL Online Magazine*, and they have a history of following me around, I assume the photographer was on their payroll."

"Oh, great," Blair said sarcastically. "So some guy followed you all the way from L.A. That's really reassuring."

"He could be a local contractor," I pointed out, but a tingle of dread ran up my spine anyway. Blair was right. If they had followed me, it was a bit on the creepy side.

"Did you get a good look at him?"

"No," I admitted. "But if I see him again, I'll try to take a picture and send it back to Jeff."

"Good." He sighed. "I worry about you."

My heart clenched. I hated knowing that. He had enough on his plate without me dumping my personal issues on him too.

"There's nothing to worry about," I assured him. "Everything is fine."

"Have you talked to Liam?"

"Uh." I hesitated. "Yes, but not about the past."

"Right." He scoffed. "Let me guess. He still won't listen?"

That pretty much summed it up, but I hadn't exactly tried to press the matter recently either.

"I thought so," he said when I didn't answer. "Why don't you come home for Christmas, Kenz? It feels wrong not having you here."

I pursed my lips. "It's a bit late for that."

"Not if you buy a plane ticket and leave right now."

He had a point, but timing wasn't the only thing holding me back.

"I need to be here. I know it doesn't make sense to you, and I'm sorry if you feel responsible for the family's Christmas, but I can't come back now."

"Hmm." He didn't say anything for so long that I

checked to make sure the call was still connected. "What about if we all fly over there? It'd be difficult to get flights for all four of us, but not impossible."

For a moment, my heart filled with longing. I'd love to see them all and to be at the center of a family hug, but I knew Blair was only doing this because he was concerned about me. The others wouldn't appreciate being asked to board a flight with no warning. Especially not Mina, who was terrified of flying.

"That's really sweet, but you guys stay there. I'm a big girl. I can manage one day by myself."

He sighed. "I don't like it."

"Blair…."

"Fine." He wasn't happy, but he was accepting my decision. "Love you, Kenz."

"I love you too, baby brother."

Chapter Sixteen

KENNEDY

Merry Christmas Liam,

This was our first Christmas without Mom and Malcolm. I didn't know what to do. It seemed like we were all missing them, and I wasn't sure whether to talk about them or try to distract the others with fun and games. I couldn't make up my mind, so I discussed it with Blair, and we decided for a bit of both. In the morning, we had presents and pancakes, and the younger kids played. Then, in the evening, we sat together, and each said something we missed from Christmas with our parents. There were a lot of tears.

I'm still not sure if I made the right decision. I feel like every day is a battle not to do anything that will screw them up. It's so hard. For a brief moment, I wished I was with you instead, enjoying a summer Christmas under the sun, without a care in the world. I felt so disloyal. I love these kids more than anything, but it's so hard to keep it together when I'm crumbling inside.

Love,
K xx

. . .

"Merry Christmas," I said as Grace opened the door.

"Merry Christmas, Kennedy." She gave me a hug that felt warm and welcoming. "Desdemona is already here. Come on. I'll show you through."

She led me down the hall and into the private living area. Grace's place had two distinct sections: one guests could visit, and another they couldn't. The private area was homier. Grace's laptop and a few bits and pieces were scattered on a table in the corner, and a small tree stood beside the window, adorned with tinsel and smelling strongly of pine. Wilding pine trees grew on the side of the road up to the ski resort, and I wondered whether Grace had cut this one down herself. She may look somewhat aristocratic, but she was a very capable woman.

My gaze fell on Desdemona, who was seated at a round four-person table, and I couldn't help smiling.

"It's so good to see you, Kennedy." Desdemona stood up and pulled me into an embrace with strength that belied her thin frame. The scent of potpourri followed her, and her iron-gray hair—with its two colorful dreadlocks on each side of her face—smelled faintly of herbal oil. "Destiny Falls has missed you, and I sense that you have also missed us."

"I have." But she was the first person who seemed to have accepted and believed that immediately. Even Grace had been cautious. "I'm glad to be back."

She kissed my cheek and reached into the folds of her faded purple outfit—which could have been either a robe or a dress, it was difficult to tell—to withdraw a tarot deck wrapped lovingly in purple satin.

"May I do a reading for you, dear?"

"Breakfast is ready," Grace reminded her.

Desdemona seemed unconcerned. "A simple single card draw. It won't take more than two minutes."

Grace sighed. "Go ahead."

"Okay." My stomach flip-flopped. I'd never been sure whether I believed in Desdemona's psychic abilities, but the woman had a way of knowing things, and it was difficult not to put stock in what she said.

Desdemona shuffled the card deck and spread it for me. "Take one."

I ran a hand over the assortment, choosing one from near the middle of the deck. "Here." She took it from me and turned it over. "What is it?"

She smiled, running her fingertips over the beautiful illustration. "The Fool."

I pulled a face. "That can't be good."

"To the contrary." Desdemona took one last look at the carefree figure depicted in the image and tucked it among the others. "The Fool symbolizes the beginning of a new adventure for you to explore with childlike glee. In this case, I would consider it a very positive card."

"Thank you. I'll keep an eye out for that new adventure."

"Oh, don't worry." She studied me intently. "The adventure will find you."

A shiver rippled down my spine, but it wasn't unpleasant. More like a thrum of anticipation.

Grace set a platter on the table. It contained an array of croissants, fruit Danishes, cream puffs, and even a couple of eclairs along with plump blueberries, strawberries, and sliced pineapple and mango.

"Looks delicious," I told her. "Thanks for including me." I'd probably be eating pancakes drowned in syrup and moping otherwise.

"You're welcome. Dig in."

We ate until we were stuffed, chatting about Grace's books—she was an author—Desdemona's store, and my acting career. Unsurprisingly, they were both interested in hearing what Hollywood was like, but I was equally eager to know more about what had happened here over the years.

By the time we'd cleared the dishes away, we still hadn't run out of conversation. We were sitting in the living room when my phone rang. I answered without looking, assuming it would be one of my siblings.

"Hello," I said.

"Kennedy."

I sat bolt upright at the distorted voice. It sounded almost mechanical. Pulling the phone away from my ear, I checked the screen. It was a private number. "Who is this?"

Grace stiffened at my tone, raising an eyebrow as if asking whether everything was okay. I held up a finger, indicating for her to wait a moment.

"Someone who cares about you." After hearing a full sentence, there was no doubt that whoever was on the other end of this call had disguised themselves electronically.

"What do you want?" I asked, my voice shaking. The delicious food I'd eaten sat like a rock in my gut.

"I left you a gift."

"You what?"

"At your cottage door," they said. "Go and look. I hope you like it."

The call disconnected.

What the hell was that?

I lurched to my feet and stumbled across the room.

Could this be the person who'd been stalking me back in Los Angeles? Were they now in Destiny Falls?

"What's wrong?" Grace asked, and I heard footsteps as she and Desdemona followed me down the hall. I hesitated at the door, wondering whether this was a trap. If I opened it, would he be there, waiting for me?

"I have a stalker," I confessed. "Or at least, I had one. I'd hoped to outrun him, but I think that was him on the phone." Although how he got my personal number, I had no idea. "He said he left me a gift at the cottage."

Desdemona gripped my wrist. "Call Nathan. The police need to be involved."

I shook my head. "Wait. First let's make sure there's actually something to report. I don't want to interrupt his Christmas for no reason."

I opened the door and peeked out, but I couldn't see anybody around. A hand slipped into mine. Grace's. I sent her a grateful look. Slowly, we walked down the path. As we drew near the cottages, a package sitting on the front doorstep of the one I was staying in came into view. A gift perfectly wrapped in red paper with green polka dots and tied with a silver ribbon. I reached for it.

"Wait!" Grace cried, intercepting me before I could touch it.

I flinched. "What?"

She grabbed my shoulder and drew me away from it. "What if it's a bomb? Or something poisonous?"

I wanted to laugh. That was ridiculous, wasn't it? *Crazy.* Nobody would do something like that. But then, whoever this stalker was, they weren't sane if they'd followed me halfway around the world.

"Okay," I agreed. "Let's back away and call the police."

Chapter Seventeen

LIAM

Nate brought a date to Christmas this year. It was weird as hell. I always thought he and Grace would get together. But at least having his new girlfriend there distracted me from the fact that you weren't around. - Unsent text message from Liam to Kennedy

Since it was a gloriously sunny day, with blue skies and a pleasant breeze, my family had chosen to sit outside. Two picnic tables had been arranged end to end to fit us all. We were one member down, since it was Tess's year to spend Christmas with her mother, which meant Nate was a little mopey. He loved spending holidays with his daughter. Unfortunately, while Maddy and Nate were on good speaking terms, they weren't interested in spending time together. Something about maintaining boundaries and not letting Tess get confused about where things stood. In my opinion, Tess had more of a clue about that than they did, but that didn't stop them from trying to shield her, and who could blame them? If I had a little girl, I'd want to protect her too.

We were halfway through the meal when a phone rang. At the head of the table, Mum's eyes narrowed. She scanned us one by one, waiting to see which of her children had dared to bring a phone to Christmas lunch. Across the table, Nate's expression turned sheepish as he fumbled in his pocket.

"Nathan Martin Braddock," Mum said sternly. "What do you call this?"

Nate gave her an apologetic look. "I'm on duty. Sorry, Mum." He stood. "Give me two seconds."

He walked a few meters away, speaking under his breath. I kept my lips firmly zipped, relieved it was him who'd caught Mum's wrath and not me. I was also technically on call and had my phone in my pocket. It was a hazard of being a first responder in a small town.

With a muttered oath, Nate stalked back. "I've got to go. There's a situation that needs my attention."

"On Christmas Day?" Mum asked with an arched brow. "During lunch?"

"I'm afraid so."

"Is it anything serious?" I asked, curious about whether I'd be receiving a call shortly too.

"A problem at Grace's."

Mum's expression instantly morphed from frustration to concern. "Is she okay?"

"She's fine." He hesitated, apparently debating whether to add more. "It seems like someone is messing with Kennedy. Could be dangerous. Probably not, but they called me as a precaution."

At Kennedy's name, everyone at the table stiffened and swung to look at me. She'd become a nonsubject in recent times. With the exception of Summer, we avoided talking about her whenever possible. Summer, on the other hand, had urged me once again this morning to hear Kennedy out.

"What do you mean by 'messing with her'?" I asked, irritated to hear the concern in my voice. It wasn't because she meant anything to me, I assured myself. It was just that seeing her with puffy eyes the other day had reminded me she was human, and I didn't want any human to be in danger.

"Can't share details; you know that."

I gritted my teeth. "Can you give me a hint?"

He didn't bother to answer as he headed to the front of the table to drop a kiss on Mum's cheek and give Dad a one-armed hug. "I'll be back as soon as I can. Save me some dessert."

My chest burned as I watched him go. My stomach threatened to mutiny and throw up the food I'd eaten so far.

"Wait." I was on my feet before I'd made a conscious decision. "I'm coming with you."

Nate's expression darkened, but he didn't argue. Perhaps he realized it was pointless.

"Talk to her!" Summer called after me.

We got into Nate's car and he got us to Grace's place quickly but without using lights and sirens. From the outside, the property looked peaceful, but as we made our way down the path, I saw three women clustered outside the cottages.

"Nothing has happened so far?" Nate asked Grace as we drew near.

She shook her head, her gaze flitting to me. She didn't ask about my presence, which I was grateful for because I had no idea how to explain it. "The package is on the doorstep."

Package?

Nate hadn't explained anything to me on the way over,

but now I saw a gift-wrapped box sitting on the doormat of Kennedy's cottage.

Nate turned to Kennedy, who was even paler than usual. "Did the person on the phone tell you what it was?"

"No," she replied shakily.

Nate nodded and drew out a notepad. "Do you know who they were?"

"No." Tears filled her eyes. "I'm sorry. I know that's really unhelpful."

"It's all right." I could tell it grated on Nate to comfort her, but he'd fallen into the role of sturdy, reliable cop, and that meant more to him than any dislike of Kennedy. "Could you tell whether it was a man or woman?"

Her teeth sank into her lower lip. I stared, certain that she was going to puncture it at any moment. "A man, I think, but they were using something to mask their voice, so I can't be certain."

Nate made a note. "So you received a call from a private number. The caller told you they'd left you a gift. You then proceeded out here and found the box?" He gestured toward the package. "Is that correct?"

"Yes."

"Okay." Nate pocketed the notepad. "A constable is on his way with Snuffles, who is a trained bomb and drug detection dog. Once he's cleared the scene, we'll open it and see what we're dealing with."

If possible, Kennedy paled further. "B-bomb?" she stammered. "Surely there's no way...."

Grace wrapped an arm around her shoulder. "It's probably just a precaution."

"There's no need for a dog," Desdemona announced. "It's not a bomb."

Nate rolled his eyes. While he liked Grace's aunt, I knew he didn't have much patience for her theatrics. "Better safe than sorry."

While we waited for the constable and Snuffles to show up, I joined Kennedy. "You okay?"

She made an unhappy sound. "I'm sorry I disturbed your family lunch. I'm sure there's nothing to worry about."

At that, I snorted. "Some crazy person left you a mysterious gift, and you don't think you should be worried?"

She shrugged. "It wouldn't be the first time it's happened. It's probably something unpleasant but not illegal. Dirty photos, a bottle of wine, a love letter—you know what I mean."

I frowned at her cavalier attitude. "You get that kind of stuff?"

"Oh yeah, all the time. But my assistant has always intercepted it before now."

Anger began to simmer low in my gut. What kind of world did we live in that assholes thought it was all right to harass people simply because they'd seen them on TV?

"I'm sorry you've had to deal with that."

She glanced at me, her eyes widening. "Thank you."

It almost seemed like she might add something more, but at that moment, a car pulled up, and Constable Shaun Trafalgar led an excited Snuffles down the path. Shaun was wearing shorts and a T-shirt with cartoon reindeer printed on the front, suggesting he'd also been summoned from a casual Christmas event.

"Thanks for coming," Nate said, then turned to the rest of us. "Please keep your distance so Snuffles has space to work."

I watched with interest as Shaun and Snuffles did their thing. It only took a few minutes.

"No indication of either explosive materials or drugs," Shaun announced.

My shoulders relaxed. "Good."

"Do you want me to hang around, boss?" the constable asked.

"No, get home to your family." Nate scratched Snuffles behind the ear. "I'll take it from here."

"Thanks, Sarge." The younger cop took the dog and left.

"I told you so," Desdemona said smugly.

"Aunt," Grace hissed.

Desdemona sniffed. "Well, I did."

Nate approached the box cautiously. I followed behind him, Kennedy keeping pace with me. She looked ready to bolt at any second but also seemed determined to see whatever was inside. Nate donned a pair of latex gloves from the emergency kit he kept in his car, then pulled a pocket knife out and used it to cut through the top layer of wrapping. It fell away, revealing a plain brown box. He sliced through the second layer and eased the cardboard open.

"It's safe," he called out.

We clustered around as he reached in and pulled out a small gift basket containing body lotion, soap, a bottle of perfume, and scented bath crystals. The fear that had been plaguing me loosened. Nothing dangerous, just an over-the-top gift, as Kennedy had said. But when I looked at her, her mouth had fallen open on a gasp.

"What is it?" Nate demanded, instantly on alert.

She raised a trembling finger. "That's the soap I use. My favorite perfume and body lotion. The bath salts I buy when I want to treat myself..."

Ice settled in my veins. Not a random gift, then. A very specific gift from someone who must have intimate knowledge of her preferences.

"He knows what I use," she whispered to herself. "He's been in my home."

"Hey, now." Nate's voice was calm and firm. "Let's not get ahead of ourselves. Have you spoken about the products you enjoy publicly? Perhaps had an endorsement deal?"

Kennedy was shaking her head. "For the perfume, yes. But the others…. Only someone who's been in my house, or whom I've spent a lot of time with, would know about them."

Nate said what we were all thinking. "Fuck."

"Have you noticed anybody in or around the cottage?" I asked, my heart hammering forcefully in my chest.

"No one." Her eyes were still locked on the basket. "And there haven't been any signs of an intruder. Besides, no one knows I'm here."

"No one?" Grace asked.

"Not here at the cottage, specifically, but people know I'm here in Destiny Falls, I guess, thanks to those online articles."

Nate straightened. "I'm going to need a list of names of people who have this as a contact address for you." He turned to Kennedy. "As well as anyone else you can think of who could realistically have found out where you're staying. Unfortunately, as far as we know, no crime has been committed, so my ability to react is limited, but this makes me concerned. I'm going to take the box and see if we can collect any fingerprints from it. That way, we have them if this person contacts you again."

"I appreciate that." Her shoulders were rigid. "If you find any, can you let me know? I employ a security company and I'd like to keep them informed."

"Of course." Nate picked up the box. "I'm sorry this has happened." To my surprise, he actually sounded it. "Do you mind coming in next week to give a full state-ment? I want to have as much information as possible on record. If the person calls again, contact me immediately. Otherwise, you probably shouldn't be left alone."

"She can stay in the house tonight," Grace said.

"Thanks, Grace." Kennedy didn't even try to argue. "I'm so sorry to have ruined your Christmas like this."

It was the same thing she'd said to Nate and me, and I frowned. I knew she'd never been one to want to put others out, but surely she realized that even if I didn't approve of what she'd done all those years ago, we cared enough about her not to want her to land in any kind of trouble.

"*You* didn't," Grace said fiercely. "This asshole did."

My eyebrow shot up. So did Nate's. Grace wasn't much for swearing, but clearly this was a hot-button topic for her.

"I'm just going to clear the cottages," Nate said. "Make sure the stalker isn't in there and didn't leave anything else. Is that all right with you, Kennedy?"

"Yes." She curled in on herself. "I didn't even think of that."

"It's just a precaution." He drew his taser as he tested the door handle and let himself in. A few minutes later, he was back. "Everything seems to be in order. Why don't you take a quick check while I look in the other cottage?"

Kennedy and Grace entered the cottage together. I waited outside with Desdemona.

"She drew The Fool," Desdemona said meaningfully.

"And?"

She waggled her eyebrows. "Don't play coy with me, Liam Braddock."

I gave her an awkward smile, once again not sure what she was talking about. When Kennedy and Grace re-emerged, they confirmed that nothing seemed to have been taken or left behind. Nate exited the other cottage and locked it behind himself. He instructed us to wait by the road while he checked the perimeter of the property. When he'd completed the circuit, he packed his taser away.

"Right. I should get this to the station," he said, gesturing to the package, which he'd retrieved from the cottage doorstep during his check. "Are you going to be okay here?"

"Yeah." Kennedy smiled, but I could tell it was forced. "Thanks for coming."

"It's my job."

The forced smile vanished, and for some reason, I wanted to wrap her in my arms. I hated to see her looking so upset. She must be holding a lot of emotion inside. Whether or not anything illegal had happened, she'd been violated, and that wasn't okay. But I also couldn't comfort her the way I used to. That wasn't who we were anymore. So instead, I reiterated Nate's statement about calling if they ran into any more trouble, and I left.

Chapter Eighteen

KENNEDY

Hi Liam,

I don't have anything to say today. Just that I wish I was with you.

Love,

K xx

Once the Braddock brothers had left, I took my phone from my pocket. "I need to call my security company."

"Come inside," Grace urged. "You can use the guest living room if you want privacy."

"Thanks." I followed her in, grateful not to be left alone. I wasn't a clingy person, and I didn't want to put her out, but knowing that my stalker had been right here scared me. It was one thing when I was in L.A. and had an expensive security system and other people around the house, but here I was a lot more vulnerable. If he could drop off a gift, he could get to me in other ways.

In the hall, I turned left into the guest living room while Grace and Desdemona continued deeper into the house. I found the contact for my security firm's number and dialed.

"Hi, Kennedy." Jeff, my security point person, sounded alert and focused. "Did you need more background on that Waldron guy?"

"No. I wouldn't have called you on Christmas Eve for that. Something happened." I gave him the rundown on the events of the day and waited for his response.

"If you're not going to hire a local for personal security, you should be back here where we can keep you safe," he said. I wasn't surprised. He'd tried to persuade me of this before, and while I knew it would be easier for them to do their jobs if I was home, I wouldn't let this stalker control my life.

"You know how I feel about that, Jeff."

"In the abstract," he agreed. "But if the stalker followed you to New Zealand, then this is more serious than we thought. Your life could be in danger."

I considered that. "It's a big 'if', to start with. He may have arranged for the box to be delivered. And even if he's here, I don't think he wants to hurt me."

"Kennedy…."

"Hear me out. I think he believes himself to be in love with me. The weird letters, the disturbing videos, and now this. He left me a basket of the things I use to relax and feel good." I'd been toying with this theory since I'd seen what was in the box, and while it didn't make the gift itself less creepy, it did make me a bit less terrified of him doing something awful to me. "I don't think that was random or a mistake. I think that was his way of trying to show he wants to take care of me."

"Eh." He didn't sound convinced. "You an amateur psychologist now?"

I sighed. "I'm just thinking about character motivation. Acting isn't a practical life skill in many ways, but it does help you get inside someone's head. If he wanted to hurt me, I've been alone in that cottage every night, yet he hasn't made a move. Yeah, it scares me to know he could be somewhere nearby, watching me, but he hasn't done anything to harm me."

"You can't know for sure that'll continue."

"You're right. But I'm staying in a house with others tonight, and I'll look into alternative options tomorrow. It's already Christmas Day here, so there's not much else I can do."

He made a sound of disapproval. "Will your landlady agree to install a video feed of the cottage for us to monitor?"

"Probably. I've also asked the police to let me know if they find any fingerprints."

"Good. Do you have a photo of what was left for you?"

"Yeah." I'd taken a couple on my phone. "I'll send them through now."

He waited on the line while I did it.

"Thanks," he grunted. "I know you think you're safe, but be careful, will you? Pain in the ass or not, I like you, and I'd prefer you stay alive."

I smiled. "I will. Thanks, Jeff."

We ended the call and I slumped onto the sofa. It wasn't as comfortable as the one in the private living area. I squeezed my eyes shut, then opened them again, reluctant to leave myself vulnerable for even a few seconds. That creeping sensation of eyes on me hadn't gone anywhere. It would be great to call Gray and talk it over. He'd understand in a way others didn't, having been stalked himself. But he'd be enjoying his first Christmas with Mikayla, and I didn't want to ruin yet another person's holiday festivities. It could wait until later.

I rubbed my temples, wishing the throbbing behind them would fade. I knew I probably only had a few more minutes before either Grace or Desdemona came to check on me, but I was stuck in this strange mental space of wanting quiet and solitude yet needing to not be alone.

In my hand, my phone rang.

Jeff calling back? Or Nate, perhaps?

But no, it was Blair. Had he grown a sixth sense for when I was in trouble? Considering our bond, it didn't seem out of the realm of possibility.

"Happy Christmas Eve," I said when I answered.

"Merry Christmas," he responded automatically. "Is everything okay?"

I hesitated, wondering whether to be truthful with him. I didn't want to lie, but I'd hate for him to spend the night worrying about me. "Why wouldn't it be?"

"Because I got a message from Liam on social media suggesting I get in touch with you."

"Oh." Hope fluttered in my belly. Liam cared about me enough to reach out to my brother and make sure I had the support I needed. That must mean something, right? "That's surprising."

He snorted. "Tell me about it. So, what's up?"

I debated whether to be honest and decided he deserved the truth. "I received a gift from the stalker."

"Shit. Does that mean they're definitely in Destiny Falls?"

"I'm not sure. A courier could have delivered it."

"Still." He sounded tense. "That's serious, Kenz. What did he send you?"

"I know it's serious." My heart was heavy. "Nothing dangerous or threatening, but it was still disturbing."

"I'll say. Why didn't you call me?"

"The police were here, and I only just got off the phone with Jeff from the security company."

"The *police*?" He was quiet for a moment. "I'm not gonna lie—what you're saying doesn't sound good. Are you sure you shouldn't come home?"

There it was. I'd been expecting it.

"I understand where you're coming from, but I'm not letting this person run my life. Especially when we don't know for sure he's here. I know I need to take precautions, but what if he's trying to frighten me into running back to L.A.?" The possibility hadn't occurred to me until now, so I unraveled the thread of thought to see where it went. "If he's over there and can't follow me for whatever reason—perhaps he can't afford it, or he has a job or dependent he can't leave—then making me think he's here would be a great way to get me to return home."

"You have a point," Blair said. "But at least here you'd have support. Over there, you're on your own."

"Not quite—" I started to say, but he interrupted.

"Your angry ex doesn't count."

"I have Grace too." I heard the defensiveness in my voice, and I was sure he could as well.

"She's not a trained personal security professional. Just think about coming back. Please."

"I'll consider it." But I doubted it was going to happen.

"And the others deserve to know what's going on."

I groaned. If Mina, Joel, and Jamie heard about the stalker, I'd never get any peace. Mina would want to bubble-wrap me and the twins would go looking for some heads to bust. "I don't want to worry them."

"They deserve to know," he repeated.

"Ugh, fine. Next time I talk to each of them, I'll mention it. But I'm not calling a virtual family meeting to freak them all out right before Christmas. Deal?"

"I guess so."

I'd take that begrudging acceptance. "Thanks for calling, Blair. It means a lot to know how much you care."

"Anytime, Kenz. Look after yourself."

Chapter Nineteen

LIAM

Yesterday would have been our one-year anniversary. I got drunk off my ass and fell asleep at Asher's place. When is every-thing finally going to stop reminding me of you? - Unsent text message from Liam to Kennedy

On the morning of Boxing Day, the last thing I'd expected was to be hours from home, shopping for security equipment. Yet I found myself driving back with a haul worth a good chunk of my savings just before lunch. I'd barely slept the night before because I kept thinking about Kennedy.

Worrying about her, if I was honest.

I'd realized that much as I may want to keep my distance, I wouldn't get any peace until I knew she had a better security system in place. I was hardly an expert in the field, but I could muddle through, and with assistance from the store manager, I'd found what I needed.

I parked outside Taste of Destiny and headed in, drawn by the scent of coffee and cinnamon. There was a line, so I stood in the back, waiting for my turn to order. The pair of women in front of me—Liz from the convenience store and someone who might be her sister—were talking in low voices. I tried to tune them out, but the sound of Kennedy's name caught my attention.

"…you know the police were at her place yesterday?" Liz was saying. "I heard a deranged fan trashed the cottage."

"Really?" The other woman sounded intrigued.

"Or maybe she did it herself," Liz added. "To get attention. You know how much those Hollywood types love drama."

My hackles rose. I didn't like what she was implying. I'd seen Kennedy yesterday, and she'd been genuinely distraught. But I could hardly disagree when I might have had the same thought only a few days ago.

"I heard she's a diva," Liz's friend said in a hushed tone. "Awful to work for. Rude to everyone beneath her. If something nasty is going on, it's no wonder."

Now that really wasn't okay. I opened my mouth—to say what, I didn't know—but Eden, the barista, beat me to it.

"Excuse me, ladies, but we don't tolerate that kind of vicious gossip in this cafe." She sent them a sugary sweet smile across the counter. "Especially not about someone who has only ever been friendly toward the staff here. I'd appreciate it if you could refrain from saying anything else unkind that you might regret later."

Wow. I fought the urge to clap. Eden had always been fiery, and the fact that she was choosing to stand up for Kennedy meant something. I'd wondered previously whether Kennedy had been the type of person to let fame go to her head, and based on Eden's defense of her, the answer was no.

Eden met my eyes, and one side of her mouth curled, as though she wasn't sure how I'd react. Perhaps she thought her intervention had been disloyal. But Eden and I weren't friends. She was a nice kid but much younger than me. She didn't owe me anything, and I wasn't upset, so I gave a slight tip of my head and a smile to show there were no hard feelings.

"Now, what can I get you?" she asked, turning back to Liz and her companion.

By the time I had my coffee and had driven to Grace's place, I'd put the encounter to the back of my mind, pleased to see that Kennedy's Subaru Outback wasn't parked on the curb. I'd rather avoid her if possible. Coffee in hand, I walked to the front door of the main house and knocked. It took a few seconds for Grace to answer. Her hair was loose around her face, which was uncommon for her, and she was wearing a tank top and a pair of denim shorts that showed off long, shapely legs. Not for the first time, I wished Grace was my type. She'd have been a much easier woman to care for than Kennedy. Although Nate might have torn me apart if I'd ever made a move on her.

"I'm hoping you won't mind if I upgrade the security for the cottage," I said as she gave me a knowing look. "I picked up some equipment earlier today."

"What kind of equipment?" She leaned against the door frame.

"A couple of cameras, motion sensors, and a keypad for the entrance." I fidgeted, knowing she'd read into the fact I was here, and that she was right to. No matter how much I wished I didn't care about Kennedy, I did.

"Just for the cottage?" she asked, cocking an eyebrow.

"Yeah." My cheeks heated. "Say whatever you need to. I'll wait."

Her lips quirked. "There's nothing to say, Liam. I've been thinking about having the security upgraded anyway, so it was timely of you to drop by. Why don't we head out there, and you can show me what you have in mind?"

I stared at her, waiting for the other shoe to drop. Could it be that simple? I'd basically told her I still cared for Kennedy, and she hadn't pried. Hadn't demanded more information or made me feel uncomfortable. In fact, she seemed to be going out of her way to make it easier for me. "Sounds good."

"I'll just put some shoes on." She slipped on a pair of boots with a low heel that made her even taller. "Kennedy is out at the moment."

I nodded, a lump dislodging from my throat. While Grace might be willing to let me off the hook, I doubted Kennedy would do the same, so I was grateful to know I wouldn't have to explain to her. Hell, if I was in and out before she got back, I might be able to prevent her from knowing I'd been here at all.

"The keypad is self-explanatory," I said as we walked. "And I thought we could pair it with a motion sensor that will go off if the keypad isn't deactivated within twenty seconds of opening the door. Then perhaps another motion sensor at the bedroom window, which she could switch on at night to alert her if anyone tries to break in or sneak up to spy on her." I ran through the other ideas I had, and Grace nodded along.

"Where will the video feeds go to?" she asked as she unlocked the door. "I have to ask because she's my tenant. Legally, I should get her go-ahead before we start making changes, but I can't see her disagreeing. I need to know who'll have access so I can be sure they won't abuse it."

It made me sick to even think about the idea of someone abusing a camera feed into Kennedy's safe space. "Of course. It will go to a secure server, which you'll get access to as her landlord. If you're comfortable with it, she'd also be able to share the link with her security firm and access it herself."

"That all sounds good." Grace rubbed her palms together briskly. "Is there anything I can help with?"

I shook my head. "I think I've got it covered, but I'll let you know if I need a hand with anything."

"Great." She paused, then added, "You're doing a good thing."

I pressed my lips together and nodded, not wanting to examine the motivation behind my actions too closely.

"Right, well." She backed away. "You know where to find me if you need me."

Chapter Twenty

KENNEDY

Hi Liam,

I don't think I ever really appreciated how genuine you were. These days, with the exception of my family, I seem to be surrounded by people who have made a career of not being who they say they are, and I'm as bad as the rest of them. I spend so much time pretending to be someone else that sometimes I'm not even sure who I really am anymore.

I miss the version of myself I was with you.

Love,

K xx

I'D BEEN OUT FOR A WALK ALONG THE MAIN STREET, TOO wired from the incident yesterday to risk walking further afield by myself, when I returned to the cottage and found the door open. I froze, completely certain I'd locked it when I left.

My pulse thudded wildly at the base of my throat, and

I backed away, hoping whoever was inside hadn't seen me. There was a chance it was Grace, but I'd told her I preferred to do the housework and laundry myself, and so far, she'd respected that. I dashed to the door of the main house and rang the doorbell. When Grace opened it, I hustled past her.

"There's someone in the cottage," I panted. Based on the way her eyes widened, I looked as shaken as I felt. "The door is open. We need to call the police."

"No, we don't." Her expression gentled. "It's Liam. I'm sorry, I should have thought to warn you. It didn't occur to me how much having someone in the cottage might concern you."

"Liam?" I straightened because for some reason, I'd hunched in on myself during my retreat from the cottage. In a subconscious attempt to be small and unnoticeable, perhaps. "Why would he be here?"

"Because he's upgrading the security system for me."

"Huh." It made sense that Grace might want a better security system considering what had happened on her property, but I felt a twinge of guilt. She probably wouldn't have had to go through this for any other tenant. "Why Liam, though? Surely Nate would be better suited to that." Not to mention better qualified.

"Liam was available." Grace's expression was cagey, making me wonder if she was telling the truth. Was it possible that Liam had decided to do this of his own volition and she was covering for him? He'd always been protective, and this was exactly the sort of thing he would have done for me when we were together. But we weren't dating now. Far from it. So why would he bother? Unless he still cared.

I smiled at that thought. God, I hoped he still cared. Even a little. I could work with that.

"Do you mind walking out with me?" I asked Grace. "Just to make sure it's him."

"Sure."

We retraced my earlier steps. When we got to the cottage's entrance, I knocked loudly and called out, "Hello?"

There was a flurry of noise, then Liam appeared, a tool belt slung low on his hips and something electronic in his hand.

He flushed beneath my scrutiny. "Hi."

"Hi. What are you doing?"

He glanced at Grace as if to ascertain what she might have already said. "The security system here has needed work for ages. I've been meaning to get to it, but it keeps slipping to the backburner. Now seemed like a good time."

His eyes kept flicking downward as he spoke. He was lying. And it amazed me how pleased I was about that. He was doing this for me. To keep me safe.

"Thank you," I said.

He lifted one shoulder and didn't say anything.

"I'll leave you two to it," Grace said, making a quick exit. I couldn't blame her. The tension between Liam and me was thick. In her shoes, I'd want to escape too.

"Have you had lunch?" I asked, still in shock that he was here, in my cottage, protecting me.

"Not yet." He shuffled from one foot to the other. "I should only be another ten minutes, and then I'll be out of your hair."

I nodded. "Would you like a sandwich? It's the least I can do since you've gone to all this trouble."

At first, I thought he might refuse, but then he gave an almost imperceptible nod. "Yeah, that'd be nice. Ham and cheese?"

"Done."

He vanished back into the other room, and I went to the kitchen and made a sandwich for him and a few crackers with avocado and tomato for myself. I was curious about what exactly he was doing but didn't want to check because I didn't want to risk being alone with him in my bedroom. That would bring back too many memories. And ideas.

I'd finished eating my crackers by the time he returned. He removed the tool belt and placed it by a stack of empty cardboard boxes, which I assumed had held whatever equipment he'd set up around the cottage.

"Thanks," he said, claiming the sandwich. "I'll show you where everything is after this, and we can set up the secure server you can use to access the camera footage. You'll be able to send a link to that security company you mentioned as well."

"That would be great, thanks."

The sandwich disappeared in a few large bites, and Liam rubbed his flat stomach. "I needed that."

"Big day?"

"Not bad, but I ate breakfast early."

"Ah, right."

Now that I had him in my temporary home, I so desperately wanted to spill everything to him. The truth about the accident and all that had followed. But I also didn't want to break our truce. Waiting a little longer for the chance to explain wouldn't be difficult in the grand scheme of things. I'd waited eleven years, after all.

"Come on." He stood up and wiped his palms on his jeans. "I'll show you."

He gave me a tour of the equipment he'd installed, then waited while I booted up my laptop and showed me how to access the feed. I had to admit, having the additional security measures did make me feel safer.

"Thank you," I said as I walked him to the door. It was just as well my arms were full of boxes needing to be stashed in the recycling bin or I was afraid I'd hug him. "You have no idea how much this means to me."

He smiled tightly. There was a hint of genuine emotion in his eyes, but he tamped it down. "No problem. Like I said, we've been talking about doing it for a while anyway."

Bullshit.

But I didn't call him on it. If he wanted to continue the pretense, that was fine by me. One day soon, we'd talk, but it wouldn't be today.

"Thank you for moving up the timeline, then."

"You're okay here?"

What would he do if I said no? I was tempted to find out, but we'd pushed our tentative truce enough for one day.

"Yeah."

"Good." He cleared his throat. "Look, if anything happens to scare you, call me." He raised his eyes, gifting me with another flash of that emotion. "Everyone deserves to be safe in their home. You call, I'll come."

My heart gave a pathetic squeeze. I didn't trust myself to speak, so I just nodded.

Then he was gone.

Chapter Twenty-One

LIAM

WE LOST SOMEONE AT AN ACCIDENT SCENE TODAY. HE WAS just a kid. I promised him everything would be all right, then had to watch as the light faded from his eyes. Sometimes life is just really fucking unfair. I wish I could talk to you about it. - Unsent text message from Liam to Kennedy

ON MY FIRST SHIFT AFTER CHRISTMAS WEEKEND, I ARRIVED at work to find Asher already in the staff room and a holiday-themed romantic comedy starring Kennedy on the television.

"What's this?" I asked, pouring myself a mug of poorly made instant coffee and pulling a face as I sipped.

Asher slung an arm along the back of the sofa. "I heard Kennedy ran into trouble over the weekend, and you raced in to save her like a white knight."

The coffee in my mouth became even more bitter. "She has a stalker. Nobody should have to deal with that."

He held his hands out, palms up. "I'm not arguing with you, but her problems don't have anything to do with you." He gestured toward the screen. "So I thought perhaps you could use a reminder of why getting soft on her again isn't a good idea."

"I'm not soft on her." But the thwack of anger that struck me as I watched her flirt with another man onscreen didn't support my statement. "And I don't need to be reminded why it's a bad idea. I was the one who got dumped the first time around."

Having said that, I couldn't deny feeling something toward Kennedy, even if it was only protectiveness. Having her thrust in my face like this didn't help. Not when I'd already given myself every pep talk I could think of in an attempt to leave her alone. The fact that I cared simply wasn't rational, and Asher's actions just made me pissy.

"Morning, guys! Hope your Christmases went well," Zane said as he bounded into the room, looking far perkier than usual, then stopped short, his gaze flicking from me to Asher to the screen. "Uh-oh. Bad timing?"

I drank more of the terrible coffee. "No, it's fine. Your Christmas went well, I take it?"

"Sure did." He grinned. "I introduced the man I'm dating to my parents, and they loved him."

"That's great." I infused the words with as much enthusiasm as I could muster, which probably wasn't enough. "How is the rest of your family?"

"Everyone is happy, healthy, and ready for the new year." He glanced between us. "You guys really need a pick-me-up though. You're bringing my energy down. Did something happen over the weekend?"

"Nah," Asher replied.

"We're good." I clapped Asher on the shoulder. Even if I didn't like his way of trying to make a point, he meant well.

"Great. No Igor yet?" Zane asked, taking us at our word.

"I'm sure he'll be here any moment."

"Morning, team," Parks said as he appeared in the doorway and scanned the three of us. "We have a hiker reported missing. She went out last night with the intention of walking to the falls. Her friends assumed she'd returned late until they checked her room this morning and discovered her bed hadn't been slept in. Asher, I'd like you to join the search party. If they find her, she might need urgent medical attention. Liam, I've called in Randy from night shift to cover for you so you can join the search as well. I figure you know the forest better than Zane or Igor, and we need to keep a full staff here in case there's an emergency. If you haven't found her in a few hours, the rest of the team will join the search. Connor is running point. Meet him at the ranger station. Questions?"

"No, sir." It wasn't uncommon for us to assist in search-and-rescue operations. If people from different organizations didn't come together, we simply wouldn't have the manpower to cover such a large area of terrain.

"Get to it, then."

I went to the garage and grabbed the pack we kept for these situations, shrugging it on. Inside were items such as rope, survival blankets, flashlights, a waterproof shelter, and food rations, all of which might be needed over the course of the day. Meanwhile, Asher loaded up the first aid duffel bag.

"We'll take my truck?" I suggested, knowing there was a chance he'd want the ambulance on standby.

He hesitated for a moment. "Yeah. The trail isn't far from here, so we can call for the ambulance later if we need to."

I drove to the ranger station, which was housed near the beginning of the track up to Destiny Falls, behind and to the side of Destiny Fibers. Several other vehicles were already there, with a cluster of people standing outside. Connor was in front, looking distinctly uncomfortable at being the center of attention. Fortunately, we were a well-oiled machine, so he didn't need to say much other than to give general directions.

Asher and I joined the group, waiting while we were assigned a quadrant of a map to search for the missing lady. Apparently she was in her fifties but reasonably fit, so the fact she hadn't emerged meant she might be injured. We needed to expect the worst. The track to Destiny Falls was well-marked and usually safe, but we were in the mountains, and that shouldn't be taken for granted. Anything could have happened.

We just had to hope she was okay.

Chapter Twenty-Two

KENNEDY

Hi Liam,

I saw myself in a tabloid magazine for the first time today. It was this terrible, unflattering shot of me in a bikini at a friend's private pool, speculating on whether I was pregnant. I was just bloated. But how did they even get that photo? Was someone hiding in the bushes? Or was there a drone? Did one of my so-called friends sell me out?

There are some ruthless people in this business, and I'm not sure if I'm cut out to be one of them.

Love,

K xx

I'D FINISHED ASSEMBLING MY NEW PHOTOGRAPHY equipment and figured out how to work my new camera. After a few test shots in Grace's backyard, I decided I was brave enough to venture off the property. I headed for the parking area where the walk to Destiny Falls waterfall began. I didn't intend to head up to the falls, but I wouldn't mind taking some photographs along one of the other trails in the area.

I chose one that skirted around the edge of the falls, and I started walking. I took my time, pausing every few minutes to snap a picture of a bird or a particularly lush tree. It had been ages since I'd tried taking photos of anything other than my family, so my skills were a bit rusty, but the challenge of sharpening them again would be half the fun.

A fantail landed on a tree branch in front of me, bright plumage flickering in and out of view as it flitted along the branch. I held my breath, edging closer, and aimed the camera.

"Hi!"

"Eeek!" I spun around, clutching my chest. "Don't scare me like that!"

It was Aiden. He cocked his head and grinned in a way I'm sure was supposed to be charming, but with my life still flashing before my eyes, I didn't have it in me to be anything other than annoyed.

The smile faded. "Sorry. I didn't mean to give you a fright." He sounded genuinely contrite.

"Well, you did." I drew in a deep breath, holding it in for a few seconds even as my lungs ached to pull in more air. When I released it, I felt a little better. "Seriously, be careful when you sneak up on someone."

His forehead scrunched. "I wasn't sneaking. You were distracted by that bird and didn't hear me."

He might have a point. I had been caught up in the moment.

"Are you out here by yourself?" he asked.

A shiver slid down my spine. Seeing him here on the trail with me, with no one else around, reminded me of how vulnerable I was. He could try anything, and if I screamed for help, I couldn't be certain anybody would hear.

"One of my friends is further ahead," I said, not wanting to admit to being alone. "I'm taking my time so I can get some pictures, but we'll be sharing lunch."

There. That made it sound as though someone was expecting me in the near future.

Aiden nodded. "Why don't we walk together for a while? I'll keep you company. My friends are at the tarn, but I was delayed speaking to the farmer I'm hoping to purchase land from, so I need to catch up to them."

"If you're in a hurry, you should go on without me." My smile was stiff. "I'd hate to slow you down."

"It's no problem." He gave me a friendly grin and gestured toward the camera. "You like photography?"

"It's a hobby I'm getting back into." I started walking up the trail, hoping he'd leave me alone. No such luck.

"I guess that makes sense, since you're in film."

"Was," I correct. "I'm not in film anymore."

His face fell. "Oh, right."

We walked in silence for a few moments, but it didn't last long. "I heard you had some trouble over the weekend. Is everything okay?"

"It's fine. Just a misunderstanding." Like hell was I telling him anything. At this stage, he was the most likely candidate for stalker I had. The fact that Jeff had cleared him of having a criminal history and his having a legitimate reason for being here didn't necessarily mean he was innocent. "What did you do for Christmas?"

He shrugged. "Stayed at the lodge. They put on a nice meal."

So he would have been in the area to plant the gift at my cottage. I cast a sideways glance at him, wondering if I ought to turn and start walking the other way, back toward civilization. But then I heard a voice.

"Mary!" It was a man. Somewhere nearby. I looked around, catching a glimpse of a dark green uniform through the trees. "Mary!"

"Hello," I called as the man came into view. Broad shoulders, dark hair. He turned, and I winced at the sight of his face. "Asher, hi." I supposed it was better to run into him than be murdered by Aiden and have my body hidden in the woods. "Are you looking for someone?"

Asher scowled. "There's a missing woman. Fifties. Gray hair. Petite. Have you seen her?"

"No, sorry—but I can help look."

Asher's gaze traveled from me to Aiden and narrowed, his expression distinctly unfriendly. "There's no need for that. The search-and-rescue team is currently going over the area. I'm sure we'll find her."

Thank God. That meant there were more people out here. Even though Aiden hadn't said anything to threaten me, knowing we weren't alone in the wilderness made me feel a lot better.

"Hey, Ash," another male voice called. I knew this one immediately. Liam. "Any luck?"

"Nah," Asher yelled back. "Found someone, but not who we're after."

"Oh?" Liam appeared on the trail ahead of us and stopped abruptly, running a hand through his scruffy hair. Twigs and leaves fell loose as he did so, and his gaze ping-ponged between Aiden and me. The flaring of his nostrils made me think he recognized Aiden from before. "Hey."

I opened my mouth to assure Liam that Aiden and I hadn't come here together, but Aiden beat me to the punch.

"I was out for a walk and ran across Kennedy," he said. "Must be my lucky day."

Liam grunted. I didn't miss the assessing look in his eye. "I'm not so sure about that." He stalked down the path toward us and jabbed a blunt finger into Aiden's chest. "If I find out you're the one who's been harassing her, you'll regret it."

My heart jumped for joy. He was warning this guy off. Trying to keep me safe. He *cared*. There was 100 percent no denying it now.

Aiden took a step backward. "Calm down, man. I have no idea what you're talking about.

Liam thundered past, intentionally knocking into him. "You'd better not."

Asher shot us one last look and hurried after him.

Aiden rolled his shoulder. "What's that guy's problem? And what did he mean about someone harassing you?"

I sighed. Damn. If Aiden was the stalker, he now knew I'd told others, and if he wasn't, his curiosity would be piqued. "It's nothing."

"Clearly not." He laid a hand on my upper arm, adopting a wounded puppy look when I flinched away instinctively. "If someone is bothering you, I'm happy to stay close and make sure they don't get to you. Would you like that?"

"No, thanks." I shrugged his hand off. "It's under control."

"Are you sure?"

I gave him a look. "I really am." Sighing, I dragged a hand through my hair. "Actually, I think I'm going to turn around. I've had enough of the outdoors for one day."

His brow etched with concern. "I can walk you back to your car."

"No, thanks. You go on. I'd hate for you to keep your friends waiting."

He seemed reluctant but eventually nodded. "I'll see you around?"

I was noncommittal. "Maybe."

I waved and started walking before he could decide to

accompany me after all. It took less time to get back to my car than I'd expected, and I was looking forward to sitting down after my encounters with Aiden, Asher, and Liam. But when I got to the driver's door, everything inside me iced over. There, carved into the silver paint—presumably with a key—were the words "you are mine."

Gasping, I backed away. Nausea rolled in my stomach, and I clasped it, afraid I might puke. Light flashed in my eyes. I blinked, shocked, and stumbled over my feet as another flash went off. Looking around, I noticed the photographer from the scene of the traffic accident standing a few yards away, snapping photos of me and the words scratched into my Outback's paint.

"Smile for the camera, sweetheart," he called in a faint Bostonian accent. I could see the man better now. He was of average height, late forties or early fifties, with a pot belly and thinning hair. I mentally committed his image to memory. "Come on, make it a good one."

Knowing the damage was already done, I didn't bother throwing up my hands to shield myself. Instead, I fished in my pocket for the key and hurried, shakily, into the front seat of the car, ducking as low as I dared as I started the engine. My heart hammered a million miles an hour as I tore away from the parking lot.

What the hell had that been?

Had he been following me and lucked into prime story fodder? Or had he defaced my car himself because he'd grown tired of waiting for me to do something else newsworthy?

As soon as I'd put some distance between us, I pulled over and called Jeff.

Chapter Twenty-Three

LIAM

How the hell am I supposed to get closure when I don't understand what went wrong? - Unsent text message from Liam to Kennedy

We were back at the fire station by midway through the shift, having found Mary sitting near one of the streams that broke off from Destiny River. Apparently she'd gone into the bush, chasing after what she'd thought had been a kiwi, and been unable to find her way back. She'd pushed her way through the thick forest for a while, then found the stream, where she'd decided to sit and wait for help, having finally realized that she might be doing more harm than good by staying on the move. She was cold and hungry but had at least had a good supply of water and no injuries worse than a few scratches and insect bites.

The remainder of the shift was uneventful, and after

clocking out, we went to Drunken Destiny, as we usually did after a search-and-rescue mission. Connor and the volunteer searchers were already there, and I clapped him on the back as Asher and I passed on our way to the bar. Dad was working again tonight, and he filled a couple of glasses and pushed them across the bar.

"On the house."

I grinned. "Thanks, Dad."

"I'm just glad you found that tourist."

I shrugged. "We might have been the ones to find her, but Connor organized the operation."

"And I've already given him a free drink or three." Dad winked. "Do me a favor and make sure he gets home in one piece."

"We will."

We took our drinks and joined Connor and the other members of the search party. We'd changed out of uniform before leaving the station, but I was still wearing a DFFD T-shirt, and as per usual, attracted a few interested looks from women because of it. I'd long ago discovered that women loved hooking up with a firefighter. Dating them, not so much. The hours and emotional toll the job took tended to put them off.

"Hey, bro," I said, sinking onto a chair beside Connor. "Good work today."

"Thanks." He looked uncomfortable with the praise.

Asher pulled another chair over and sat opposite us. We made small talk for a few minutes, then I felt a hand land on my head and ruffle my hair. My eyes narrowed. Only one asshole would be dumb enough to do that.

"Toby," I growled.

"What." He scooted in beside me, smiling innocently. "Messy suits you. Plus, girls love it."

"Oh, you're an expert on women, are you?" Asher

asked with a smirk. "Put your money where your mouth is, Tobes."

Toby glanced at something behind me, then bared his teeth in a sharklike smile. "Wait and see, gentlemen. There's a pretty blonde on her way to talk to us as we speak."

I didn't look over my shoulder, not wanting to make the poor girl think we were whispering about her behind her back.

There was a light touch on my shoulder, followed by a soft greeting.

"Hi."

I looked up. The woman was indeed pretty. Blonde hair in a messy bun, a wide, warm smile, and a golden tan that spoke of long hours in the sun. She looked friendly and easygoing. I should want her. But I didn't.

"I couldn't help but notice you," she said, fine lines crinkling the edges of her eyes. "Can I buy you a drink?"

Asher gave me a meaningful look. I knew he wanted me to go for it, but I just didn't have the energy tonight. Especially not when it most likely wouldn't go anywhere.

I nodded toward my beer. "I'm all set, thanks. But Toby just got here."

She glanced at my brother and obviously approved of what she saw. "Nice to meet you."

"Why don't I take care of your next drink?" Toby said, taking her elbow and guiding her away. "I'd love to hear what you're doing in our little town."

Asher shook his head at me.

"Not in the mood," I said. "Didn't seem like you were either, so stop giving me that look."

He dipped his chin. "Fair enough."

I tried to focus on the cricket match, which was playing on a TV above the bar, but something kept niggling at my mind. "What did you think of that guy with Kennedy today?"

"The American?"

"Yeah."

"Looked like a douche."

Part of me thought there was more to it than that. "I get a weird vibe from him."

Asher frowned. "You're looking for something that's not there."

"Maybe." But I didn't think so.

"Ever think that maybe you just don't like him because he's hanging around Kennedy?"

I pressed my lips together. I wanted to deny the comment, but he could be onto something. It wouldn't hurt to mention him to Nate though. Perhaps my brother could use his police resources to make sure the guy was on the up-and-up.

"Come on." Asher stood. "Let's play darts. We need to distract you before you do something you'll regret."

"Fine." I followed him to the dartboard, trying to put Kennedy, Aiden, and the entire stalker situation to the back of my mind. "You're going down, Heaton."

Chapter Twenty-Four

KENNEDY

Hi Liam,

I've ended up in this really weird space with my siblings, where I'm their sister, but sometimes it seems more like I'm their mother. I don't like that. Nobody can replace Mom, and I hate when it feels like I'm stepping into her shoes. It's difficult to navigate with Blair because he's the closest to me in age, but somehow it's even worse when it comes to the twins. Perhaps it's because I know that by the time they're legally adults, they'll have had me as their guardian for longer than Mom was, and that feels all kinds of wrong.

I hope life is easier for you than it is for me.

Love,

K xx

A BANG WOKE ME.

I jerked upright, panting, already searching the room for an intruder. None of the alarms had gone off, and there didn't seem to be anyone inside. Biting my lip, I eased my feet off the edge of the bed and tiptoed to the window. Nobody there.

Bang!

This time, I was able to pinpoint it as coming from the direction of the front door. I slipped a robe over my short cotton pajamas and treaded softly through the house. As I drew nearer, I realized somebody was knocking—a bit too forcefully. I reached for the door, then stopped. What if it was the stalker?

"Who's there?" I called, wondering if it would have been smarter to simply sneak out my bedroom window, just in case.

"It's Blair."

I yanked the door open, hardly able to believe my eyes. There, standing on the doorstep with his hair mussed, eyeliner emphasizing the green of his eyes, dressed in a Linkin Park T-shirt and ratty black jeans, was my brother. I launched myself into his arms, smiling as they closed around me. Blair might be four years younger, but he was a good deal taller and broader than me.

"God, I missed you," I told him, breathing in his usual peppermint scent. He probably had a packet of mints in his pocket. He started popping them to mask the smell of cigarettes, and even though he'd quit smoking, he'd never managed to shake the mint habit.

He squeezed me. "Missed you too, Kenz."

I pulled back, looking up at his face. "What are you doing here?"

He rolled his eyes. "Your stalker delivered a Christmas gift. Was I supposed to stay in L.A. and leave you to deal with that on your own? Hell no. I did Christmas with the others, then caught the first flight to New Zealand. I talked Tyler into coming too, so he'll be here tomorrow. He's stopping by Melbourne to visit some friends first."

"Oh, right." I wasn't sure what to make of that. Blair

and Tyler Johnson, an all-American trust funder, had been friends for a long time, although I hadn't seen much of him recently and I was surprised he'd agreed to come.

"That's okay, isn't it?" he said, suddenly looking worried.

"Of course." I tried to smile reassuringly, and then I glanced at the time. "You must be tired. Why don't we sort out bedding, and then we can catch up properly later?"

Blair grinned. "We've already rented the cottage next door. It looks nice enough, but I didn't want to wake the landlady to get the key, so hopefully you won't mind if I crash in your bed for a bit?"

"You rented the cottage?" My brain was lagging. "For you and Tyler?"

"The sofa turns into a pull-out bed," he explained. "Tyler can sleep there. He could have gotten a separate place, but it seemed pointless to send him somewhere else when we're going to be spending most of our time together anyway. By the way"—he made his way past me and into the cottage—"this place is a pain in the ass to get to. It took two flights, renting a car, and getting lost in the back-side of beyond three times over before I found the damn town."

"Yeah, it's a bit off the beaten track," I agreed. "It's pretty well signposted though, since we get a lot of tourists."

Blair scowled. "If it was so well signposted, I wouldn't have gotten lost."

I hid a grin. He was used to driving in the bustle of L.A. He probably had no idea what to do in the rural isolation of an area like this. "If you say so."

"It's a nice town though," he said, heading for the kitchen to pour himself a cup of water. He drained it in a few mouthfuls. "Quaint, I guess. Not sure it's my thing, but I can see why you like it."

"It's a special place." I went to Blair and wrapped an arm around his waist. "Come on. I'll show you the bedroom."

"I want to see the rest of town later too. Size up anyone who might be causing you problems."

I pressed my lips together to keep from chuckling. I knew he wouldn't find much, but it was sweet that he wanted to protect me. Especially after the car-keying episode, which had left me even more shaken. Jeff had managed to track down the photographer's employer and persuade them not to print the story by implying we'd sue them, since it seemed a little too coincidental that the paparazzo had been there to photograph my reaction but supposedly hadn't seen who did the damage. I'd had a police officer around to take a look and make a record, but the paint hadn't been fixed yet. Hopefully soon, because each time I saw the words carved into it, I got a chill. I shook my head to dispel the unwelcome thoughts.

"If I'm not here when you wake up, just text me. Okay?"

He pressed a kiss to the side of my forehead. "You got it, Kenz."

Chapter Twenty-Five

KENNEDY

Hi Liam,

I called you today. I waited for two rings, and then I chickened out and hung up. My phone number has changed a few times, so I doubt you'll know who it was. Or perhaps you'll see a Californian number and be able to guess.

I regret so deeply the way I ended things between us. I wish I'd had the presence of mind to lay out the situation and discuss it more rationally, but I was in survival mode. I couldn't think of anything beyond putting one foot in front of another.

There isn't a lot I regret, but I do regret that.

Love,

K xx

While Blair slept, I had breakfast with Grace and returned with the key to his cottage. When he woke, I gave it to him so he could make himself at home next door, then

I cooked scrambled eggs while he filled me in on the flight and asked for more details about the stalker.

Blair shoved a quivering piece of egg into his mouth and scowled. "If I get my hands on this guy…."

"You won't do anything because your loving sister would hate to see you get into trouble."

He grumbled, and then continued eating. I sipped a mug of herbal tea and waited until he was finished.

"Would you like to go for a walk around town?"

"You're on." He took his plate to the kitchen and rinsed it off. "Just give me five minutes to get ready."

I grinned, pleased that some things never changed. Even though Blair had already showered and adorned himself with a new set of tattered black jeans and a T-shirt advertising his own band, he'd no doubt want to primp his hair and touch up his eyeliner. He didn't like to go out looking anything other than 100 percent. It worked for him though. Women and men flocked to him. Whenever I'd gone to one of his band's gigs, I'd seen him sneak off home with someone afterward.

He emerged a few minutes later with everything just so. I led him out of the cottage, keyed in the code, and locked the door behind us.

"I'm glad you've had better security put in," he said as we walked down the path to the road.

"Liam did it."

"Oh." He seemed taken aback. "That was good of him."

We wandered along the footpath and turned onto Centennial Street. The Colonial-style buildings looked more yellow than usual in the warm sun, and groups of tourists clustered on the pavement, some of them spilling onto the road. While cars could drive through here, many chose to park at the edges and walk in. Destiny Falls was a pedestrian-friendly town.

"When was the town built?" Blair asked. "It looks like they've kept a lot of the original architecture."

"They have." I was pleased he'd picked up on it. The locals had a lot of pride in the fact that their buildings were beautifully restored and maintained. "I think most of it was constructed in the 1860s, during the gold rush. There used to be a gold mine in the side of Destiny Peak, and many of the local rivers are still panned for gold—not that you'd find more than the occasional fleck or nugget. But the Heritage Museum would be able to tell you more accurately." I pointed toward the building, which was across the road and down a couple of blocks. "They keep a lot of information about the town's heyday there. Destiny Falls was a big deal at one point, and Arthur Emerson, who runs the museum, is a font of local knowledge."

"I'd like to see the museum," Blair said, earning a smile from me as we changed course to cross the street.

We paused outside and I fished in my pockets for a coin to drop into the donations box as we entered the museum. There was nobody in the foyer, so we passed into the main part of the building, which was a rabbit warren of rooms and corridors with glass display cases built into the walls. We found Arthur Emerson inside the room where they kept a collection of old mining tools.

"Guests." The small man clapped his hands in delight, his perfectly trimmed gray mustache jiggling with the motion. "Are you happy looking or would you like the full tour experience?"

"Hi, Arthur," I said, hoping he'd recognize me after all this time. And not hate me.

Arthur took a pair of spectacles from the front pocket of his striped shirt and propped them on his nose, then a smile spread over his face. "Kennedy, my dear!" He stepped forward with open arms, and I gave him a quick hug, pleased to have received a warm response rather than the cool reception I'd been granted in other parts of town. "I've been keeping up with your career. I always knew you were meant for big things, although I had hoped you might stay here."

My smile faded. "Things happened that made it pretty much impossible, but I'm here now and I plan to stay."

"Yes, I think I know a little about that." His expression was sympathetic. "Many people made it their business not to know, but I've always been the curious type." He looked me up and down. "I'm glad to see you've been eating since you arrived. Whenever I saw you on the television, I wanted to hand you a piece of pie. You were too thin, dear."

"Tell me about it," Blair grumbled. "That's what the film industry does to women. Chews them up and spits them out with an eating disorder and a drug addiction."

I shot him a look. The last thing I needed was for him to start rumors. "Fortunately, I avoided both of those." I gestured at Blair. "This is my brother. He's visiting for…." I trailed off, realizing we hadn't discussed time frames.

"A few days," Blair filled in. "Maybe a couple of weeks. As long as I'm needed, really."

"Blair." I huffed. "You have a career. You can't just walk away from it indefinitely."

His chin set mulishly. "Can and will. You're more important."

Arthur smiled and offered him a hand. "I like you," he said. "I think we're going to get along well."

Blair's expression was smug.

"Now that we're introduced, indulge an old man." Arthur led us to one of the display cases. "I want to take you on a historical journey."

"Go for it," I told him. "We have nowhere else to be."

As we followed Arthur through the rooms, he gave a practiced spiel, pausing every now and then to add facts or clarify. I was amazed, once again, by how much knowledge he held. I didn't pay much attention to the stories themselves, since I'd heard most of them before. It was a photograph, and the accompanying note, that caught my eye.

"Wait," I interrupted before he moved on to another point. "You're saying the couple in that picture are the ones who started the mythology around Destiny Falls being a destination for young lovers wanting to pledge themselves to each other?"

"They are." His expression wistful, he took the framed photograph off the shelf so I could see it better. "We don't know much about them other than they were married at the waterfall and the photographer referred to them as Rocky and Jewel. I have no idea if those were nicknames or their real names."

"Wow." I studied the photograph, which showed a pretty brunette with a beauty mark not dissimilar to Marilyn Monroe's, and a slightly older man with his arm around her. His face was craggy, but there was no denying the devotion in his eyes as he gazed down at her. It was a powerful picture. I understood why the story had captured people's imaginations. "Rocky and Jewel." I wondered if there was more evidence of them around the township. "I'd love to find out what became of them."

"Don't go getting all mushy on us," Blair warned. "They were just a couple who got married and didn't leave much of a paper trail. Hardly some small-town Romeo and Juliet."

"We'd all like to know, dear," Arthur said. "If you ever find out, I hope you'll come to me first."

"Of course."

We finished the tour and lingered in the exit.

"I'm keen to get back outside," Blair said. "Didn't you say there are walking trails around here?"

I nodded. "There are maps at the information center if you'd like to have a look."

I hadn't been into the information center since I'd returned. I'd been too much of a wimp to face Heather Braddock. With Blair at my side, acting as guard dog, maybe I could manage it.

We said our goodbyes to Arthur and walked the short distance to the information center. I froze in the doorway, spotting a small group of people at the front desk.

Liam.

His golden arms flexed as he gestured animatedly to his mother. I swallowed and backed up a step. A woman stood beside him. Based on her blonde hair, I'd guess it was Summer, but I couldn't see her face from where I stood. Standing to the side was Asher, smiling for once—although perhaps that was because he hadn't seen me yet.

"Um," I murmured, about to suggest we come back later, but words escaped me.

"Shit," Blair said, noticing the same thing I had. He wrapped an arm around me. "Come on. You can do this."

The Braddocks looked up as one. Asher's expression distorted into that familiar scowl. Summer's eyes lit up with excitement. Heather pursed her lips. And Liam....

Well, if I didn't know better, I'd think Liam looked jealous. But then Asher grabbed him by the arm and dragged him out the side exit. Summer followed them, mouthing an apology.

Damn. I guess things hadn't improved all that much between Liam and me after all.

Chapter Twenty-Six

LIAM

Sometimes I wonder whether I'd give you a second chance if you begged me to take you back. Some days I don't think I could say no. - unsent text message from Liam to Kennedy

"What was that?" Summer called from behind us. "Why did you walk out? I thought you guys were working out your differences."

"They're not 'working out their differences,'" Asher snarled. "She's wrapping him around her finger all over again, and he's letting her. He needs to keep his distance."

Summer jogged around in front of us, cutting us off. "Don't you think you should both be more mature about this? You're grown men. Why not just hear her out and then decide what to do next?"

"Because—" I started to reply, but Asher had already launched into a response of his own. I stood and watched while they argued over what I should do next. Asher was clearly in a mood, but Summer had taken exception to his attitude and wasn't about to back down. They raised their voices, waved hands, poked fingers, and I looked around, realizing we'd garnered more than our fair share of attention.

"Guys," I said. "Maybe we need to move."

"What we need is for you and Tweedledum to act like adults," Summer snapped.

Asher's complexion was bright red. "We don't need to hear whatever bullshit That Woman has to say."

"But what if—"

"*Enough!*" I roared, quieting them both. "Both of you need to calm down. You know what? It doesn't matter what Kennedy has to say. Nothing would change the fact that she broke my heart so she could stay in Hollywood and become a goddamn icon. The type of person who does that isn't someone I want anything to do with."

It was the hitched breath that alerted me we weren't alone.

I turned.

Kennedy and the man she'd arrived with were standing a few yards away. She had her hand clasped to her mouth, silent tears rolling down her cheeks.

Fuck.

She'd heard everything. And based on the thunder-cloud expression of her companion—whom I now recognized as her brother, Blair—so had he. I meant what I'd said, but I'd never wanted to hurt her. Not like this, and especially not in public.

A sob burst from her chest, and she pivoted and ran. I took a few steps after her, but Blair blocked my path.

"I need to—"

"You need to leave her the fuck alone," Blair rumbled. He had a raspy voice and a build that was difficult to reconcile with the scrawny fifteen-year-old kid I remembered. Apparently he'd been a late bloomer, because this guy looked like he could crush me one-handed—and had every intention of doing so. "You have no idea what went on in Kennedy's life." His chest heaved with emotion. "She had to go through shit that nobody that age should have to deal with. You think she dumped you for the Hollywood dream?" His face twisted with distaste. "The past decade has been far from a fucking dream." He shook his head. "You don't have a clue, and I'm ashamed I ever looked up to you."

My lips parted, but I had no idea what to say. What the hell was he talking about? Kennedy had been the one to leave me. She'd ditched me in this town that was too small for her while she went on to earn millions of dollars and become a household name.

"You don't know anything about it," I told him, but I sounded as unconvincing as I felt.

Blair leaned forward, baring his teeth. "No, Liam. You're the one who doesn't know anything."

"Fucking hell." Anger surged through me. Anger at his attitude, at my best friend and sister for starting this debacle, and at myself for feeling like I couldn't make sense of a really simple situation. "If I missed something, it's because she never told me."

Blair laughed. It sounded bitter. "Maybe not. But it's not as though you made an effort to find out, did you?" He looked at me in disgust. "I thought you loved her."

"I did," I protested. "She. Dumped. Me."

He shook his head. "You don't deserve her."

Then he took off after Kennedy. I watched them go, questions seething through my mind, my stomach churning.

What the hell was going on? With just a few sentences, Blair had challenged everything I thought I knew.

What had he meant?

"Where do they get off talking to you like that?" Asher demanded, sounding confused rather than angry. He hesitated. "That was weird, right?"

"It was," Summer mused, rubbing her chin thoughtfully. "Any ideas what he was talking about?"

I shrugged. "None."

But damn, I was going to have to find out.

Chapter Twenty-Seven

LIAM

Isn't time supposed to make me miss you less? - unsent text message from Liam to Kennedy

I left Summer to smooth things over with Mum, and Asher and I headed back to the fire station.

"Seriously," Asher said as we crossed the road. "Any idea what he meant?"

"None." My tone was short, which I felt bad about, but I also couldn't erase the memory of Kennedy's tearful gaze from my mind, and if Asher and Summer hadn't been arguing like children, I might not have reacted so poorly and upset her that way. "What does it matter to you anyway? Aren't you the one who's been saying all along to keep my distance?"

"Yeah." He huffed in exasperation. "But I figured anything she said would be a useless excuse."

"Sounds like there might be more to it than that." And

I needed to know what. Especially when Blair had looked like he might genuinely want to kick my ass. But I couldn't go after her without clearing it with Parks first, considering I was due back from lunch in a couple of minutes. Technically, we weren't supposed to leave the station at all during shift, but it was only a couple of blocks to the cafe and town center, so he usually didn't mind as long as we made sure our phones were on and our gear was ready to go at a moment's notice.

"What are you going to do?"

"Find out what they're talking about." We entered the garage attached to the fire station, and Igor glanced up from where he was doing some maintenance work on the hoses. I nodded to him in greeting. "Need to get the okay from Parks to leave for a bit longer."

We parted ways in the corridor. Asher went to the staff room, and I knocked on Parks's office door. Unfortunately, after pleading my case, he refused to give the go-ahead for me to leave long enough to talk to Kennedy. Frustration simmered beneath my skin for the rest of the shift, but I understood his refusal. If anything were to go wrong, he needed me here. But that didn't make it any easier to wait out one of the most uneventful shifts of my career.

As soon as I was off the clock, I drove to Grace's place and took the path past the house to the cottages. I rapped my knuckles against the wood and stood back, waiting to see if Kennedy would let me in. But when the door opened, it wasn't Kennedy standing on the other side. It was Blair. I scanned him from head to toe, noticing the differences a decade had wrought. He'd filled out, and he looked more confident in himself than he had as a sullen teenager. Once upon a time, he'd been moody and distant, but we'd bonded over music, and I'd earned his approval. Now, it was obvious any trace of his past warm feelings toward me was long gone. He glowered, arms folded over his chest, and waited for me to speak first.

"Is Kennedy here?" I asked.

"What's it to you?" he demanded. "Didn't think you cared what she did or said because it wouldn't make a difference."

I winced, hearing my own words reflected back at me.

"It seems like we're overdue for a conversation," I said as levelly as I could. If I responded to his aggression with my own, it would only make things worse.

Blair scowled. "I'm not letting you in just so you can hurt her. She deserves better than that."

"I have no intention of hurting her," I assured him. "I just want to talk."

"You've had three weeks to talk, but you haven't been interested." He glanced over his shoulder, then lowered his voice. "As far as I can tell, nothing has changed, so why now?"

I shifted uncomfortably. "I thought I had all of the information, but I'm starting to think maybe I don't."

"Because that's what I told you," he snapped. "If I hadn't said anything, would you ever have listened to her on your own?"

Shame burned in my gut. I couldn't say yes because I wasn't sure. I liked to think I would have eventually given her a chance to say her piece, considering how we'd been slowly getting more comfortable with each other again, but I couldn't say for certain.

"Please." I appealed to Blair. "Five minutes is all I'm asking for."

"What's going on here?"

We both turned at the question spoken in Kennedy's accented tone from behind Blair.

"Liam is here," Blair told her. "I'm getting rid of him."

He gave me a look that threatened bodily harm if I didn't do as he said and leave.

A hand appeared on Blair's arm, then Kennedy moved him aside and stepped forward.

"What do you want?" Her voice was rougher than usual, and the puffiness of her eyes showed she'd been crying. My hands twitched, aching to comfort her.

"Five minutes of your time," I replied.

She considered me for a moment, head cocked. "Okay."

"*Okay*?" Blair stared at her as if she was crazy. "But he—"

She clapped her hand over his mouth. "Shush."

He glared mutinously.

"I'm not fragile," she said to her brother. "I appreciate you looking out for me, but I can make my own decisions. What I need now is for you to go back to your cottage. Spending five minutes with Liam won't break me."

Blair narrowed his eyes at me, then turned back to Kennedy, his expression softening. "All right. But I'll be back over here in fifteen minutes to check on you."

She nodded, clearly willing to accept that. I supposed that meant I'd better make sure we covered all the important stuff within fifteen minutes, or I had no doubt Blair would be kicking me out with a smile on his face.

He traipsed past me and into the cottage next door. Kennedy waited until he'd closed the door before going back into her own place and gesturing for me to follow. She settled on the sofa. I took the armchair, afraid that if I was too close to her, logic might fly out the window.

"So," she said, studying me warily. "You've got five minutes."

Suddenly, my tongue was tied. I didn't know where to start or how to find out what I somehow knew I needed to know.

"I, uh." I thought back over the events of the day. Caught her bloodshot eyes. "I'm sorry for upsetting you earlier. I didn't mean to say what I did—especially not to yell it in the street. Ash and Summer were arguing, and I just wanted them to stop."

She sighed. "It's fine. Honestly, I think it was the wakeup call I needed."

My muscles clenched. Perhaps it was ridiculous, but hearing how defeated she sounded made me feel sick. I didn't want her to give up. I didn't want her to let me go.

"What did Blair mean when he said I didn't know the whole story?" I asked, hating the wobble in my voice.

Kennedy rolled her eyes. "You've made it obvious you aren't interested in what I have to say. As you said earlier, it won't make a difference, so why bother?"

Her expression was distant. Even seeing her pain had been better than the mask she was pulling on now. I could sense her slipping away emotionally, and somehow, I knew that if I didn't stop it, it really would be too late.

"Please." I lurched out of the chair and across the room, dropping onto the sofa beside her and taking her hand. "Please tell me what he meant. I need to know."

Chapter Twenty-Eight

KENNEDY

HI LIAM,

I've written a hundred different emails explaining what happened, and I deleted every one of them. I can tell you the facts, but there's nothing I can do to make you understand how scared and alone I felt when I found out my parents had died and I was suddenly guardian to four children. It was as if I'd been treading water for days, and at any moment I might sink beneath the surface. I didn't want to drag you into the deep end with me.

Love,
K xx

I FELT AS THOUGH EVERY ONE OF MY NERVES HAD BEEN rubbed raw, and now Liam wanted to smother them with salt.

I didn't need him to hammer the point home. I already got it. All of my dreams of a big reconciliation had been just that: dreams.

But then, I owed him the truth, didn't I? Even if it didn't change things, he deserved to know why I'd done what I had so he could finally see that it had nothing to do with him.

"You really want to know?" I asked. "If I start talking, you're not going to leave halfway through?" Because I wasn't sure I could handle that.

"I'll stay until you're finished," he confirmed.

"Okay." I stood and went to the kitchen where I filled a glass with water, then another. One for myself and one for him. I passed him the extra and sat down, cradling my glass between my palms. My mouth was dry, so I took a sip. "When I returned to Los Angeles, I had every intention of coming back here as planned. I'd almost finished organizing everything." His eyebrows drew together, and I could see he wanted to say something, but I held up a hand, hoping he'd give me time to get through the full story. "But then Mom and Malcolm were in a car accident. They died."

"What?" His face twisted in a combination of shock and disbelief. "You mean, while you were getting ready to come back?"

"Yeah."

"You never mentioned it." He looked like I'd slapped him. "I'd have remembered that."

"It happened while I was sorting out the last few things." I sipped the water again, more for something to do than because I was thirsty.

"Is that why you fell off the radar for so long before you ended our relationship?"

I nodded. "I didn't know what to say, or how to tell you. And everything was crazy. I had to arrange their funerals, sort out the will. Then there were the kids to consider. They were old enough to understand but young enough that they'd never imagined they might have to live without their parents."

He shook his head. "I wish I'd known." His hands clenched at his sides. "I wish I could have been there for you. That must have been hard on you, especially after you'd already lost your dad."

"It wasn't easy." I set my drink on the floor and wedged my hands beneath my thighs. They were trembling badly, and I'd prefer he not see that. "Mom and Malcolm had been intending to update their wills, but they hadn't gotten around to it." I drew in a slow breath and allowed it to flow out between my lips. "We didn't have any close relatives, so I became their legal guardian."

"You what?" He blinked rapidly, clearly taken aback.

"If I didn't take them, they'd have either gone to a distant relative they'd never met or into the foster care system. I didn't want that for them. Things would be difficult enough without having to leave home, their school, and live in a situation I couldn't be sure was safe. So I stepped up."

A muscle ticked in Liam's jaw. He looked much like I'd felt at the time. Confused, sad, and a little angry. "So, you're telling me that you became the legal guardian of your siblings?"

"I did."

Emotion flashed in his midnight blue eyes. "When did you find that out?"

"Pretty soon after their deaths. But we finalized the arrangements the day I broke up with you."

He pressed his lips together. I couldn't read him. Had no idea what was going on in his head. "I could have helped you. I would have flown over to be there for you."

A rock sank to the bottom of my stomach. "Yeah, you could have. But I'd already decided I couldn't move them halfway around the world after what they'd been through. I knew how you felt about L.A. and that you never wanted to leave Destiny Falls. My plans were already in shreds, and I didn't want to ruin your life by asking you to come be with me." I chewed my lip. "I knew you might feel obligated, and then you'd be miserable and resent me." Tears burned in my eyes. I blinked them back. "I couldn't be selfish like that."

I pulled one of my hands out from beneath my thighs and swiped my hair away from my face. "In hindsight, I wish I'd handled things differently, but I was still a teenager, and I was suddenly in charge of four children. I did the best I could at the time, and I'm sorry for hurting you. I've always regretted that. I went about things wrong, and I've been sorry for it ever since."

When I stopped talking, Liam seemed to be processing my words. I stayed quiet, even if it was killing me not to know what he was thinking. Eventually, he seemed to arrive at a conclusion.

"I can't imagine how lost and alone you must have felt," he said slowly and carefully. "But you shouldn't have made the decision for me. You should have given me the opportunity to decide for myself what I wanted to do. If I'd gone over there to be with you and ended up unhappy, that would have been on my shoulders, not yours."

He wasn't wrong.

"I'm sorry," I repeated. "I meant well. I thought I was saving you from a life you wouldn't want, and if I'm completely honest, I was also saving myself the heartbreak I'd have experienced if you decided I wasn't worth it."

"I get it." He sounded resigned but not angry. "You were young and overwhelmed, and couldn't see a way out."

"Yes," I said, relieved he'd managed to sum up so many mixed emotions with one sentence. "I took the route I thought would be best for you and least complicated for me, but I was wrong."

His hand landed on my knee, the warmth of his palm soaking through the fabric and defrosting my cold soul. I felt like I'd been numb for so long, and tingles of sensation were finally returning.

"This was years ago. What made you come back?"

"A friend of mine asked when I was last happy, and it got me thinking." I was quiet for a moment, trying to determine how best to express the fact that while I'd had moments of happiness—some of which I'd never give up for anything—I hadn't been content with myself since I'd been in Destiny Falls. "The last time I could remember being completely at peace, without worries dragging me down and without feeling like I had to play a part for someone else's benefit, was when I was here. With you. So I came back."

I was almost afraid to look at him. I'd opened up so much, and I wasn't sure how he'd react. He'd been good so far, but I wasn't used to making myself so vulnerable.

"Wow. That's… wow." He glanced at me. "You've had a crazy eleven years."

"Yeah."

"I'm amazed you seem to have come through every-thing so well." He eyed me curiously. "So, how did the fame happen? I always figured that was part of the reason you stayed in L.A. That you must have secretly had dreams of making it in Hollywood but had never shared with me because you knew I wouldn't have approved."

I snorted. "Hardly. One of Malcolm's former clients needed a last minute fill-in for a minor role in a movie he was filming. It wasn't the kind of thing I'd ever thought of doing, but it paid well, and I was beginning to worry about how quickly we were going through my parent's life insur-ance payout. It was nice to have the chance to earn some money of my own. It all spiraled from there, and somehow, I ended up going to fancy parties, wearing designer clothes, and starring in big films without ever having consciously made the decision to be an actress. Before I knew it, I'd set aside college funds for the kids, and I figured I may as well go with the flow, since everything seemed to be working out well enough."

He shook his head. "It's hard to imagine that happening when you always hear how difficult it is to have a career in the industry."

I grimaced. Yeah, I knew how privileged I'd been, and that some people had it much harder. "It really is about who you know. I'm a decent actress because I spent a lot of my childhood around actors, but I became popular because I had the right connections and a reputation for being easy to work with."

"You can't say you didn't enjoy the parties and premieres though," he remarked.

I shot him a look. "There were definite upsides. I won't deny it. But I never sought them out. I went out of obligation more than anything else. Production companies like their actors to be publicly visible. But getting back to the point—the kids are all grown, they have money to set themselves up, and I don't have to play a part anymore. I can finally be myself again, and do what makes me happy."

Liam gave a half-hearted laugh. "Strange to think you could effectively retire at age thirty."

It was. I considered myself incredibly lucky to be in that position, and I wasn't going to waste it.

"I feel so stupid for not seeing that there was more going on." He squeezed my knee gently. "My girlfriend was going through a major crisis, and I missed it. I should have flown over there regardless of what you said, but instead, I let fear and a bruised ego get the better of me.

We had something real, and I shouldn't have let it go so easily."

I pressed my lips together. The last thing I wanted was for him to beat himself up. That wouldn't solve anything. Especially not when I couldn't know how I'd have reacted if he did turn up on my doorstep in Bel Air.

"Do you think we could start fresh?" I asked, feeling the full force of more than a decade of longing build within me.

He met my eyes. Confusion roiled in the depths of his dark irises, but a lot of his bitterness seemed to have dissipated. "I'd like that." He took a breath and turned to face me completely. "Will you get coffee with me before my shift tomorrow? It can be our official new beginning."

My lips curled into a faint smile, and I let myself feel a little hopeful. "It's a date."

Chapter Twenty-Nine

LIAM

I was wrong about so many things, and now I'm not sure where to go from here. - unsent text message from Liam to Kennedy

I wasn't sure of the proper etiquette for getting coffee with an ex who I'd spent years hating in a way that was apparently unfounded, and whom I maybe wanted to date again. *Maybe.* I wasn't committing to that. With how mixed my feelings were, I wasn't even sure I should have suggested coffee, but if I'd allowed a few more days to pass, we'd have been caught up in the New Year's Eve rush, and I wouldn't have had a free second. So while this wasn't ideal, it was the best of the options available.

I pulled up outside Taste of Destiny, glancing around to see if Kennedy's Outback was already parked nearby. When I didn't see anything, I locked my Ute and headed in. This early in the day, the morning rush hadn't yet begun, so I spotted Kennedy in the corner as soon as I entered. She was sitting on her own, reading the newspaper with a coffee at her elbow. I greeted Eden with a nod and made my way over to join Kennedy.

She looked up, and her features creased into a smile that looked as uncertain and hesitant as mine. "Hi."

Butterflies fluttered in my stomach. I grimaced at the realization this felt like a first date.

"Hello." I sank into the chair opposite her and waited while she closed the newspaper and set it aside. I scanned her face for evidence she'd spent more time crying and was pleased to see she looked back to normal. "How are you today?"

"I'm good. And you?"

"Good too." I interlaced my fingers to stop myself from fidgeting. Damn, this was awkward. I searched around for something to talk about. "So, how long has Blair been in town?"

She gave me a look. "He just arrived yesterday."

Ah. Yeah. Of course he had. Because on the weekend, he hadn't been around while I'd installed the extra security, and he sure as hell hadn't been there on Christmas.

"Was it a planned visit?"

"No. He's worried about me."

I nodded. As he should be. I'd been worried even when I'd told myself I should hate her guts.

"One of his friends should be arriving soon," she added. "Tyler. Apparently he agreed to join Blair in New Zealand, but wanted to drop by Australia to visit some friends first."

"Huh." My chest burned at the thought that Blair had felt the need to call in reinforcements. It was good that he was looking out for her, but no other guy could protect her the way he and I would. "Have you met Tyler before?"

"Of course." Her smile was a little too fond for my liking. "He and Blair have been close for quite a few years, so we've spent a lot of time together. I haven't seen much of him recently though."

"Oh?" Why did that please me more than it should? I shouldn't be getting possessive over a woman I'd done my best to leave in the past.

"Good morning." Eden stopped beside our table, wearing an overly bright smile. "Would you like to order anything?"

I glanced at Kennedy, who nodded.

"Yes, please," I said. "I'll get a breakfast bagel and a cappuccino with cinnamon. What would you like, Kenz?"

"Waffles with chocolate syrup and whipped cream on the side, please. Another trim latte too. Thanks, Eden."

Eden grinned, her nerves seeming to fade. "Good choice." She hesitated, then added, "I'm glad you two are talking."

Fortunately, she left before either of us had to respond. I looked around, suddenly realizing that a few other people had arrived, and many of them were watching us with interest.

"So…." I cleared my throat. "Apart from the fact you have an acting career, I know nothing about your life over the last eleven years. You've probably realized that Destiny Falls boycotted all things Kennedy Cox, so I haven't even heard the usual celebrity gossip. You raised your siblings?"

Kennedy smiled. "Blair, not so much. He was only a little younger than me. But Mina, Joel, and Jamie, yes. I was their primary caregiver through middle school and high school. Now Mina is at Stanford studying criminal law, and Jamie and Joel are living their best lives at the Kappa Lambda Mu frat house at U.C."

I raised an eyebrow. I remembered the twins being high-energy and not particularly academic. "Those little terrors are at university?"

She laughed. "It continues to shock me each time they

get a passing grade. Fortunately, they're aiming for the NHL. I'm hoping they get scooped up sooner rather than later because I'm not sure they'll make it to senior year. They're great kids. They have massive hearts, and I'm proud, but working in a corporate setting wouldn't be right for them. They need to be constantly challenged and on the move."

The warm way she spoke about them stoked a fire deep within me. I'd forgotten how big her capacity for love was and how wonderful it was to be the recipient of that love. She clearly adored her siblings. I'd thought I might feel bitter toward them, since she'd effectively chosen them over me—even if I knew that way of thinking wasn't entirely rational—but I was surprised to discover I didn't. I was glad things had turned out well for them. The family had been through a lot and deserved good fortune.

"And Blair?" I asked. "What's he do?"

"He's a musician." Her expression was fond, her tone soft. Blair had held a special place in her heart, and it seemed he still did. "He's incredibly talented. His band could already have a contract with a recording studio if he'd take advantage of Malcolm's or my connections, but he's determined to do it on his own."

"I understand that." I had a lot of respect for people who didn't want a handout or shortcut. Not that I thought poorly of Kennedy for the success she'd had because of her own contacts. "He's grown up a lot."

"Yeah." She sounded wistful. "But he's still overprotective of me."

"That's not a bad thing. From what I can see, you need a little protection."

Her smile faltered. "Yeah. Maybe. But hopefully all I'm dealing with is an overzealous fan who somehow got Grace's address." Based on the worry etched into her forehead, she didn't believe that, and neither did I. "What about your siblings?" she asked, deftly switching the focus of the conversation. "Nate is the local sergeant. Max is a doctor. I assume Summer is working at the veterinarian clinic because she was wearing one of their shirts yesterday. What about the others?"

"Summer is the primary small animal vet at the clinic," I told her. "They have another vet who works with livestock and wildlife. Connor is a park ranger. Toby works as a ski instructor at the resort and picks up a few odd jobs to cover the rest of the year."

"Nice." She nodded to herself. "Summer is young to be a primary vet. Your parents must be proud."

"They are." Of course, with a doctor, a cop, and a veterinarian in the family, they had a lot to be proud of.

"Park ranger suits Connor. He always did like his own space. Being a ski instructor sounds perfect for Toby too, if he's the same as I remember. It means he can have fun all day and flirt with any pretty girls staying at the resort."

I grinned. "Spot-on."

Our breakfast arrived, and we fell silent for a few minutes while we ate.

"This is amazing." Kennedy moaned, and my body perked up in response, recalling how fantastic it felt to be buried inside her while she made that same noise. "They have the best food here."

"It's pretty good." I sounded breathless. Shit. I swallowed a mouthful of coffee and told myself to calm the fuck down. Back to the sibling talk. No way could that be sexy. "Are any of your siblings partnered off?"

"No." She licked her lips, missing a fleck of cream above her cupid's bow. "The twins are probably working their way through the freshman population at U.C., but they never mention it to me. Mina is married to her study. Blair dates, but he's not seeing anyone at the moment. Yours?"

"Nah. Nate was married briefly, but it didn't work out. He's got a beautiful daughter though."

"Nate has a kid?" For some reason, that seemed to surprise her.

"Yep. Her name is Tess. She loves to read."

Kennedy's mouth twitched. "Must take after her mom."

"You'd think so, but Maddy isn't much of a reader either. Not sure where Tess got her love of books from. Grace, maybe."

"Tess is the only grandchild?"

I nodded. "Max is chronically single. Same with Connor, but I don't think he cares, whereas Max would like to be with someone if he could find the right person. Summer dates occasionally, and Toby always has a new flavor of the month."

She looked like she might ask more. Perhaps she wanted to know if there had been anyone special for me. But she didn't, and I swallowed my disappointment. She was right to be cautious. We were taking baby steps. It wouldn't do to jump into things before we'd had time to work out where we each stood with each other now.

We talked for a while longer. But when breakfast ended and Eden cleared our plates away, I didn't want to say goodbye. On impulse, I reached across the table and took her hand.

"I'm going hiking on Sunday," I said. "Would you like to come with me?"

Kennedy's mouth curled into a shy smile. "I would."

"Good. I'll see you then." God help me if I wasn't enchanted with her all over again.

Chapter Thirty

KENNEDY

Hi Liam,

This is going to be the last email I write to you. I don't think it's healthy to hold on the way I have been. I've used my imaginary letters to you as an outlet for too long. Years have passed. I'm a different person, and my life looks nothing like it used to. You can probably say the same. It's time for me to accept the way things are.

I'm going to keep these private communications in case I ever want to look back. This has been cathartic. Like a journal, almost. I like to tell myself that maybe one day I'll see you again, and I'll share everything I've written to you, but I doubt that will happen.

So, for now,

Goodbye.

K xx

WHEN I GOT BACK TO THE COTTAGES, THE DOOR TO THE other one was open, and Blair and Tyler bounded out. Tyler grinned, and it lit his square-jawed face.

"Hi, Kennedy," he said. "It's good to see you."

Blair's friend was wearing jeans that would probably cost a month's rent for most people, and a designer T-shirt. With tousled blond hair and deep brown eyes, he had the kind of easy good looks that always attracted attention. I liked him, but I'd never been interested in him romantically, and I was glad he had a girlfriend now and seemed to have gotten over the crush he used to have on me.

"Hey, Ty." I gave him a quick hug. "You really didn't have to come all this way."

He released me and stepped back. "When Blair explained what was happening, and the fact that he was worried for your safety, I knew I needed to be here at least for a while to see you with my own eyes and make sure you're okay. Plus—" A dimple popped in his cheek. "—I've always wanted to visit New Zealand, so it didn't take much convincing."

I laughed. "Well, there's plenty to see in this area of the country. Perhaps you and Blair can do a bit of a tour while you're here."

"I'd like that." He smiled. "I already know I like Destiny Falls. It feels like such a welcoming community."

"Mm," I replied noncommittally. "Welcoming" wasn't exactly how it had felt recently, but I knew I had some ground to make up.

"How did your meeting with Liam go?" Blair asked.

My heart lightened. "It went well. We talked. Had breakfast together and caught up."

"Good." He still looked wary. "So, what now?"

A smile crept over my face. "We're going hiking on the weekend."

"Cool." He glanced at Tyler. "We were just talking about heading up to see the falls now. Do you want to come?"

"No, thanks." I still hadn't been there since that last

time with Liam, and I didn't want to return unless it was with him. "I might see if Grace is home. I told her I'd explain things once I'd talked to Liam, and I've talked to Liam, so I think it's about time she gets the full story."

"Fair enough."

"I'll see you guys later though. Have fun."

"You too," Blair said as I performed an about-face and went to the main house.

I knocked and waited a few moments for Grace to answer. When she did, she was wearing a soft sweater over yoga pants, and her cheeks were flushed.

"Do you have a few minutes?" I asked. "Or are you in the middle of something?"

"Oh, uh." She looked caught off guard by the question. "I have time. I've been writing, but I can get back to it when we're done." She stepped away from the door. "Come in. Would you like a drink?"

"No, thanks. I just had coffee and breakfast with Liam. I'm plenty caffeinated."

Her eyes widened. "Breakfast with Liam?"

She led me into the private part of the house, and I celebrated at the realization that she considered me more than just a guest.

"Yeah, we had a talk yesterday and cleared up a few things from the past, so now I'd like to do the same with you, if that's okay."

"Of course."

We sat on her sofa, and she reached over and squeezed my hand. The gentle reassurance was all I needed to start talking. I spilled the whole story in a stream of verbal diarrhea, and she listened patiently, her expression betraying surprise at certain points but otherwise giving little away. When I was done, she wrapped an arm around me.

"I'm sorry for your loss." She held me close, not letting go. "I may not know what it's like to be orphaned and have such responsibility dumped on my shoulders at a young age, but I do know how it feels to not have parents around. Mine…. Well, let's just say we have some fundamental disagreements and leave it at that." She drew back, but kept a hold of my shoulders. "You should be proud of yourself. You might not have gone about things the way you wish you had, but you did something that a lot of people wouldn't be able to, and it sounds like you raised your siblings to be healthy, well-adjusted adults. That's a pretty amazing accomplishment."

Her praise warmed my insides. "Thanks, Grace." I let out a deep breath, grateful to finally release the secret I'd been carrying around. It felt good to be honest. "I really missed you when I left."

She kissed my cheek. "I missed you too, and like I said when you got here, I always thought there was more to the story than you let on. I'm just sorry I wasn't there to offer my support when you needed it."

"Think we can be friends again?" I asked, knowing how middle-school I sounded but not able to bring myself to care.

"Yeah." She flashed a smile. "I want that."

Chapter Thirty-One

KENNEDY

Destiny Peak Ski Resort hosted an annual New Year's Eve party. Most of the locals stayed away because it was targeted at tourists, but Blair and Tyler wanted to go and refused to leave me alone at the cottage. So here I was, decked out in the type of cocktail dress I hadn't worn for weeks and silently cursing the fact I'd let my natural hair color grow out rather than speeding up the process with a trip to the salon. I was getting a lot of sideways glances from wealthy women who'd never be seen dead with hair in the state mine was. Things changed as soon as they recognized me though. I'd never get over the hypocrisy of some people.

I wandered to the window and looked out. The restaurant floor had been cleared of tables with the exception of a few bar leaners, and waitstaff circulated with platters of canapes. I was glad I'd eaten before we came because while the food was delicious—as should be expected with

Tabitha in charge—it would never be considered a meal on its own.

"Everything okay?" Blair asked, appearing at my side. He'd barely let me out of his sight since we'd arrived except to refill our drinks.

"Yeah. You don't need to worry." I turned away from the darkness outside. Midnight was still an hour away, but people had already settled into their positions for the night. Some lingered by the bar, others were on the makeshift dance floor, while others stood around the fringes and made conversation. Blair was hovering on the edge of the action with me, but I'd seen him cast longing glances at the dance floor. He wanted to be out there. He just didn't want to abandon me. "You should go dance with that cute blonde girl who was flirting with you earlier," I suggested. "Or that guy over there with the glasses. He's been checking you out."

Blair blushed and sneaked a look at the bespectacled twenty-something who was adorable in a nerdy sort of way. A pair of men approached us, their apprehensive expressions suggesting they'd been working up the courage for quite some time. I opened my mouth to greet them, but Blair wrapped an arm around my waist and swept me away.

"What was that about?" I asked when he released me.

"How do we know one of them wasn't your stalker?" he said, narrowing his eyes as he looked back over his shoulder.

"We don't." Even the thought sent a shiver up my spine. "But you were the one who insisted I come here. You can't stand guard over me all night. Go have fun."

"I wasn't thinking clearly earlier," he grumbled, his face lighting as Tyler appeared in front of us and handed me a glass of white wine and Blair a shot of something brown. They clinked their glasses and tossed the drinks back. I cringed. I could only imagine the burn. Since I'd inherited four children at age nineteen, I hadn't gone through a wild phase, but I honestly didn't see the appeal. Give me a glass of wine and a good book over a boozy party any day.

"I've been trying to get Blair to dance," I said to Tyler.

"Go on, man," Tyler encouraged, clapping him on the shoulder. "I'll keep Kennedy company."

Great.

I rolled my eyes. They meant well, but I didn't need a pair of man-children trying to manage my life.

"You sure?" Blair asked, obviously tempted.

"Go." I gave him a little push. "Let loose, but not too much because I don't want to be trying to get your drunk ass home."

He grinned and saluted, then strode in the direction of the girl he'd been flirting with earlier.

One down.

"Want to dance?" Tyler asked, offering me a hand. He sounded reluctant, so I shook my head. The last thing I needed was to make him feel uncomfortable.

"No, thanks. I don't feel like it."

"Cool." His tone was relieved. "We can talk instead." He laid a hand on my arm and gestured to the balcony. "Or we could go out and look at the stars, if you'd prefer."

"Actually, I need to go to the bathroom." I shuffled away a few steps, and his hand dropped from me. "I'll be back soon."

Or not, if I could help it.

I made a beeline for the ladies' room. I didn't really need to use the facilities, but it would give me a chance to clear my head. I ducked inside and looked in the mirror, shock hitting me all over again at the sight of my reflection. The carefully made-up face staring back at me had become a stranger. I'd grown used to seeing all the slight imperfections that were currently hidden beneath a layer of foundation, blush, highlighter, and a dozen other things. With my makeup done and my hair pinned back, I looked like I used to—except for the darker regrowth and the fact my cheeks weren't quite as hollow.

I grabbed one of the cloths kept for drying hands—no paper towels here—and wet it, then dabbed the base of my throat, needing to cool down.

"You can do this," I said to my reflection. "Makeup doesn't change who you are. You're not playing a role. Just be you."

The bathroom door opened, and I spared a smile for the woman who stumbled in, then tossed aside my cloth and left. I headed directly for the kitchen, hoping to catch Tabitha, but a man stepped into my path.

I stopped an instant before running into him. "Whoa."

He grabbed my arms to steady me. "Hey, Kennedy."

I resisted the urge to groan.

"Hi, Aiden." I glanced past him, wondering if I'd be able to make a quick escape.

"I haven't seen you in a few days," he said. "And you didn't look so great last time we spoke. Is everything all right?"

"Fine." My tone was brusque, and he frowned. "Sorry." I felt a pang of guilt. I shouldn't be taking my frustration out on anyone else. "I'm just not in the mood for a party."

"Ah." Understanding spread over his face. "Still haven't kicked whatever had you down? Do you have a ride home?"

"I'm the designated driver for my brother and his friend, so I can't exactly bail." Although I was beginning to think I shouldn't have come in the first place. I just hadn't wanted to cause a fuss and have them cancel their plans.

"Hmm." He looked thoughtful. "Listen, if you'd like, you're welcome to lie down in my room for a while. It's a private suite, so nobody will bother you, including me. I'll be out here until after midnight."

If he'd been someone else, I might have accepted, but there was something that unsettled me about Aiden. I didn't want to be alone with him because I couldn't be sure he wouldn't try something on.

"Thanks, but I think I'm going to find a quiet spot out the back."

"Want company? I wouldn't mind escaping the noise for a while."

"No, thanks." I gave him a thin smile, and this time, he got the message.

"Okay." He backed away. "But if you change your mind, the offer stands."

With a nod, I hurried to the kitchen before he had a chance to decide to follow me after all. Hopefully Tabitha needed an extra set of hands. I'd prefer to make myself useful in the kitchen than spend another moment among the party guests.

As I closed the kitchen door behind me, my phone vibrated in my clutch. I checked it, and my blood ran cold.

Private number: *Countdown to midnight, sweetheart. No kisses for us today, but soon. I promise.*

Chapter Thirty-Two

LIAM

SOMETIMES I WONDER IF YOU'VE REPLACED ME WITH ONE OF your leading men, but I can't bring myself to Google you and find out.
- Unsent message from Liam to Kennedy

AFTER TAKING SATURDAY TO RECOVER FROM A CHAOTIC New Year's Eve spent racing from one emergency call to another, I collected Kennedy on Sunday morning for our hike. She smiled as she climbed into the passenger seat, wearing shorts that showed off her gorgeous legs. A small backpack was slung over her shoulder.

"I brought a few supplies," she said, dumping the backpack on the floor. "I wasn't sure what I'd need."

"Just yourself," I told her. "And maybe some sunscreen and a bottle of water."

"Great." She beamed. "I've got those plus a first aid kit, snacks, my camera, and a change of clothes."

"Good planning. Connor would be impressed."

She sent me a shy smile. "What about you?"

Ugh, this woman did crazy things to my insides.

"I'm impressed too," I said gruffly, pulling out onto the road.

"So, where are we going?" she asked.

"There's a newish trail near the west end of town. It's only been there for a few years." I glanced at her, stunned once again by how she managed to look exactly like the girl I used to know but also completely different at the same time. "I thought it might be a good place for us to continue our fresh start."

"Is there much uphill?"

I chuckled. "Kenz, everywhere is uphill around here. You know that."

She grumbled. I tried not to think of how adorable she was. I was a thirty-year-old man, damn it, not a giddy schoolboy with a crush.

I turned onto a side road and followed it for a short while. It changed from sealed to graveled just before a farm gate.

"Are we allowed here?" she asked after I'd opened the gate to let us through and we were bouncing along the rough track on the other side.

"Yeah, but we have to leave the gates as we find them to make sure any stock grazing in the area stay safe."

We drove a little further and reached our destination. It wasn't much to look at. A stony path that climbed the side of a lightly forested hill. The view from the top of the saddle would be worth the effort though. I headed to the rear of the car and grabbed my own backpack. I pulled a cap low over my face, shielding it from the morning sun, and turned to Kennedy. She was eyeing the trail nervously, but I knew she'd enjoy herself once we got going. She just needed to remember how it felt to be in the bush.

"Shall we get started?" I asked.

"I guess so." She marched determinedly toward the trail. I followed close behind. A few hundred meters later, she paused. "My thighs are already killing me."

I winked. "Hollywood made you soft."

Her eyes narrowed. "Did not."

She continued upward, but stopped with a gasp at the first small lookout. She took her bag off and rummaged in it until she found her camera, then fussed around with the controls, aiming it at the view over Destiny Valley. Green trees and bush stretched for miles, fading into the yellower shades of tussock in the distance. I moved closer, eager to see what she was capturing on the screen.

"I'm glad you brought your camera," I said as she lined up another shot, this one with a branch from a nearby tree artfully framing the image. "Have you kept up with photography?"

"I wish." She lowered the camera and kept it out while she zipped her bag and slung it over her shoulder. "Unfortunately, I didn't have time to, and once I started acting, the shine wore off. Being in front of a camera all the time is exhausting. But I'm getting back into it now."

"I'm glad." There was a twinge in my heart at the knowledge she'd had to give up something she'd enjoyed so much, but I suspected it was only one of many things she'd sacrificed for the sake of her family.

We continued walking, stopping every now and then for Kennedy to take photographs. When we reached a small waterfall beside the trail, she insisted I stand beside it and pose for her. She leaned back, her forehead furrowed as she tried to find the best angle. I heard the scrape of rock, and then one of her legs slipped out from under her. I lunged forward, catching her around the waist. The air whooshed from her lungs, and she gripped my upper arm, staring at me with wide eyes, her camera still clutched in her other hand.

"Whew, that was close," she breathed.

My grip tightened on her waist. I should let her go. I knew that. But her slender curves were pressed against me, and holding her felt so right. My heart thudded loudly, drowning out everything else. Her eyes locked on mine and darkened with heat. She swallowed, then her body melted against me, her lips parted, and we were kissing. It was soft, chaste, and over almost as soon as it began, but my mind could scarcely comprehend that it had happened. After all this time, I'd kissed Kennedy Carter, and it had been everything I remembered.

"Thanks for catching me," she whispered.

"Oh." I straightened, helping her right herself. My cheeks blazed with heat, and I was sure they must be red. "No problem."

"I think I've got enough photos for now." She switched her camera off.

Apparently we were going to pretend the kiss hadn't happened. I shook off my disappointment. I could live with that. For now.

Chapter Thirty-Three

KENNEDY

I couldn't stop smiling. The hike to the saddle had taken most of the day, but if my muscles were rebelling, I couldn't tell. I was too busy floating on air. The brief kiss I'd shared with Liam had filled me with a sense of hope I hadn't experienced in too long. It made me think there was a chance we could find our way back to each other. As we returned to the start of the trail, I watched his sexy back as he strode ahead of me. Shoulders broad, butt definitely worth ogling. Mm.

Being with him was exactly what I needed. I'd been in a funk yesterday after receiving that New Year's Eve text. I'd initially hoped that Nate would be able to run some kind of trace on the number even though it displayed as private—but apparently that was only something that happened on television shows, unless the police had either a full phone number or could run an active trace with a bunch of very expensive equipment during an ongoing call. When I'd showed Nate, he'd had to gently break the news that there was nothing they could do with it. He'd pointed out that the way the message was phrased, coupled with the fact the sender was hidden, meant we couldn't be sure they were even in the country. It could be someone from back home. But then, it concerned me that someone had my phone number to begin with. It wasn't listed. In fact, it was very, very private.

But I wasn't thinking of that today. I was thinking of Liam's gorgeous blue eyes, his cautious smiles—which were harder to earn than they used to be and more valuable because of it—and the future we might be able to build together. I imagined fair-haired babies with faded denim eyes. A cute house with none of the pomp of my place in Bel Air, and maybe a dog. I'd always wanted a pet, but with the kids around and work sending me all over the country, it hadn't seemed prudent. Now, if I wanted a dog, there was nothing stopping me. I smiled to myself. Perhaps I'd adopt a rescue. I'd heard a newcomer might be opening a shelter on the outskirts of town. I could be their first customer.

I laughed out loud. I was getting ahead of myself. I wasn't even sure if this was a date, although it felt like one.

"What's so funny?" Liam asked, looking back over his shoulder.

"Nothing." My cheeks heated. "Just thinking how lucky I am to be here and how excited I am about finally being able to live the life I want."

"Those sound like good thoughts." He smiled and kept walking. "So, no regrets coming back to Destiny Falls?"

"Absolutely not." Up ahead, the trees parted, and I could see the clearing where we'd parked. "Hey, Liam?"

"Yeah?"

"Would you like to come to my place for dinner? I promise I'm better at cooking than I used to be."

He chuckled, and the sound warmed all of the hidden

recesses of my soul. "You couldn't have gotten much worse, but yeah, I'd like that."

"Great." I was so pleased, I didn't even grump at him about the potshot at my cooking skills.

The drive home seemed to take less time than it had to go in the opposite direction—perhaps because I was trying to decide what to cook for Liam. While I was much better than I used to be, I was also far from perfect, so it was best to take anything fancy or time consuming off the table. I tried to recall what was in the cupboards at the cottage. By the time we arrived, I'd thought up a menu.

"Come on in," I said, grateful I'd done a quick cleanup before leaving that morning. I was generally pretty tidy, but Blair and Tyler had spent much of yesterday in my living area and still hadn't got the hang of leaving rooms as they'd found them. I glanced at the other cottage, relieved to see that the windows were dark. The boys must be out somewhere. Hopefully they wouldn't turn up and give me a hard time about inviting Liam back after our hike.

"You can sit over there while I cook," I told him, waving toward the sofa.

"Nuh-uh." He rubbed his palms together. "I'm not sitting around while you do all the work. Just tell me how I can help."

"If you're sure." I wasn't going to turn down assistance. I went to the fridge and pulled out a carton of baby tomatoes. "Chop these."

"Yes, chef." His wink made my tummy flip.

While he cut the tomatoes, I boiled water on the stove and measured out a portion of pasta. I added the pasta to the water and retrieved the container of pesto sauce from the fridge along with a bag of mozzarella chunks.

"What now?" Liam asked, finishing with the tomatoes.

"Can you do the same with the olives?" I handed him a jar. "I'm going to grill a few strips of capsicum."

We worked well together over the next fifteen minutes, and when we were done, we had a Greek-style pasta salad. I served the meal onto two plates and packed the rest away for tomorrow. We sat side by side on the sofa while we ate.

"This is really good," Liam said, and the comment filled me with pride. I'd had to learn to cook so I could feed the family, but there was still a certain buzz I got from someone enjoying food I'd made—or, in this case, food we'd made together. It had come out well.

"Thanks. Have you told your family about my parents?"

His fork clattered against the porcelain. Apparently the question had taken him by surprise. "I've told Mum, so I assume Dad knows as well. Asher too, since we see each other every day. I haven't mentioned it to anyone else, but it's possible they all know by now. Mum is the worst gossip in town. I hope that's okay. We never discussed whether it was private."

"You can tell anyone you like." Maybe it would stop them hating me so much. "I told Grace, so there's a good chance she said something to Nate."

"Yeah, those two share everything."

I pursed my lips. In my opinion, there were a few things they hadn't shared. I could have sworn Grace had feelings for Nate, but that was none of my business, so I kept my mouth shut.

"I'm sorry I was such an asshole when you first arrived in town," he said after a moment of quiet. "It can't have been easy for you to come back, and now that I know what happened to your parents… I feel terrible about how I reacted."

"Don't." I smiled so he'd know I meant it. "I hurt you. Whatever my reasons were, that fact doesn't change. I just hope the past won't get in the way of the future."

Liam put his plate on the coffee table and reached over

to take my hand. "It won't. We have a lot to work through, I can't deny that, but I don't intend to lose you again."

I squeezed his hand, the back of my throat tightening with emotion. "Neither do I."

I set my plate aside and scooted closer. He draped his arm around my shoulders, and I rested my cheek on his chest. I loved the scent of him. Fresh mountain air, a little sweat, and a delicious undertone that was all Liam. I closed my eyes and let the comfort of being near him wrap around me. It was on the tip of my tongue to invite him to stay the night. I didn't want to say goodbye. But our relationship was starting from scratch. It wouldn't be wise to run too fast into something. We needed to learn to walk again first.

Chapter Thirty-Four

KENNEDY

On Monday morning, I rose early and walked the length of Centennial Street past the still-closed shops and Taste of Destiny, where people were lining up for their coffee fix. When I reached the end of the commercial part of town, I looped around the block and made my way back home. I wandered up the path, enjoying the signs of life in the garden, then stopped abruptly, stumbling to catch myself before I tripped and hit the ground.

Written across the cottage door in bright red lettering was a single word.

Whore.

My hand flew to my mouth, and I choked out a sob.

Someone must have done that while I'd been out for my walk because it sure as hell hadn't been there when I'd locked up. A chill crept over me, and I looked around, realizing they could still be here. I hadn't been gone for long. Half an hour, at most. What if they were watching me right now?

Cicadas chirped. Birds cheeped. Flowers swayed in the breeze. And all of it took on a sinister tone. I felt as though the world was closing in on me. Splotches appeared in front of my eyes, and I clutched at my throat. Somehow, I'd forgotten to breathe.

I sucked in a lungful of oxygen. Then another.

I looked around. Nobody was here. At least, no one that I could see. But I didn't trust that. I rushed to the other cottage and hammered on the door. It opened a moment later.

"Hey, whoa, whoa—what's up?" Blair asked as I fell against his chest. His arms curled around me.

"We need to call the police," I gasped. "He was here."

"He, who?" His eyes darkened. "The stalker?"

I nodded frantically. "I think so. He… I…" I tugged his hand. "I'll show you."

He let me lead him to the door, calling back over his shoulder, "Tyler! Get your ass out of bed!"

I dragged him to the other cottage's front porch and held his arm as he swore a blue streak. He reached toward the red lettering, but I snatched his hand away.

"Don't touch it. The police might be able to use it for evidence."

"Shit, sorry. I didn't think." He leaned close and inhaled. "It's spray paint. Looks like it's still wet."

"They were right here," I whispered. Right here. In Destiny Falls.

"It still could be someone paid to do it," Blair pointed out.

I nodded, but I was beginning to get the feeling that we were denying the obvious. It made more sense to acknowledge the fact that my stalker was most likely somewhere nearby.

And why hadn't the alarm gone off? Or did the ones

Liam had set up only get triggered if someone actually entered the building?

"Holy crap," Tyler said, arriving behind us, tugging a sweater over his bare torso. "Are you okay?"

"Yeah." But I wasn't. Not even close.

"You got your phone on you?" Blair asked him.

Tyler scowled. "Dude, I didn't even have a shirt on until a second ago."

"I have mine," I said, fishing it from my handbag with shaking fingers. I found the number Nate had given me and called it. When the sergeant answered, he sounded wide awake. I gave him a quick rundown, and he promised to be here as soon as he could.

"Well, that cements it," Blair said. "I'm not leaving this place until I know you're safe."

For once, I didn't argue. I couldn't imagine how frightened I'd have been if I'd discovered it without him here for support.

"Should we wake Grace?" Tyler asked.

I considered that. "Yes, she'll probably want to know what's happening. Would you mind doing it?"

"No problem." He gave me a reassuring smile. "I've got it. You just focus on the police."

Only a couple of minutes later, a police car pulled up to the curb. Blair and I waited while Nate and a uniformed officer got out. They headed up the path, wearing identical black expressions as they took in the vandal's work. I couldn't help glancing at it too. I wondered whether the culprit simply mean to hurt me, or if this was a sign they didn't like the fact Liam and I were rekindling our relationship. If the stalker considered me to be his, as he'd indicated before, then I doubted he liked having another man on the scene.

"Rough way to start the day," Nate said, coming to a stop in front of us. "You'd been out for a walk?"

I nodded. "It wasn't there when I left."

"That means they were most likely waiting for you to go," he said, resting one hand on his hip. I closed my eyes at the thought that while I'd been waking and making breakfast, someone might have been lingering nearby, waiting for the opportunity to strike.

"You're going to find them, right?" Blair demanded. "This isn't acceptable. They can't get away with it."

Nate gave a long sigh and pinched the bridge of his nose. "We'll do the best we can. At least on this occasion, they've broken the law by trespassing and vandalizing personal property, so if we do find something that makes a connection to the stalker, we can haul them into the station and rake them over the coals." He looked at me. "We probably can't charge them with any crimes against you, but Grace could press charges if she wants."

"I do," Grace said, hurrying toward us with Tyler in tow. She must have taken the time to dress, because she was wearing jeans and a blouse, but her hair was a mess. "You find him, and I'll press whatever charges I can."

"Thanks," I murmured, feeling torn between relief that we could pin a crime on the guy for once and frustration that despite the messages, videos, the weird gift, and the word that stared out at me from the place that had been my refuge, there was still nothing the police could do about me being harassed. Unless I was directly threatened or harmed, or unless they managed to find evidence of who had damaged my car, they couldn't arrest a stalker just for taking an unhealthy interest in me. It was so damned unfair.

Nate nodded toward the uniformed officer. "This is Constable Mehrtens. She's been trained to gather evidence from crime scenes. We're not able to get crime scene technicians out here, so Mehrtens will gather what she can. While she does that, why don't we head into the main house, and you can talk me through everything again?"

"Yeah, okay."

I leaned against Blair as we went inside. Grace busied herself in the kitchen, making tea and coffee. Meanwhile, Nate asked for permission to record our conversation, and I granted it. He might be a hothead when it came to his friends and family, but I trusted him to do things by the book.

While Grace served hot drinks, I recounted the whole story from start to finish. By the time I stopped talking, Grace had brought her laptop over and was replaying the video recorded by the security cameras that morning. We all watched, glued to the screen, but only a few minutes after the video showed me leaving, the image was blotted out, as if something had been used to cover the camera lens. A short time later, whatever was blocking the lens vanished, but there was no one visible in the recording. Grace rewound and played the feed at quarter speed, but we couldn't see enough for it to be useful. Whoever had spray-painted the door had been incredibly careful.

"I want a copy of this," Nate said. "With our tech, we might be able to isolate part of the perp while they're covering or uncovering the camera lens."

"Absolutely," Grace agreed, and I echoed the sentiment. Whatever he needed, he could have.

Nate turned to me, his expression solemn. "We're going to do as much as we can to find the person behind this. In the meantime, don't take any risks with your safety. It would be best if you could stay, at all times, with someone you trust." He hesitated, then added, "Have you told Liam about this latest development?"

"Not yet."

He caught my eye and held it. "You should. He'll want to know."

Strange how that statement felt like a taciturn acceptance that things had changed for the better between me and Liam.

"I'll call him when we're done here."

Chapter Thirty-Five

LIAM

Sometimes, I pick up my phone to tell you something and realize I don't even know your number anymore. - Unsent text message from Liam to Kennedy

I sauntered into work, feeling like everything was sunny-side up on Monday morning. I'd spent an awesome day with Kennedy, and if I hadn't been reading things wrong, I think she'd been tempted to invite me to stay for longer last night.

In the staff room, I unpacked my gear and went to the kitchen to start coffee brewing. That done, I flopped onto the sofa.

"You look pretty pleased with yourself," Asher said, joining me.

I grinned like a goof. "I had a really good weekend."

"Must be nice," he grumbled. "What did you get up to?"

"Went hiking with Kennedy." I took in his morose expression and frowned. "What's wrong with you?"

He sighed. "My folks have been talking to some friends of theirs whose son recently got engaged and they were on at me all Sunday to find a nice girl and settle down." He jabbed a finger in the air. "I already know every girl our age in Destiny Falls, and I've dated half of them. If I haven't found the one yet, I guess I'll just have to double down on flirting with the tourists who come through. Maybe one of them will fancy moving to the middle of nowhere to live with a sexy paramedic."

I laughed. I knew all about that well-intentioned parental pressure. "Can't help you there."

My phone buzzed. A quick check of the screen showed Kennedy was calling.

"Hi, beautiful," I said, getting to my feet and putting some distance between Asher and me because I didn't trust him not to eavesdrop. "Don't tell me you miss me already."

Her breath hitched. The silence became awkward. Damn.

"Um, I wish that was the only reason I was calling." Her voice was strained, instantly putting me on alert.

"What's the matter?"

"Someone spray-painted the cottage door this morning. I think it was the stalker. Nate has been here already, but I thought you might want to know. You said to call if anything happened."

My hands curled into fists. "I'm glad you let me know." Even if it made me want to beat the crap out of someone. "How are you doing? Is Blair with you?"

"I've been better." She sighed. "I've also been worse though. Blair is here and threatening to never let me out of his sight again."

My tension eased. Things may be strained between Blair and me at the moment, but I trusted him to be there for whatever she needed. "Listen, I—" A siren rang through the station, and I cursed my rotten luck. "Damn it, I have to go. It's work. Sorry."

"Of course." She sounded falsely cheerful. "I'll talk to you later. Stay safe."

"You too." I hung up, still cursing. Damn. Mornings were almost always quiet. Why did today have to be different?

———

IT WAS NINETY MINUTES BEFORE I GOT BACK TO THE FIRE station and was able to check my phone to see if Kennedy had sent any updates. There were no messages from her, but there was one from Nate.

Nate: *Braddock family working bee at Grace's place tonight. We're going to clean up the spray paint and check for any weak spots in the cottage's security because the asshole managed to avoid being caught on camera.*

I sent a quick reply.

Liam: *Thanks for organizing. I'll be there as soon as my shift ends.*

I pocketed my phone and returned to duty.

The rest of the shift seemed to drag. Whether it was because of my impatience to finish, or just because it was a slow day, I didn't know, but by the time my twelve hours were done and I clocked out, every instinct I had was screaming at me to get to Kennedy and make sure she was all right.

I drove straight to Grace's place, noting a number of Braddock family vehicles parked along the frontage, and headed up the path to the cottages. The left one stood empty, the door open, but the right one, where Kennedy was staying, was a hive of activity. The door looked to have been freshly painted, and Grace was sitting on the top stair, clad in paint-flecked overalls. Nate and Toby were messing with the camera I'd installed on the front porch. I raised a hand to greet them as I approached.

"Hey, bro," Toby said. "Connor couldn't make it, and Dad is at work. The others are inside."

I gave him a one-armed hug and did the same with Nate, then reached down to touch Grace's shoulder. "Thanks. I appreciate it."

"No big deal." Nate's expression was dark. "It pisses me off that we haven't got the jerk locked up yet though."

"You're doing the best you can. It's not as if you have many resources."

He scowled. "Yeah. I'd like a few more, but it's hard to get manpower for a stalking case."

"It's just wrong," Grace said. "Everyone should have a right to safety and privacy."

"I know, Gracie." Nate sighed. "But some fuckers just don't understand that, especially when it comes to celebs."

"I'm going to go see Kennedy." I ducked past them and into the cottage, getting a strong whiff of paint from the door on the way. In the living room, Mum, Kennedy, and Summer were clustered on the couch. They all glanced up as I entered, and I met Kennedy's eyes. The haunted look in them made my soul ache. I went to her, pulled her to her feet, and hugged the crap out of her. My lips ghosted over her temples, and I buried my face in her hair and breathed her in. She whimpered, and a shudder wracked her body.

"I've got you," I murmured. "I'm so sorry this is happening."

"It's bullshit," she muttered against my chest.

"I know, baby."

We both stiffened. She tilted her face up toward me, a question in her eyes. I didn't take the endearment back, and we gazed at each other for a long moment before someone coughed loudly.

"Liam." Blair sounded a little friendlier than he had the other day, but not by much.

I released Kennedy and nodded at him, then forced myself to acknowledge his friend, Tyler. We'd met once before in passing, and he seemed nice enough, but I didn't like him being around Kennedy. He was a little too handsome, and he'd spent years as a part of her life. Truth be told, even though Kennedy had assured me there was nothing romantic between them, never had been, and that Tyler had a girlfriend, I was envious because the younger man knew Kennedy in ways I didn't.

"Big day?" Max asked, a smile creasing his face as he offered me a chocolate chip cookie from a platter on the coffee table. I took one. Where Max's twin was a wall of muscle with close-cropped hair and a rugged complexion from spending time outdoors, Max himself was leaner, and his features were more gentle.

"Not too bad," I replied, smoothing a hand down Kennedy's back. "How are you holding up?" I asked her.

"All right." She glanced around the room. "I can't believe everyone turned up like this," she murmured for my ears only. "Last week, they hated me, but now they're here to help."

I drew her to my side, erasing as much distance between us as I could. "Learning the truth probably helped on that front, but when it comes down to it, you're one of us, and we support each other."

Her smile was hopeful as she looked up at me. "You really mean that?"

"I do." God, I wanted to kiss her. But now wasn't the time or the place.

"Kennedy," Mum called. "You haven't tried the fudge chunk cookies yet, have you?"

I grinned. My family had rallied around Kennedy regardless of our rocky past, and I loved the hell out of them for it.

Chapter Thirty-Six

KENNEDY

A SHRILL RINGING DRAGGED ME FROM A PLEASANT DREAM where I was floating on a cloud above Destiny Falls, gazing down on the township while birds flew past in bright flashes of color. I flopped an arm out of bed and reached for my cell phone, which was on the nightstand.

"Hello?"

"Kennedy, it's Owen."

Ugh. Owen was my agent. The one I'd tried to let go when I'd flown to New Zealand, but he'd insisted I'd be back and in need of his services, so he'd refused to be dropped.

"It's five in the morning," I groaned. "I was sleeping."

"Oh." He sounded surprised. "Sorry, I hadn't thought about the time difference."

I forced myself to sit up and flick on the light. "No one ever does."

He ignored my comment. "I've been talking to Jeff."

I stiffened. "Oh?"

"It's time to come back," he said imperiously. "For your own safety, if nothing else. We can take care of you here."

Despite my annoyance, I smiled. He'd like me to see this as him protecting me, but even if there was a degree of that involved, his call was driven more by self-interest than anything else. He wanted me back in Hollywood, making movies, so he could collect his cut.

"Not happening." No matter how muddled my morning brain was, I wasn't wavering on that point.

"Please, Kennedy. Be reasonable."

"I'm being perfectly reasonable," I told him. "My career as an actress was an unplanned detour from what I really want to do with my life. I appreciate everything you've done for me, and I'm grateful for the chances I had because they mean I'm financially set for life, but I'm ready to get back to the original plan now."

Owen scoffed. "That 'detour', as you put it, is the kind of happy circumstance most people dream of."

"I know." I gentled my tone. I knew how blessed I was and didn't ever want to forget that. "I appreciate that I was able to support my family and provide a secure future for each of them because of it, but it's never been *my* dream."

"Fine." Owen sounded defeated. "Can't blame a guy for trying. Keep in touch? I do care about you, you know."

"I know. Bye, Owen." I ended the call and stretched, then looked around the room. After yesterday, Blair had wanted to sleep on my couch, but I'd convinced him to stay next door. Having people around in the evening had soothed my nerves. They'd all been so determined to make sure the cottage was safe, and even though I'd been over-whelmed by their presence at first, I'd felt reassured by the company and the fact they'd double and triple checked the security systems.

I sat up, too awake after my conversation with Owen to consider trying to sleep again. I padded out to the living room, collected my laptop from the coffee table, and brought it back to bed. I'd discovered that Destiny Falls Heritage Museum had a website, and I felt the urge to look up the photograph Arthur had shown us near the end of our tour. The one of Rocky and Jewel near the waterfall.

I brought the webpage up and studied it for a long moment. There was an energy about the couple. A sense of love and devotion. Perhaps I was reading too much into things, but I really understood how Destiny Falls had become a romantic destination based on this photograph. I copied the image and tried a reverse image search through a browser, bringing up dozens of tourist pages and blogs with copies of the photo and various versions of the story Arthur had told us. None of those blogs named the couple though. Wistfulness curled through me. I'd love to know who Rocky and Jewel really were.

Then a smile stretched my lips. I opened my inbox and typed a quick email to a private investigator I'd hired to do background checks on staff. I sent him a link to the photograph and a request for any information he could find about them. It was a long shot, but I had the money and the interest, so why not? That done, I opened the files for some of the photographs I'd taken during the weekend and started touching them up.

A couple of hours later, I'd showered and was making a hot drink when there was a knock at the door. My adrenaline spiked and I tiptoed over and peered through the newly installed peep hole. When I saw Grace standing on the other side, I relaxed and disarmed the alarm.

"Morning," I said as the door swung open.

"Hi." She scanned me. "Been up for a while?"

I made a face. "Got woken early by someone back in L.A. who didn't think to check what time it was here."

"That's no good." She shifted her weight from one foot

to the other. "Would you like to come up for breakfast? We've got fresh fruit, yogurt, and pastries."

I smiled. "Sounds great. Is this your way of checking up on me?"

"Maybe." She looked embarrassed. "I promised Nate I'd report back about how you are."

Sweet that he'd care. "I'll be there in a moment. I just need to turn off my laptop. I was editing some photos and doing a little research on the couple who started the commitment tradition up at the falls."

"Oh, really?" Her eyebrows rose. "Have you found anything interesting?"

"Not yet, but I'm hoping to. It's caught my attention, and it's not as though I have a job to distract me, so I may as well indulge myself."

"I'd love to hear about whatever you find." Grace tucked a lock of hair behind her ear. "I'm a closet romantic."

I grinned. "I totally could have guessed that. Yeah, I'll pass on whatever I find. Why don't you come in? I'll be back in two minutes."

She followed me inside and stopped in the living area. I headed to the bedroom, smiling at the prospect of spending more time rebuilding my friendship with Grace. Everything was coming together. If not for the pesky issue of the stalker, I'd be utterly content.

Chapter Thirty-Seven

LIAM

I TOOK A DATE TO THE MIDSUMMER DIP AT DESTINY TARN. She thought the whole thing was provincial and stupid, which made me think of you and wonder whether you might have secretly agreed with her. - Unsent text message from Liam to Kennedy.

OVER THE NEXT WEEK AND A HALF, I SPENT MOST OF MY free time with Kennedy, getting to know her all over again. There weren't any more stolen kisses, but there were plenty of moments when our lips could have connected if either of us had been willing to close an inch-wide gap. It seemed we were both reluctant to move too fast.

On a Saturday in the middle of January, I collected Kennedy from her cottage in the morning, ready for our walk to Destiny Tarn for the annual midsummer dip. Everyone in town who wasn't working and had the physical ability to make the hike would be on their way to the trail for the traditional swim. I'd packed a towel, a change of clothes, sunscreen, and snacks. I already had my swimming trunks on, since they'd be perfectly fine for hiking in.

"Hey," Kennedy puffed as she jogged toward me. "Thanks for waiting. Blair and Tyler are planning to come, but they only just got up. I told them if they weren't here by the time we buckled in, we'd go without them." She yanked the passenger door open and hurled herself—pack and all—into the seat. "Come on. I want you to myself. Let's get out of here."

My eyebrows shot upward. "You want to leave them behind?"

She waved a hand, mischief in her eyes. "They'll catch up. They've got a car and they know where they're going. Quickly!"

"Yes, ma'am." I jumped behind the steering wheel, checked the road, and pulled out just as Blair came belting down the path.

"Go, go, go!" Kennedy cried, laughing in a way that made me wonder about her state of mind.

I side-eyed her. "He's going to be pissed at you later."

"He'll get over it. I've been trying to convince him to leave, since the stalker has been keeping his distance, but he needs a nudge. He can't put his life on hold forever just because something *might* happen."

I reached across the console and took her hand, keeping the other firmly on the steering wheel. "He wants to keep you safe. There's nothing wrong with that."

"There is if he's missing out on his own life," she grumbled.

I sent her a look of disbelief. "Says the woman who put everything on hold to raise her family."

"They were kids, and I was an adult. It's not the same. Blair and I are both adults now. He doesn't have to take care of me, and I feel guilty knowing that he might be missing out on career opportunities because of me."

I wanted to argue, knowing Blair would disagree with her interpretation of the situation, but I kept my mouth shut, not wanting the day to get off to a bad start. I knew Kennedy didn't like other people being put out because of her. After all, wasn't that the whole reason we'd broken up for eleven years?

We reached the start of the walking trail in only a few minutes. I leaped out of the Ute and rounded the hood to open her door. She'd been looking for something in her backpack but stopped when she noticed me.

"Did you happen to bring extra sunscreen? I put some on before we left, but I'll need more once we're at the tarn."

"I have plenty," I assured her.

"Good." She slid out of the Ute and shouldered her bag.

I put my own on and looked around at the other vehicles that were already here. "We're lucky we found a spot."

"Yeah. I should message Blair and let him know to hurry." She took her phone from her pocket and tapped at the screen, then put it away again. "Ready?"

I gestured for her to lead the way. "After you."

As we started up the trail, the sound of voices filtered through the trees, and the imprint of shoes in the dirt showed that plenty of others had already been here this morning. I glanced at Kennedy out of the corner of my eye and tried not to think about the fact that in a couple of hours, I'd be seeing what was underneath her clothes for the first time in over ten years. I felt like a teenage boy who was finally getting the chance to go past first base. Not that I necessarily expected anything to happen between us, but my body stirred at the thought of seeing all of her creamy skin with droplets of moisture beaded on it.

Fortunately, it didn't take long for my legs to feel the burn of hiking uphill, distracting me from my fantasies.

During the hike, we passed a few older members of the community, pausing briefly to chat with some of them. We weren't in a hurry. The dip officially happened at midday, but people would be hanging around the tarn for a while before and afterward, although in keeping with tradition, no one would venture into the water before the clock hit twelve.

We rounded a bend that took us through a clearing in the trees. Up ahead, I spotted a familiar little girl with dark blonde hair that fell messily over her shoulders.

"Tess," I called.

She spun around and smiled. "Hi, Uncle Liam." She grabbed the arm of the kid beside her, who also looked over at us. "Look, Skye, it's Uncle Liam." Her eyes landed on Kennedy and widened, then she shrank back.

"Hi, Skye." I glanced at the woman beside her, Skye's mother, Nikkita. "Hey, Nikki. Are these two ragamuffins behaving themselves?"

"As much as they know how," Nikkita said wryly. "Tess is fine. It's my little munchkin you need to be wary of."

"Mum!" Skye protested. She was the more outgoing of the pair, and Tess tended to let her take the lead. Her eyes narrowed at Kennedy. "I've seen you in a movie."

"You probably have," Kennedy agreed, giving her a little wave.

Skye looked intrigued, but Tess seemed to be trying to sink into the earth and disappear. What was with that?"

"This is my friend Kennedy," I told them both.

Tess beckoned for me to come closer. I crossed to her side and bent so she could whisper in my ear.

"Daddy always says bad words when he sees her on TV. Is she a criminal like the ones he puts in jail?"

My eyes widened. Good old Nate and his hot temper. I could tell why Tess was concerned. She didn't want to talk to Kennedy if it would make her dad angry.

"You know how sometimes you and Skye fight?" I asked her quietly. She nodded. "Well, your dad and Kennedy had a disagreement a really long time ago, but they've apologized and forgiven each other now, so you don't need to worry."

"Okay." Her shoulders relaxed, and she sent Kennedy a tenuous smile.

I straightened and turned to Nikkita. "Want to walk with us the rest of the way?"

It wasn't far from here to the tarn.

She shook her head. "Nah, we're just taking our time. You go ahead, and we'll see you there."

"All right."

We waved them off and soon crested another hill, bringing the tarn into view. It stretched out in front of us, clear, blue-tinged water with round stones on the bottom. A few children played on the shore, and several groups had set up picnic blankets on the ground to lie or sit on, since the tussocks weren't very comfortable. I dropped my bag and pulled out the blanket I'd brought, laying it down. I checked the time. Eleven fifty.

"Not much longer until we jump in," I said.

Kennedy sat and crossed her legs. She was wearing shorts and a tank top. I really wanted to know what was beneath them. Had she opted for a bikini? A one-piece?

"I'm looking forward to it." She mopped her face on the hem of her shirt. "It's hot out here."

I grinned at her. "I thought you were a Cali girl. Not afraid of the heat."

She rolled her eyes. "It's a different kind of heat. You can really feel that hole in the ozone layer."

"True. Speaking of." I dug into my back and handed her a bottle of sunscreen.

"Thanks." She applied it to her face, then set it down while she worked on her arms. I squirted some onto my palm and did the same. She shed her tank top, revealing a black bikini with barely-there straps, and my jaw dropped. I couldn't look away as she slathered sunscreen on her belly and the curves at the top of her chest. She turned and offered me her back. "Do you mind helping?"

I fumbled with the sunscreen, my hands clumsy as I rubbed the lotion into her skin.

Smooth, Liam. Super smooth.

Her back was unblemished and sexy as hell. Her skin was like silk beneath my fingers, and it was all I could do to make myself stop touching her.

"There. All sorted."

"Thanks." She smiled over her shoulder, then looked up, and her expression faltered. "Hi, Aiden."

Damn.

When I turned, the persistent jerk I'd seen with her several times now was standing on the edge of our blanket with a beer in each hand.

"Hey, Kennedy." His gaze lingered on her in a way that made my blood heat with anger. He spared a glance for me. "Sorry, I don't remember your name."

"Liam," I growled.

But he'd already dismissed me. He offered Kennedy a beer. "Here. My friends got a prime spot by the edge of the water. You're welcome to join us." He flicked another look at me. "Your buddy can come too."

Buddy. Yeah, he wishes that's all I am.

"Thanks," Kennedy said, and for a moment I thought she might accept the beer, but she didn't move from her spot on my blanket. "That's a nice offer, but I'm comfortable here."

Aiden's lip curled down in obvious disappointment. "Well, I'll be there if you change your mind."

She nodded, but it took a few seconds for him to actually leave. Perhaps he'd been waiting for her to leap up and chase after him.

"What was with that?" I asked when he was out of earshot.

She shrugged. "Not sure. I think he means well, but I kinda wonder if he's one of those guys who wants to be able to say they've hooked up with a celebrity."

The back of my neck prickled. "You don't think he's the person who's been harassing you, do you?"

She caught her lower lip between her teeth. "It crossed my mind, but when I had a background check done on him, it came back clean. Besides, he's here on business and was in the country before me, so he couldn't have followed me over."

"A clean background check doesn't mean he's never done anything wrong," I reminded her. "Just that he's never been caught. But yeah, I get your point with the other things." It was certainly something to think about.

She shivered, and I regretted making her anxious during what should be a fun, relaxing event.

"Hey." I grabbed her hand. "Let's strip off. Only a couple more minutes until swim time."

"Yeah, okay." She stood up and shimmied out of her shorts. The bottom part of her bikini matched the top, and rode high over the curves of her ass. I gulped, suddenly wishing we were already in the water so it'd be less obvious if I sprang a boner. She gestured at me. "You too."

I whipped my T-shirt over my head, satisfaction coursing through me as her gaze lingered on my chest and heated with desire. I had more tattoos than I'd had when we first got together, but she didn't look as though she minded. To the contrary, the way she studied me made me think she wouldn't mind dragging me somewhere private to trace them all with her tongue. I'd be totally fine with that, but I also didn't want her to miss out on a big Destiny Falls tradition, so I guided her away from our blanket and toward the shore, where locals and tourists alike were crowding at the water's edge.

"One minute," a voice boomed over a loudspeaker.

Bodies pressed close around us. I caught Nate's eye through the crowd from where he stood behind Tess and Skye. Beside him, Nikkita was stealing peeks at his torso in a less than subtle way. I grinned. She was happily married, but also the kind of woman who had no qualms ogling whomever she wanted to.

"Is it going to be cold?" Kennedy asked.

I wondered if I should lie, but I decided not to. "Probably. It's fed by a glacier. Even in midsummer, it's still going to be chilly."

"Can we get on with it then?" she muttered. "Before I decide this is crazy."

"Ten," the voice boomed out. "Nine, eight…"

The crowd started chanting the countdown. Kennedy met my eyes, smiling widely as she called out the numbers. When we hit one, a horn blared, and we raced into the water. I gasped as it hit my toes and splashed around my ankles, then cringed as the water drew up the insides of my thighs. I could almost feel my balls trying to crawl up inside me.

"It's so cold!" Kennedy cried, leaping into my arms— presumably to escape the water, but it backfired, since she toppled me off balance and we crashed into the tarn together. Water closed over my head, and I struggled upward, panting as I broke the surface. I looked around and grabbed Kennedy, hauling her up with me. She spluttered, her eyes round with shock. Icy streams of water trickled from her hair over her shoulders and down her breasts. She clutched my chest while she caught her breath. When she'd finally recovered, she started to laugh. Her eyes crinkled with mirth, and I loved the sound of it so much, I joined in.

Then, all of a sudden, her mouth was against mine. Her cool lips pried mine apart, and I yielded easily, reveling in the taste and feel of her. I drew her closer, fit my body against hers, and tried to get more of her.

A wolf-whistle ended the moment.

We broke apart, staring at each other with a combination of need and surprise.

"Want to get out of here?" I asked, my voice rough. I wasn't sure if it was too much too soon, or if the question would frighten her off, but she nodded eagerly and pushed me toward the shore.

"Let's go home."

Chapter Thirty-Eight

KENNEDY

LIAM AND I PACKED AS QUICKLY AS WE COULD AND RACED down the trail, away from the tarn and back toward the township. I wished I could snap my fingers and have us back at the cottage, but sadly, that didn't work in real life. During the time between leaving the tarn and arriving at Liam's Ute, I had plenty of opportunity to reconsider. Perhaps that was good because it meant neither Liam nor I would be able to say we'd been completely caught up in the moment.

As we reached the parking area, Liam stopped, drawing me into a brief, fiery kiss, then we hurried across the clearing to the vehicle. I shoved my stuff into the back seat and climbed into the front. Liam buckled up and got the engine revving in record time.

"To the cottage?" he asked.

I hesitated. "Yeah."

I still hadn't been to his place yet, but I didn't want to

push. Especially not now. That would happen when it happened.

He steered us out of the parking area and took the shortest route to Grace's place. When we arrived, he pulled over, and we both leaped out, abandoning our gear. We could come back for it later. At the cottage doorstep, I found the key in my purse to let us in and deactivated the alarm. Liam closed the door behind us and pushed me up against it. I moaned as his mouth met mine.

"You are so fucking sexy," he groaned, pressing closer.

I shivered, partly from desire and partly because I was starting to cool down after our swim and dash.

"Shower." He pulled away and steered me into the bathroom.

I turned the shower on and stripped out of my remaining clothes, baring myself fully to Liam. His hungry gaze ate me up. Forget any sensual photoshoots I'd done, this was the sexiest I'd ever felt, with the love of my life's eyes on me like a caress.

Since he didn't seem to be moving, I stalked over and grabbed the waistband of his board shorts. With my eyes locked on his, I snapped the button open and let them fall to the floor. Beneath the board shorts, a pair of briefs barely contained his erection. I peeled them down and lowered my gaze. A drop of precum beaded at the head of his cock, and I wrapped my hand around his shaft and pumped.

"Whoa." A shudder rippled through him, and he gently pushed me away. "Enough of that or this will be over in two seconds."

I kissed him softly and let go. He was right. There was no need to rush.

I opened the glass shower cubicle and stepped inside, holding the door open for him to join me. I wet my hair and turned to grab the shampoo, but Liam already had it.

He gestured for me to turn my back to him, and when I did, he lathered shampoo in my hair, raking his fingertips over my scalp. I leaned into his ministrations, loving his touch and the pure bliss of a head massage. When he stopped, I rinsed and applied the conditioner myself.

Everything clean and shiny, he backed me against the tiled portion of the wall and dipped his head to kiss the side of my neck. Kiss. Kiss. Then he latched his mouth onto my pulse point and sucked. I arched away from the wall, heat blazing to my core at the knowledge that he was marking me. He brushed another gentle kiss over the spot, soothing it with his mouth, then trailed kisses up the side of my neck and across my cheek.

With another deep, throaty groan, he claimed my mouth. I melted against him, trusting him to hold me up. One of his hands curved around my neck to position me where he wanted, and the other skimmed down my side and rubbed over the mound of my sex. He slipped two fingers between my thighs and stroked.

"Oh!" My hips gave a stuttering thrust. It had been so long since someone touched me like this, and I was sensitive.

"You like that?" he murmured against my ear. His warm breath sent shivers cascading over my skin.

"Yes," I whimpered. "More, please."

He nuzzled the side of my face and slicked his fingers through my folds, over the bundle of nerves at the top, until I was quivering, begging, and more turned on than I could remember being in, oh, say, eleven years or so.

"I need you," I told him.

"You have me, sweetheart."

One of his fingers probed my entrance and pushed inside. I gasped as he crooked the finger and stroked the inside of my channel. His palm clasped tight to my body, the pressure was absolutely delicious as I rubbed against him shamelessly.

"Just like that," he urged. "You feel so good, and you're moving so sweetly for me."

Oh my God. He knew just what to say and how to touch me to drive me out of my mind.

"Please," I begged.

His mouth settled over mine in a messy, heated kiss. "What do you want?"

"You inside me. Over me. All around me."

"Yeah?"

"Like, right now."

He gave a strained laugh. "I think we'd better take this to the bedroom." He stiffened. "Do you have condoms?"

"In the nightstand," I admitted. "I wanted to be ready, just in case."

He brushed a tender kiss over my temple, his lips moving against my skin as he murmured, "Being prepared is sexy as fuck."

I reached for the shower knob and shut the water off. We spilled out of the cubicle, each grabbing a fluffy towel but not pausing to dry ourselves properly as we ran, giggling, to the bedroom. My heart was light. I couldn't remember the last time I'd felt so giddy and completely present in the moment.

I dragged the towel over my body while Liam rummaged in my nightstand and victoriously held up a condom. He tore the foil wrapper, rolled it on, and stalked toward me. I ran my hands over his muscular chest and around his shoulders, loving his strength. The tattoos weren't bad to look at either. I didn't get the chance to explore more though because he guided me back onto the bed and lowered himself between my thighs.

"You want this?" he asked, his voice low. "There's no going back."

My gaze caught his, and the banked fire in his eyes fueled my own desperation. "Not want. Need."

"Then I'm all yours." With one slow, sure stroke, he entered me. "Then. Now. Probably forever because I'm goddamn addicted to you."

"I'm yours too," I told him, needing him to understand. "Always have been. Always will be."

"God, Kenz." He lowered his forehead to mine and moved inside me, his eyes never leaving mine. We didn't kiss, but somehow sharing panted breaths seemed even more intimate.

Every thrust hit just right, sending sparks of pleasure along my nerves, but I held on as long as I could, wanting the moment to last forever. I bit my lip and rolled my hips, floating in the soulful blue of his eyes.

"So good," he growled out. "So fucking sweet."

I cried out, shattering into a thousand blissful pieces, my eyes squeezing shut as a beautiful release washed over me. Above me, Liam's breathing was ragged. His cock jerked inside me, and he shuddered, my name on his lips as he came.

We lay holding each other, both of us apparently content to exist in the private world we'd spun together until Liam pulled away for long enough to dispose of the condom. But then he was back, wrapping me inside his embrace, and it felt like a long-lost puzzle piece finally slotting into place.

Chapter Thirty-Nine

LIAM

THERE WAS NOTHING BETTER THAN THE FEELING OF HOLDING you. Some mornings I wake up and expect you to be in my arms. — Unsent text message from Liam to Kennedy

WHEN I OPENED MY EYES AND INHALED THE SCENT OF Kennedy and sex, my first thought was that I must still be dreaming. Then she wriggled and I got a mouthful of hair. No way would that be happening in my dreams. I wrapped my arms around her and buried my face in the back of her neck. I'd deal with her hair in my face all day long if it meant I got to keep her. I might have made the mistake of letting her go once, but I had no intention of doing so again. She and I were meant to be together. It had just taken us a while to get there.

"Hi," Kennedy murmured, nestling into the curve of my body. "Good nap?"

"Excellent nap." I leaned over and kissed her cheek. "By the way, I'm serious about this. I want to be with you."

She rolled over so we were facing each other, and a shy smile curved her lips. "This wasn't just a bit of fun for old time's sake, then?"

"Absolutely not." I kissed the tip of her nose. "I care about you, and I want to see where this goes. Are you on the same page?"

She rolled her eyes. "I literally flew to the bottom of the world because I want another chance with you. If that doesn't spell out my intentions, I don't know what can."

I chuckled, warmth fizzing through me at the thought that I brought her here. She wanted to be happy, and she came to me. That was kind of amazing. "Some of us don't do subtlety. We need the words."

"I want a future with you," she whispered.

"Thank you." I pecked her on the lips again. Things weren't as comfortable and easy between us as they used to be, and I was sure we'd both need extra reassurance while we fell into a rhythm of togetherness again, but I was confident we'd get there—or to somewhere new and better. After all, we were both older, with more life experience. Surely that meant we could make an even deeper connection if we worked at it.

"In fact," she continued with more certainty, "I think it's about time I start looking for a house of my own."

My heart skipped a beat. "You what?"

"Well, I've been here for six weeks, and I don't plan to leave, so I should find a more permanent living situation. It's not as though I can't afford to buy a home here. I just wanted to come to the cottage first because of nostalgia, I guess. Or maybe because I'd hoped Grace would be more accepting of me than others might be."

"Pretty safe bet," I said. "Grace is something special."

"Yeah, she is."

Looking into Kennedy's vivid eyes that were slightly blurred by sleep, it was on the tip of my tongue to suggest that she make use of the key I gave her all those years ago and move in with me. But I forced myself to swallow the words. It was best to take things slow, no matter how much I might want to run into a relationship with her at top speed. I just hated the thought of all the years we wasted.

Outside the bedroom, there was a series of loud knocks followed by heavy footsteps. Then another set of knocks on the bedroom door.

I stiffened, immediately going on the defensive, but a voice called out.

"Kenz, you'd better not be naked, because I'm coming in." It was Blair.

"Totally naked!" she yelled back at the exact moment the door swung open and her brother appeared. Kennedy yanked the covers over herself and I shifted to make sure all the good bits were covered, but if Blair hadn't wanted an eyeful of my chest, then he should have been more considerate of Kennedy's personal space.

"First you left us behind, then we got there just in time to see you two running off together. What's up with that?"

Kennedy and I exchanged a look.

"We wanted private time," she said.

His hands went to his hips. "So, everything is worked out between you now?"

"More or less." I took Kennedy's hand and gave it a comforting squeeze.

"Good." His scowl faded. "I'm happy for you." His gaze locked on me. "But you'd better treat her right."

"I will," I promised. We hadn't had the maturity to work through life's challenges last time around, but this time we did, and I wouldn't give up on us.

"Okay." He inched backward and jerked a thumb over his shoulder. "We'll be next door."

"Hey, Blair," I called impulsively as he began to leave.

"Yeah?"

"Thanks for being here for Kennedy when she needs you."

He shrugged one shoulder. "That's what family is for."

Chapter Forty

KENNEDY

LIAM AND I SPENT THE REST OF THE AFTERNOON IN BED, kissing, snuggling, and talking about the future. When dusk fell, we shared another shower and dressed.

"Would you like to stay for dinner?" I asked.

Liam glanced at his phone. "I'd better go home. I think I left a few windows open, and I don't want the place to fill up with insects."

"Oh." I deflated.

"Why don't you come with me? I can cook for you."

A warm glow began in my heart and radiated throughout my chest. "I'd like that."

"Great." He tangled his fingers with mine. "Should we head over now?"

"I'll grab a sweater." And perhaps I'd pack a small overnight bag, just in case.

I sorted my things and made sure the security camera and motion sensors were in place, then Liam and I set the alarm and locked the cottage. We got into the Ute, where we'd left the bags we'd discarded earlier, and Liam started the engine. We cruised around a slight bend in the road toward a T-intersection. But as we approached, the vehicle didn't slow.

"You planning to brake?" I asked, getting fidgety as we drew closer. There were cars going the other way. Not many, because this was Destiny Falls, but some.

"I am braking." His jaw tightened. "It's not doing anything."

My stomach clenched. "Pull over."

"I can't," he growled. "I'll hit one of the cars on the side of the road."

"Better than a moving car."

"Fuck."

We were nearly level with the intersection. He slammed his hand on the horn so it blared, and he tried to turn, but we had too much momentum. I gripped the edge of the seat, my heart in my throat as we slid across two lanes of traffic—miraculously not crashing into any vehicles—and toward the concrete wall of the Destiny Falls Motors building on the far side.

Liam spun the steering wheel as fast as he could, and the car angled to the left. We smashed into the concrete wall driver's side first.

Glass shattered. Metal crumpled. I screamed.

We jolted to a stop, and my head whipped back. Pain flashed up the back of my neck.

"Are you okay?" Liam asked, reaching across the space between us to run his hands over my body.

"I'm fine," I assured him, though my neck hurt. "I'm more worried about you."

His last-minute maneuver meant the impact had centered on his side of the vehicle. I could already see that the door was damaged, the frame no longer fitting properly. I looked down at his legs to see if they'd been crushed or injured. There was a cut on his thigh, blood soaking his shorts. I grabbed a discarded towel from the back seat and pressed it to the wound.

"Fuck," he muttered. "It's just a scratch, but it hurts like a bitch."

The door on my side was yanked open, and a bear of a man with wild brown hair and worried eyes loomed over us. It took a moment, but I eventually recognized him as Warren, the auto mechanic who'd fixed the paint on my car after it had been keyed.

"Anyone injured?" he asked in a low, rumbly voice.

"Not badly," Liam replied. "But we'll need to be checked over by a paramedic."

"I've already called," Warren said. "An ambulance is on its way. Police and fire too." He unbuckled my seatbelt. "Let's get you out of here." He wrapped an arm around my shoulders and helped me out of the seat. He set me against the side of the Ute. "Wait here while I help Liam. He's going to have to climb over. His door won't open."

I nodded, but he was already back at it. When he emerged a moment later, pulling Liam with him, I gave a sigh of relief. Except for his bloody thigh, Liam seemed unharmed.

Sirens wailed nearby, and lights illuminated the darkening street as an ambulance and a fire engine pulled to a stop a few yards away. Asher jumped out of the ambulance and hurried over, a bag clutched in his hands.

"Shit, man, you scared me," he said to Liam. "What hurts?"

"My leg, mostly," Liam replied.

"Excuse me, miss." I turned to find a female paramedic waiting for my attention. "Were you in the accident?"

I nodded. "I'm okay. My neck hurts a bit, and my back and chest too, but Liam is the one who needs help." I couldn't believe he'd intentionally turned the vehicle so he'd take the brunt of the crash. He'd avoided hitting the wall head-on, which could have injured us equally, and pulled around to protect me from the impact.

"Asher is with Liam," the paramedic said soothingly. "You're my concern. Let's give you a check-over just to be sure you're as fine as you think you are. Okay?"

I nodded, paying her little attention as she checked each of my limbs and asked a few basic questions. I was focused on Liam. Asher had pushed his shorts up and was washing the wound. Did it hurt? Was it bad? I couldn't tell from here.

Another siren announced the police's arrival. Nate and Constable Mehrtens got out of the marked vehicle and hurried over.

"What happened?" Nate demanded. "The emergency caller said you cut through two lanes of traffic and hit a concrete wall."

Liam looked up, his expression grim. "The brakes didn't work."

Nate frowned. "When was the last time you had a maintenance check?"

"Just before Christmas," Warren cut in. "Everything looked fine then. No indication of wear or damage."

Nate's frown deepened. "So, when you say they didn't work," he said to Liam, "were they weak or completely gone?"

"Completely gone."

Nate swore. "Warren." He turned to our rescuer. "Can you check the brake lines? Mehrtens will oversee. Turn on your camera," he added to the constable.

"Yes, sir."

A chill zapped down my spine. They were checking the brakes. Would they do that if this was a typical traffic accident?

"You don't think this was random." My tone was

accusatory, and Nate's gaze snapped to me. His eyes were hard at first, but they softened after a moment.

"I think we need to keep an open mind." He moved closer to Liam, surveying the now clean wound on his thigh. "Considering the problems you've been having, it seems like a pretty big coincidence for Liam's brakes to fail when he usually maintains that crappy old Ute like it's his baby."

"How's your head?" the paramedic asked. "Does it feel woozy and muddled?"

"It's fine," I told her, but my stomach lurched at the thought of someone sabotaging Liam's vehicle. "I think I'm gonna be sick."

"Brakes have been tampered with," Warren called.

My stomach roiled and bile burned up the back of my throat. Oh my God. Someone had done this intentionally. They wanted to hurt us, and they'd succeeded in injuring Liam.

I closed my eyes and took a slow breath, begging the world to stop spinning so much. And here I'd thought the stalker wouldn't actually hurt me. That they'd cared, in some twisted way. If this had gone differently, Liam and I could be dead. If a truck had been coming the other direction and swiped us off the intersection, we'd have been goners. All because of me.

"This is my fault," I said quietly. Forcing my eyes open, I bent beside Liam as Asher covered his cut with tape. "Is it bad?"

"He got off lucky," Asher said. "It's shallow. Won't even need stitches."

"Thank God." I stretched up to kiss Liam's cheek. "I'm so sorry. This must have been my stalker. I'm the reason you got hurt."

"Hey. No, you're not." He grabbed my chin and tilted

my face up so I had to meet his eyes. "This is on them, not you."

"But it might not have happened if we weren't together." I let all of the love that had always been in my heart for him shine through my eyes, hoping he could see it even if we hadn't said the words. "I want to keep you safe. Maybe you need to stay away from me for a while."

"Hell no." He brushed his lips over mine. "I wasn't able to be there when you needed me in the past, but I damn well will be now. Some asshole with an obsession isn't going to stop that."

Chapter Forty-One

LIAM

I heard you've been nominated for a Golden Globe. I'm not sure how I feel about that. - Unsent text message from Liam to Kennedy

"You mean that?" Kennedy whispered, her eyes shining with emotion.

"With all my heart." I was mad as hell that some guy thought he had the right to endanger our lives, but I wasn't about to leave her to deal with him alone.

Asher cleared his throat. "We're going to head out. The engine is returning to the station too. Call later?"

"Yeah." I gave him a hug. "Thanks for patching me up."

"No worries." He lowered his voice. "Take care of your girl."

"I will."

He left, and I circled an arm around Kennedy, careful

not to be rough in case she was feeling as battered as I was. I suspected I'd have some nasty bruising in addition to the laceration on my thigh, but it could have been much, much worse. We were lucky I hadn't been driving fast and that we were in town. If the brakes had malfunctioned else-where, I could easily have slid off the side of the road and down a gully.

Kennedy jerked all of a sudden. "I need to call Blair. If he hears about this from someone else, he's going to be worried sick."

"Do you have your phone?" I asked.

"It's in the car."

Nate handed her his. "Use this."

She took it and dialed the number by heart, wandering further away while she spoke with her brother.

"We're going to need to record a formal statement at the police station and keep the car in lockup so a forensic analysis can be undertaken," Nate said, his voice low. "If this was the stalker, it's a serious escalation. The sooner we uncover the scumbag, the better."

"Agreed."

Kennedy returned, her expression strained. "Blair and Tyler are on their way."

"Would you mind directing them to the police station instead?" Nate asked. "If you're feeling up to it, we'll head over there and run through everything that happened."

Her jaw firmed. "Absolutely."

Nate retrieved her phone from the Ute, cautioning us to stay back, and handed it over, then we packed into the back of the patrol car and he drove us to the police station. Similar to the fire station, the police were located on a side road adjoining Centennial Street. Nate led us inside, past a receptionist, and into a small room out the back. The walls were white, and a round table occupied most of the room. The floor was concrete, the table bolted down. I sank onto one chair, and Kennedy pulled up another beside me, reaching for my hand, seeking comfort via touch. Nate set his phone on the table, and Constable Mehrtens withdrew a notepad and pen from her pocket.

"You mind if we record this?" Nate asked.

"Go for it," I told him, and Kennedy nodded too.

He set the phone recording and stated his name and the names of everyone else present, then asked us each to say our name in turn so any listeners would be able to recognize us by voice.

"Can you walk me through the events leading up to the accident?" he asked.

Kennedy and I exchanged a look. I wasn't sure if she'd prefer to take the lead. But then she gave a slight nod and started speaking. She ran through a highlight reel of the day's activities, a faint blush coloring her cheeks as she mentioned our time at her cottage. Mehrtens took notes. Nate simply listened and asked for clarification. When Kennedy finished talking, we sat quietly for a few seconds before Nate spoke.

"As I see it," he said, "the car was fine when you drove back from the tarn, but it had been damaged when you left the cottage, so it was most likely tampered with while you were inside the cottage. Was it out of sight at that time?"

"Yes," I confirmed, but even if it hadn't been, I doubted we would have noticed anything out of the ordinary. We were too wrapped up in each other.

"Was it on the road or in the drive?" he asked.

"On the road."

He pulled a face. "So, anybody could have accessed it."

My stomach dropped. "I guess so."

"That's unfortunate." He ran a hand over the bristles of his short hair. "Okay, here's what we'll do—"

A ringing phone cut him off.

Kennedy's cheeks flamed. "Sorry," she muttered,

fishing the phone from her pocket. She swiped the screen and was about to end the call when she stopped. "It's a private number." She looked at Nate. "It might be him."

"Answer it," he barked. "Put it on speaker."

With trembling hands, Kennedy followed his instructions.

"Who is this?" she asked when the call connected.

"Consider that a warning," a distorted, mechanical voice said through the phone. "End things with your boyfriend, or next time will be worse."

What the fuck?

I bolted upright. "Go to hell, you psychotic asshole!"

The connection cut out.

"Liam." Nate was fuming. "That was our chance to talk to him, and you blew it."

"He needs to know he can't get away with it."

Nate dragged a hand down his face. "And people call me the hothead."

"I told you." Kennedy's voice was thin and reedy. "I said we should separate for a while. Not forever, but what if he really hurts you?" She was pale, dark splotches of purple beneath her eyes. "I couldn't live with that."

My back teeth ground together. "I'm not playing along with him. We're a package deal now, through good and bad. You got that?"

She nodded, teeth scraping her lower lip, her eyes worried.

"This is serious," Nate said. "They've sabotaged your vehicle, possibly attempted to injure or kill you, and we have a threat on record. We'll be moving on it as soon as we can. Ideally we'd have an officer accompany Kennedy 24/7, but it's not feasible with our current staffing situation. I'll try to get more bodies from neighboring towns, but for now, we need other arrangements."

"I'll stay with her," I said.

"You have to work," she pointed out. "But perhaps Blair can help too."

"I'm sure he will." Blair would want to wring the motherfucker's neck when he got all the gory details. "In the meantime, you can move in with me. He's clearly watching your cottage."

"But that's where all the security is." She made a good point.

"What do you think?" I asked Nate. "You're the expert."

He considered for a moment. "Take her to your place, but I want you two to have eyes or ears on each other at all times. Kennedy isn't the only one who might be at risk."

"I hope the weasel comes after me." I'd teach him to terrify the woman I loved.

Nate reached over and switched off the recording. "That's enough for now."

Chapter Forty-Two

KENNEDY

Everything was spiraling out of control, and I didn't know what to do about it. I felt like the atmosphere had become pressurized, and I might burst out of my body.

"Shaun is picking up your car and bringing it here," Nate continued, speaking to Liam. "We'll test it for fingerprints and other trace evidence and canvas Grace's neighbors to see if they remember any strangers in the area during the time you were in the cottage and the car was unattended." He turned to me. "Meanwhile, can you compile a list of any enemies you might have, or anyone who might wish you harm?"

I nodded, the sensation of pressure lessening now that I had a task, but it left me cold. "That's not going to be easy," I told him. "It could be any fan who's gone over the edge."

He nodded, considering that for a moment. "Do the best you can. Any people you know personally, or anybody who's sent you threatening or inappropriate correspondence in the past, or whom your security may have had to remove from a show. Do you have access to that information?"

"I can get my security company to send it through."

"Tell them it's urgent. We need it ASAP."

"I will," I promised, although I dreaded having to go through another conversation where Jeff would try to convince me to come back to Los Angeles. "We might be looking at someone who has targeted me both here and in L.A., which narrows the pool."

"True," Nate said. "I assume we can rule Blair out, unless you've had any problems with him before?"

"Not at all! He's my brother."

"Family is sometimes the most motivated to do someone harm," he said. "I had to ask." He got his phone out and navigated the screen. "I've run a background check on your buddy Aiden. Nothing popped, but that doesn't mean he isn't responsible. We'll look into his whereabouts this afternoon. I followed up on the paparazzo who photographed you after your car was keyed. His company has told us they recalled him to L.A., but we haven't had confirmation he's boarded a flight yet. I'll get someone to check." He glanced at Mehrtens, who jotted a note. "How much do you know about Blair's friend, Tyler?"

I frowned. "He and Blair met in high school, and he's been around the family for years. They're really close. There's no way this was him."

"Are you sure?" Liam asked, shocking me. "I think he has a thing for you."

I laughed. "That's ridiculous. He had a crush on me a few years ago, but I haven't seen any hint of that in ages. Besides, he's crazy about his girlfriend."

"That doesn't necessarily mean anything," Nate said.

I rolled my eyes. "What about the fact that he wasn't

here when that gift was delivered on Christmas Day? He was in L.A. The only reason he's here at all is because Blair talked him into it."

"He could have paid someone to deliver the gift," Nate pointed out.

My stomach dipped for a moment, but then a thought struck me. "He was with Blair, on his way here, so he couldn't have made the phone call."

"Damn," Liam muttered, his idea thwarted.

"Hmm." Nate scratched his chin. "Good point. There are other angles to look at here though. The stalker isn't necessarily in town. They could have paid someone to deliver the gift, vandalize the cottage door, key the car, and damage the Ute. Or the car incident might have been instigated by that paparazzo—we can't rule it out. Alternatively, it's possible someone else from L.A. is in town but lying low. We'll check with the accommodation providers and see if anyone is willing to share their customer list, but most will be worried about privacy regulations, so I'm not holding my breath."

"Can't you get a warrant for that?" Liam asked, sounding frustrated.

"Not with what we've got to go on." Nate's tone was apologetic. "I wish we could, but no one would approve it."

Mehrtens tore some pages from her notepad and passed them to me, along with a pen. "You can use this to make a start on the list," she said. "If you think of anyone else later, you can send us their names."

"Thanks." I picked up the pen and stared at the blank page, hating what they'd asked me to do. I didn't want to think of reasons why people might dislike me. After all, I didn't cause drama, sleep around, or party, except for when it had been encouraged for the sake of my career. But that didn't mean others didn't resent me or that I hadn't ever rubbed someone the wrong way. I pressed my lips together, steeled my jaw, and started writing.

Mehrtens left the room a few moments later. Liam put an arm around me, obviously sensing my discomfort, but he didn't watch over my shoulder, which I was grateful for. He and Nate spoke in low voices. I tried to tune them out so I could focus on thinking of who might want to hurt me. I jotted a few names, feeling disloyal, then wracked my brain for more. Finally, I pushed the notepad toward Nate.

"This is all I can come up with off the top of my head, but I'll have Jeff send you the details of any overly enthusiastic fans, and I'll keep thinking."

"Thanks, Kennedy." He touched my hand briefly. "This will help us make the best start we can."

There was a knock at the door. Nate stood, opened it a crack, then stepped back. Blair and Tyler spilled into the room.

Blair's eyes were frantic as they landed on me. "Are you okay, Kenz?"

I hugged him. "I'm fine. Liam took the worst of it."

Blair let me go and laid a hand on Liam's shoulder. "Thank you."

"I'll always do what I can to keep her safe." Liam's words were directed at Blair, but his eyes were locked on mine, and a shiver ran through me. I liked knowing he cared, but I'd rather he didn't put himself at risk.

"You're not injured?" Tyler asked from behind Blair, an air of concern about him.

"Nothing other than a few bruises," I replied.

"Thank God. You gave us a scare."

"Yeah, well, we gave ourselves one too."

"I bet."

Blair placed his hands on my shoulders and looked me in the eye. "The stalking only escalated when you came over here. I know you love Destiny Falls, but they don't have the means to protect you the way we can back home. Maybe it's time to consider returning to L.A."

"*No.*" My immediate response had more bite than intended, and I instantly felt bad about it. "I see where you're coming from, but I'm not letting some asshole run me out of town."

"It wouldn't have to be permanent," Blair said reasonably. "Just until things quiet down."

"But what if they don't?" I challenged. "What if any time I try to do anything, my stalker turns up? I can't let that stop me from living my life."

"She has a point," Tyler said to Blair, who glared at his friend.

"Aren't you supposed to be on my side?"

"I am." He shrugged. "I'm just saying."

"She's not going anywhere," Liam said firmly, looking as if he was prepared to argue the point as far as necessary.

I glanced at Nate, aware the conversation was going off the rails. He appeared to be following it with interest but didn't seem inclined to interrupt. Perhaps he wanted to see the dynamics of the group in action.

"Look." I thrust my shoulders back and hardened my voice. "I appreciate your concern, but I'm not leaving. If you want to get back to your lives, please do. I'd hate to stand in the way of that. You know I don't like it when anyone makes a fuss over me."

Blair and Tyler both looked like they wanted to disagree, but for a long moment, neither of them spoke.

"Fat chance of me leaving when you need support," Blair finally said.

Chapter Forty-Three

LIAM

I heard a rumor you're engaged. Tell me it's not true.
- Unsent text message from Liam to Kennedy.

"Now that that's sorted," I said before anyone could begin debating the point again, "why don't we get Kennedy back to my place so we can make dinner and catch up on some much-needed rest after the chaos of this evening?"

Kennedy sent me a grateful smile. "Yes, please."

"Shouldn't she be at the cottage?" Blair protested.

"Most of the incidents have happened in or around the cottage, so we're going to stay away for a couple of days," I explained. "I have to work on Monday though, so I'm hoping you might keep Kennedy company then."

The tension in Blair's shoulders eased. "Of course." He sounded disgruntled that I'd felt the need to ask.

She leaned over and kissed his cheek. "Sorry this stuff

keeps happening. Hopefully it'll be over soon, and you'll be able to return to your life."

Blair's smile was soft and only for her. I felt like an intruder witnessing it. "Being here can't come close to repaying everything you've done for me. I'm just glad I can finally do something for you."

"You've done more for me than you think," she whispered back.

I turned to Nate. "Are we all good to go?"

He nodded. "Check in with me tomorrow. I'll be in touch if we have any news."

"Thanks."

We said our goodbyes to Nate, and Blair and Tyler gave us a ride back to Grace's cottage where we picked up Kennedy's car. Before we left, I performed a check to make sure the brakes and steering were in working order.

"Everything seems fine," I announced.

"I want a message as soon as you're safely there," Blair said.

"No problem," Kennedy replied.

As we pulled away from the curb, Kennedy pumped the brakes a couple of times to make sure they were functioning correctly before speeding up. She seemed to remember the directions to my place without any assistance, which pleased me more than it should. We didn't have any incidents on the way over, but when she pulled up the drive, it took me only seconds to notice something was amiss. The front door, which I'd locked when I'd left in the morning, sat ajar.

"Stay here," I said. "Something is wrong."

I debated calling Nate, but I wanted to be sure it was worth dragging him away from his office, so I opened the car door as softly as possible and eased out. I grabbed a metal rake from the lawn and wielded it like a bat as I headed toward the entrance. I paused when I heard movement behind me and glanced back to see that Kennedy had followed with a cannister of pepper spray clasped in her hand. I gave her a look, and she raised her chin, indicating she had no intention of backing down.

Fine.

I tiptoed through the small foyer, the rake poised above my shoulder, and into the living room.

My feet stopped so suddenly I nearly tripped.

Holy shit.

The place had been trashed. The glass coffee table had been smashed, and the sofa had been torn open, with stuffing strewn everywhere. Behind that, the dining table was upended.

Kennedy gasped. I spun to her and touched a finger to my lips, mouthing, "Quiet."

She nodded.

We progressed into the kitchen where drawers had been opened, their contents haphazardly tossed about, and the appliances and coffee-making equipment from the counter had been knocked onto the floor. I nearly whimpered at the sight of my beloved coffee machine damaged beyond repair.

I guided Kennedy into each of the two spare bedrooms to find that they had received similar treatment. In the bathroom, someone had written "BACK OFF" on the mirror in what looked to be black permanent marker.

But my bedroom was the most shocking. Paper of some sort had been torn into confetti-sized pieces and spread over nearly every surface with the majority of it on the bed. In the center of the mattress, with a pair of scissors buried in its cover, was a photo album.

Kennedy cried out, racing past me to reach for the album. Seeing that she meant to touch it, I grabbed her around the waist and stopped her before she could.

"Let me go!" she screamed, kicking at me. "That's my scrapbook!"

"Stop," I ordered, as calmly as I could. "You can't touch it, or you might mess with any evidence the stalker left."

"But that's… Oh my God."

She buried her face in my shoulder. A moment later, a sob wracked her body. My heart wrenched, and I held her close, murmuring comforting words that were meaningless when I didn't know exactly what had upset her. Clearly the book meant something.

"I've got you," I said, brushing my lips across her cheek. "Why don't you tell me what it is?"

She pulled away and looked up at me with watery, red-rimmed eyes. "After I left Destiny Falls, I made a scrapbook about our first year together. I was going to give it to you when I came back, but then the accident happened, and I never got the chance to. I kept it and used to look at it when I needed to be reminded of good memories."

My innards clenched at the thought of her carefully creating a book that chronicled our relationship, her heart full of hope, then having to pack it away when her life turned upside down. I hated that she'd been in that position, but I was glad she'd found strength in memories of us.

I scanned the shredded paper, noticing glimmers of color among the wreckage. Flashes of green and skin tone. "You kept it all this time?"

"And brought it here with me," she confirmed, her words like a jolt of electricity to my heart. "I was keeping it in the closet in my bedroom, which means the stalker was in the cottage."

Oh fuck.

"How could they have gotten in without setting off the alarm?" I asked. "When was the last time you saw the scrapbook? Could they have stolen it weeks ago?"

She shook her head. "It must have been during the past couple of weeks because I last looked at it soon after Blair and Tyler arrived in town."

"Which means it happened after we installed extra security." I reached for her hand, needing the contact. "They shouldn't have been able to get to it."

Kennedy hesitated, and when I glanced at her, she was biting her lip. "Well, there is one way they could have gotten access without setting off the security system."

I frowned. "What's that?"

Her eyes lifted to mine, wide and frightened. "If they did it while I was there. I usually deactivate the alarm when I'm home."

I closed my eyes. "He was there at the same time as you. Shit."

She clutched at my arm, and I curled it around her body. "That's not everything."

I swallowed. What else could there be?

Her entire body was tense, her muscles rigid. Her jaw muscle flickered a couple of times, and then she opened her mouth. "I still have the key you gave me back then. I kept it inside the scrapbook. So that might be how they got into your place. I didn't notice any broken windows out front."

Part of me wanted to freak out. Whoever the stalker was, they might now be able to enter and leave my home at will. But the knowledge that Kennedy had kept my key all this time prevented me from going over the edge. I liked the thought that she'd held onto hope that we'd return to each other. She'd never given up on us, even if I had.

"I'm sorry," she whispered. "I never thought this would happen."

"It's okay." I tucked her against my chest. "I'm sorry you're being targeted like this. It's sick."

Was I angry my house had been trashed?

Hell yes.

I was devastated. I'd spent years trying to turn this place into a home, and my progress had been set back. But on the other hand, perhaps a fresh start was what Kennedy and I needed. It sucked that it had to be this way, but if I thought of this as cleansing my old life, getting rid of bitterness and regrets, maybe I could get through the rest of this God-awful evening without screaming.

"I need to call Nate," I said, letting her go. Yet another mess to hand over to my brother. He wasn't going to be impressed.

Chapter Forty-Four

KENNEDY

After Nate and Constable Mehrtens arrived at Liam's place and declared it a crime scene, we weren't able to collect any of his belongings to take with us. I could tell it bothered Liam, and I hated that I'd brought this mess into his life. He'd been settled here in Destiny Falls, and then I'd come along and turned everything upside down.

"Where to now?" I asked as we stood outside his house.

"Well, if we want to be absolutely sure there's no chance of you being left alone at any time, I know one place we can take you."

I raised a brow. "Where?"

"Mum and Dad's place."

A breath got caught in my chest. Heather and Eugene had both been friendly to me recently, but I was still the woman who'd broken their son's heart. I wasn't sure they'd want me under their roof. "Are you sure that's a good idea?"

He grimaced. "It's the best we've got unless you want to go back to the cottage."

"No, thanks." A ripple of dread skated along my nerves at the thought that the stalker had been in my home while I was there. If they'd wanted to hurt me, I'd have been a sitting duck. I'd been completely oblivious while they'd pawed through my things and taken my most precious belongings in the world. How had I not heard or sensed that something was wrong?

"Let's go, then."

I offered Liam my keys. "Do you mind driving? I'm having trouble focusing."

My mind was too busy conjuring all sorts of alternative scenarios and what-ifs.

"Of course." He took the keys and kissed my forehead. "I know this is hard, but we're going to find a way through."

I really hoped so because I didn't know how much longer I could keep going when I knew that someone might be watching me from the shadows. What if, next time, they opted for a more violent route? My stomach hardened. If that were to happen, I wouldn't want to leave Liam wondering how I'd felt about him.

I touched his arm to stop him getting into the car and stretched up to kiss him. "I love you," I told him. "I always have. Every beat of my heart has been for you since the first time we met."

His eyes widened. He pocketed the keys and cupped my face between his palms. His eyes searched mine. I felt no fear that he wouldn't reciprocate. I didn't need him to. I loved him anyway. His gaze softened, and he captured my lips in a slow, toe-curling kiss. I smiled against his mouth.

When we separated, he spoke softly, his breath ghosting over my lips. "I've been terrified of opening my heart again, but when I dig deep, I don't think I ever really shut you out of it. I love you too."

My heart filled to the brim. Despite the horrible events of the past couple of hours, the tears that prickled in my eyes were happy ones. "Really?"

He nodded. "No more pushing you away or trying to pretend I don't feel that way."

"And no more of me suggesting I should do things on my own," I said wryly. "We're a team."

"Always, baby." His fingers tangled with mine. "Everything that comes, we deal with it together."

I released a shuddering breath. That sounded pretty perfect to me.

He led me to the car and helped me into the passenger side, then rounded the hood and got behind the wheel. We drove to his childhood home on the western outskirts of town near the golf course, our hands connected the entire time. When we arrived, he kept an arm around me as we approached the door. It flew open and Heather raced out, her arms outstretched. They closed around Liam and me, and she pressed a motherly kiss to both of our cheeks.

"I heard what happened," she said, looking shaken. "Nate called. I'm so glad you're both okay."

Eugene wasn't far behind. He seemed just as anxious as his wife, tugging Liam into a hug and then scanning me from head to toe to make sure I was unharmed.

"What happened to your leg?" Heather demanded, reaching for the hem of Liam's shorts and lifting it to reveal the taped gash.

"It was cut in the accident," Liam told her. "It's not a big one though. No stitches."

She covered her mouth with her hand and whimpered. "You could have died."

"But I didn't," he soothed. "We're both all right."

"No thanks to that psycho," Eugene grouched. "What the hell do they think they're playing at?"

Guilt swelled in my chest. "I'm sorry," I said, suddenly regretting my agreement earlier to back off from trying to do things on my own. These loving people had been dragged into a nasty situation because of me. They didn't deserve to have me disrupting their lives. "I never meant for Liam to get hurt."

"Oh, sweetheart." Heather pulled me into an embrace, shocking me so much I didn't know how to respond. "We know you didn't. Please don't feel guilty for this. The only person responsible is the one who destroyed the brakes and broke into Liam's house."

My lower lip wobbled, and for a disastrous moment, I thought I might burst into tears, but I managed to school my emotions.

"Come in." Heather placed a hand on both of our backs and guided us toward the entrance. "You're welcome to stay for as long as you need. As soon as I heard what happened, I put fresh sheets on one of the spare beds, and there are brownies in the oven."

"Brownies?" Liam perked up.

Eugene clapped him on the shoulder. "She wanted to rush down to the police station, but Nate said to give you time, so she stress baked instead."

"There are cookies too," Heather assured Liam, "and enough dinner for everyone."

My heart warmed, and the trepidation I'd been feeling about their reaction to us turning up unannounced melted away. They'd expected us to come here. They'd prepared for us. Because that's what family did. And it felt so good to be part of their family once again.

Chapter Forty-Five

KENNEDY

LIAM AND I SPENT SUNDAY AT HIS PARENT'S HOUSE, PLAYING Scrabble and fielding visits from every one of his siblings except Connor, who sent a message but didn't turn up in person. It warmed my heart to know they cared.

At the end of the day, Nate informed us that the police were still going over Liam's house, but that he'd arranged for someone to come over when they were done and install new locks. Meanwhile, we'd stay where we were. He also let us know that they hadn't been able to confirm an alibi for Aiden or determine whether the missing paparazzo was still in the country, nor had they had any luck calling around local accommodation providers and inquiring about their guests.

On Monday, Liam and Heather both had to go to work, and Eugene was called in to cover for Bailey, who was at home with a cold. He invited me to join him at the pub, but I didn't feel like being out in public, so I organized to spend time with Blair instead. He was alone because

Tyler had signed up for an adventure tour that Blair wasn't interested in.

I dropped Liam off at the fire station and drove to the cottage. Blair was standing outside, waiting for me. The moment I got out of the car, he raced over and swept me into a crushing hug.

"It's only been a day," I protested as the air left my chest in a whoosh.

"Feels like a month," he said, releasing me. "I'm glad you're still okay." He drew back and studied my face. "I hope the Braddocks are treating you well."

"They are."

"Good."

We walked up the path to the cottages and stopped outside mine. We'd decided that it made more sense to set up there since there were security measures in place, even if they hadn't been completely effective in the past. I unlocked the door and tapped the code into the alarm box but left the security camera running. I strode inside and flopped onto the sofa, then pulled my laptop out of the overnight bag I'd packed what felt like a lifetime ago.

"I've got some photos to edit," I told Blair.

"Cool. I have a song to write." He pulled a notepad from his pocket.

"Want a movie on in the background?" I asked. "Or will that distract you?"

He hummed thoughtfully. "Something we've seen before would be fine. That way it's just background noise."

"Sure."

I switched the TV on and hunted through the options until I found something we agreed on—a screwball spy comedy we'd watched several times in the past. For the next hour, we worked companionably together. Me on my laptop, and him writing on his notepad—which more often than not entailed screwing up sheets of paper and tossing them aside.

After a while, Blair stood up. "I've got to use the bathroom."

"Want me to pause the show for you?"

He glanced at the screen. "Nah. I know what happens and, uh, I might be a while, if you get my drift."

I grimaced. I got it, all right.

"You'll be okay here?" he asked.

"Of course. You're not leaving the cottage, right? If I yell, you'll hear me."

He nodded and left the room. I resumed editing the photographs, lingering on one of Liam and me walking to Destiny Tarn for the midsummer dip. It had only been a couple of days ago, but the lighthearted excitement I'd felt seemed a world away. Amazing how much everything could change in a short period of time, but I guessed that was pretty much the story of my life.

I moved on to another photo. Then another. When half an hour had passed and Blair hadn't returned, nerves started to churn in my stomach.

"Blair!" I called, pausing the TV while I waited for a response.

Nothing.

Fear tightened my gut. I tiptoed to the kitchen and grabbed the biggest knife I could find. I was probably over-reacting, but better safe than sorry.

I made my way to the bathroom and paused outside.

"Blair?"

No response.

"If you don't say something right now, I'm coming in."

When I didn't hear as much as a bump from the bath-room, I reached for the handle. To my surprise, it opened. Unlocked. The door swung inward, then knocked into something and stopped.

"Blair?" My voice shook. I eased forward to peek around the door. My instincts were screaming at me that something was wrong and that I should run, but surely I'd have heard if anything had happened.

Slowly, a pair of feet entered my field of vision, tied at the ankles.

Goosebumps erupted over my body, and I broke out in a cold sweat but forced myself to keep going. I saw my brother's thighs, his hips, and then his hands, which had also been bound with a zip tie.

I should run.

My mind howled at me to bolt. But my baby brother was in that room, and I needed to know if he was okay. I pressed my palms to the bathroom door and shoved. It opened all at once, revealing the rest of Blair's unconscious body. His eyes were closed, his mouth taped shut. And there, standing over him, was a man wearing all black, his face hidden by a balaclava over what looked to be a pair of pantyhose.

I screamed.

When the man moved, I noticed the black handgun he held steady and leveled at my chest.

"Shut up," he hissed with an American accent. "Drop the knife."

I clapped my lips together, my gaze bouncing back down to Blair sprawled on the floor. I checked for signs of blood. He wasn't dead. He couldn't be, otherwise the man wouldn't have bothered to restrain him, right?

I didn't let go of the knife.

"Drop it," he barked. "Or I'll shoot him."

I let the knife go. It clattered to the tiled floor.

"What did you do to him?" I whispered.

The man ignored me. He aimed the gun at me with one hand while he knelt and fetched Blair's lyric notepad off the floor with the other.

"Here's what's going to happen," he said, his voice hoarse and breathy, as if he was trying to disguise it.

"Aiden?" I cut in before he could finish.

The intruder stalked forward. I stumbled away, tripping over my feet and falling on my ass with a painful thump. I scrambled up as he emerged from the bathroom, and I glanced toward the exit, wondering if I could escape if I ran for it. But then what would he do to Blair?

"Don't even think about it," he growled and tossed the lyric notepad at me, the gun never wavering. I instinctively caught the notepad. "You're going to write a letter to your boyfriend, telling him you've decided to leave."

"No!" My chest seized. I couldn't do that. Assuming this guy had planned how to make it appear that I'd left of my own accord, reading a letter like that would destroy Liam. I couldn't hurt him that way again.

The intruder whipped his free hand up and smacked me across the face. Pain exploded in my cheek. My head snapped around, and the muscles of my neck screeched in protest, not having fully recovered from the accident.

"Yes, you are." The gun still didn't waver. "I know how to shoot, and if you don't do what I say within the next twenty seconds, I'm going to put a bullet in you—not to kill you, just to stop you moving—and then I'll go back into the bathroom and put one into your brother's skull."

I whimpered. Oh God. He was serious. Nothing about his tone or demeanor said he was bluffing. If I didn't do as he said, he'd kill Blair—presuming he wasn't already dead. I could survive getting shot myself, but I couldn't be responsible for another death in my family. It was my job to protect my siblings, and if this was what it took, then I'd just have to do my best to send a message to Liam that my captor would overlook.

"Okay," I relented, grabbing the notepad. "But I need a pen."

He nodded. "Don't try anything."

He followed as I retreated to the living room in search of a pen. My heart hammered wildly as I mentally sifted through options. If I followed his instructions, I'd keep him calm, but there was no telling what he planned to do, and I didn't want to make things easy for him. If I delayed, someone might notice something was amiss and send in a rescue team.

I sat on the sofa, pen in one hand, paper in the other, and a gaping pit of despair in my gut. Who knew what this guy would do to me once he had me on his own? But at least if I got him away from Blair, there was a chance my brother might be okay.

With shaking hands, I scrawled a note, praying Liam would understand what I was trying to tell him. When I'd finished, I pretended I was still writing, and reached into my pocket with my left hand to activate my phone by touch. I couldn't afford to try to look at the screen and risk him seeing, so I pictured the swipes and pushes I'd need to make to activate the location tracker function and crossed my fingers that it would work.

"Good girl," the man said after I withdrew my hand and set the notepad down. "This will only hurt for a second."

Something pinched my upper arm, and then the world went dark.

Chapter Forty-Six

LIAM

I love you. Stay safe. - Message from Liam to Kennedy, earlier today

WE WERE CRAMMED INTO THE ENGINE ON OUR WAY BACK TO the fire station after assisting at a workplace accident at a vineyard out of town when my phone rang. I glanced at Parks, who gestured for me to take it.

"Hello?" I said, raising the phone to my ear.

"Where are you?" It was Nate's voice. His abrupt tone made me sit up straight.

"Driving back from a callout. What is it?"

"Kennedy is missing."

"What the fuck?" I exclaimed. "How? Blair was with her. He'd have stuck to her like glue."

"He was drugged."

"What?" I shook my head, trying to make sense of his

words. How could Blair have been drugged if he and Kennedy were together? And where was Kennedy?

I should never have left her alone this morning, but I'd thought we'd done as much as we could to ensure her safety.

Beside me, Zane glanced over, concern in his eyes. "You okay?" he mouthed.

I looked away.

"As far as I can tell, Blair needed to use the bathroom. As soon as he was out of Kennedy's sight, the perp drugged him and tied his wrists and ankles. He doesn't seem to have been injured other than that, but he's on the way to hospital for a full tox screen."

"He agreed to leave while Kennedy was missing?" I couldn't imagine Blair willingly going anywhere.

"It was either that or I'd be forced to lock him up until he stopped threatening to commit homicide." Nate made a weary sound. "Not much of a choice. Anyway, when he came to, Kennedy was gone. There was a knife in the room, and he managed to use it to free himself so he could find help."

"How long ago was this?"

"Fifteen minutes. I called as soon as I could. We're assembling an operation. I've brought in reinforcements, and Connor is planning to gather a group of park rangers to search the forest surrounding town."

"Fuck." My mind whirled. Just like that, Kennedy was gone with no warning. It was like history repeating itself except this time, she hadn't had a choice in the matter. God only knew what the sick bastard might be doing to her. "How did they get into the cottage?"

"He knew the code. The security feed shows an average size man dressed all in black letting himself in the front door. He must have seen someone else enter the code.

Perhaps even watched as Kennedy disarmed the alarms when they arrived this morning."

My stomach dropped to my shoes. Whoever this guy was, he was prepared. If he'd been so well organized in getting into the cottage, I could only imagine he'd had his exit strategy as meticulously planned. By now, he could be out of town with Kennedy in the back of his car. Or he might have relocated her somewhere we'd never think to look.

"Did you see what condition Kennedy was in when they left?" I asked.

"She appeared unconscious. We're operating under the assumption that he gave her the same drug he did Blair, which makes it all the more important we find out what that was."

"Where are you now?" I asked.

"At the police station."

"I'll get there as soon as I can."

As soon as we were back in Destiny Falls, I borrowed Asher's car and raced to the police station. When I arrived, the receptionist escorted me to the open-plan area behind the interview rooms. It buzzed with intense conversation and activity from at least twelve occupants—many of whom were uniformed police officers.

"Liam," Nate said, hastening to my side. In his grip was a sheet of paper wrapped in a clear bag. He held it out for me to see. "This was left at the scene. Does it mean anything to you?"

I skimmed the text, my insides lurching when I recognized Kennedy's handwriting, but it wasn't as tidy as usual. I had to squint and tilt my head to make sense of it.

Liam,

I'm leaving Destiny Falls. After a lot of thinking, I've decided I'm better off elsewhere, and I've taken steps to ensure you can't find me, the same way I used to with paparazzi. I hope you can respect my decision like I respect your preference for Americanos to lattes, even though I disagree.

All the best,

Kennedy

I stared at the words, struggling to comprehend them. The whole thing was wrong. For starters, it felt garbled, as though she'd been under a lot of stress when she wrote it. But that only brushed the surface.

My mind whirred, trying to make sense of it. What did she mean that she'd taken steps to ensure I wouldn't find her, the same way she did with the paparazzi?

A memory struck me. The two of us packed into a fire engine cab with a bunch of other sweaty firefighters. Me asking her about the guy at the accident scene who'd photographed her. Kennedy telling me she should have switched off her Bluetooth and location tracker. Something clicked into place. She'd been forced to write this, but she'd tried to leave us a trail of breadcrumbs.

I grabbed Nate's arm. "I think she left her Bluetooth and the location tracker function on her phone switched on. Is there a way we can search for her using that?"

He frowned. "Maybe. I'll look into it. Anything else you get from this?"

I read it again. "That last sentence is strange. She knows I prefer cappuccinos to both lattes and Americanos. It's a weird way to say it. Unless…."

"Unless it's another message," Nate finished.

I looked up. "I think whoever took her is American."

He nodded. "It's a possibility. I'll see if we've got eyes on any of our favorite Americans." He cleared his throat. "One thing I don't understand. Why force her to write a note? He must have known Blair would be found and the security footage discovered, so it would be obvious she hadn't left of her own accord."

"Perhaps he planned to come back for Blair. Without the kitchen knife, Blair would have had more difficulty getting free. Perhaps the guy forgot about the knife and expected to have more time to return and tidy up after himself."

"Maybe."

My lips pinched together. "Or perhaps it wasn't a logical decision. They might have been angry and wanted to hurt me." I felt a ring of truth in the words, so I continued. "From what we know, it seems like the stalker wants Kennedy to himself. I'm getting in the way of that. Perhaps the note was a type of petty revenge. He knew we wouldn't believe it long term, but maybe he had hoped to fuck with my head in the meantime?"

"It's possible," Nate agreed.

But even if Blair hadn't managed to summon help, brilliant Kennedy had made sure I'd know something was up. My heart expanded. God, I loved her so much.

Footsteps marched into the room behind me, and I spun. It was Constable Mehrtens, her eyes alive with the thrill of finally seeing some proper police action.

"Sir, we made contact with the resort. They reported that Aiden Waldron isn't answering his door, and his rental vehicle isn't in the parking lot. His business colleagues are also absent, and none of them are picking up their phones."

"Thanks, Constable. Good work. Any other leads?"

"We haven't been able to get a hold of Tyler Johnson. He told Blair Carter he was going on an ATV tour, but he didn't mention with whom. We're calling around the local adventure tour companies at the moment to find out where he's supposed to be."

"Keep it up." Nate dismissed her with a nod, then

called out, "Anderson, any leads on the names Kennedy's security guy sent us?"

"Not yet, sir, but I just received confirmation that the photographer who'd been bothering her departed Queenstown airport yesterday. He flew to Auckland, where he stayed overnight, and his boarding pass was scanned at the gates of a direct flight to LAX."

"I guess that's something." Nate gritted his teeth. "Patton, have you managed to track down any witnesses who saw vehicles in and around the site of the abduction at approximately 11:00 a.m.?"

A young constable with a wisp of a mustache snapped to attention. "The neighbor across the road reports seeing no unusual vehicles or activity and says that she's usually very alert to comings and goings. Nobody else seems to have seen anything, including the homeowner, but Cross and Moore are still knocking on doors."

"We need to get out and look for her," I muttered to Nate. "This isn't getting anywhere. Do you have boots on the ground, doing a search?"

Nate gave me a look that said I was pushing all of his buttons but that he'd let me get away with it in the circumstances. "Yes, Liam, we do. But we can't send everyone out willy-nilly with no trail to follow. We need to be smart about this."

I fought the urge to hit something. "What can I do to help?"

Chapter Forty-Seven

KENNEDY

My head throbbed and my mouth was dry. I couldn't see anything. I tried to force my eyes open, but they refused to cooperate. Beyond the thump of blood in my ears, I could hear the sounds of someone moving nearby. I concentrated, trying to remember what had happened. It all flooded back to me in an instant.

Blair on the ground.

The intruder, face hidden by a balaclava.

The gun.

The letter.

Then a prick in my upper arm, which must have been a needle. He'd drugged me.

Keeping my eyes shut, I drew a slow breath through my nostrils, gathering what information I could about my surroundings. Based on the woody scent of the air, I assumed I wasn't at the cottage anymore. I couldn't feel a breeze, so we might be indoors. Not in a car because I was lying on something soft and had plenty of room to stretch my limbs. I shifted my feet and felt something coarse rub at my ankles. He must have bound them with rope. Testing my wrists, I felt the smooth, cool plastic of a zip tie around them. He'd restrained me the same way he had Blair. But what was over my face?

I tried to focus on the sensation of the fabric against my skin. It was soft. Dark. Covering not only my eyes, but my cheeks and chin as well. Not a blindfold. I moved my head ever so slightly and felt fabric brush against the back of my neck.

It was a hood. Perhaps a bag of some kind or a pillow-case. It wasn't secured around my throat, which meant that if I wriggled down, I might be able to get free of it. But I might also attract my captor's attention.

A latch clicked, and a draft swirled through the room. Something rustled, then the latch clicked again, and the draft ended. Perhaps it had been a door opening and closing. I strained my ears for several seconds but didn't hear anything, so I shimmied down the soft surface, slowly working the covering off my face. It took a few minutes, and the adrenaline surging through my veins reminded me that my captor might return at any second, but eventually, I was able to shake it off, blinking against the light.

As my vision adjusted, I realized I was in a poorly lit room, lying on a broad bunk bed. There was a wooden counter along the opposite wall and an old-fashioned fire-place standing empty. My best guess was that I was in an old musterer's cabin.

I sat up. My vision swam and my stomach rolled unpleasantly—perhaps an aftereffect of whatever he'd drugged me with. Through a small window above the counter, I could see tussock extending into the horizon with no other buildings in sight. But closer, right outside, was a four-wheeled motorcycle with a blond man sitting astride it. He had broad shoulders and tidy hair. Recognition set in an instant before he glanced around and made eye contact.

Tyler.

His mouth dropped open, and his frame went rigid. His mouth moved, but I couldn't hear what he was saying.

I threw myself backward, trying to get out of sight because I instinctively knew that this wasn't good. Tyler wasn't part of any rescue party. He was the one who'd brought me here. His eyes, burning into mine, had been cold and assessing. No sign of his usual gentle, friendly demeanor. My back hit the wall and I curled into a ball. There was nothing nearby I could use to protect myself, and even if there had been, my hands and ankles were still bound. The door crashed open, and Tyler strode in, his expression dark.

"You weren't supposed to see me." His voice grumbled like a thundercloud. I generally thought of Tyler as a nice, levelheaded guy, but it seemed I didn't know him at all.

"What do you want?" I asked, shakier than I'd have liked.

He rolled his eyes. "What every guy always wants. To get the girl." He stalked closer, watching me the way I imagined a shark would a fish right before it became dinner. "I had everything planned perfectly. When Blair got free, it put a kink in my plans, but I had it figured out. I was going to find you and be the hero. You just had to ruin it." He shook his head, but I didn't care, I was too relieved about what he'd said about my brother.

"Blair is okay?"

He ignored my question. "Fuck, Kennedy. All you had to do was lie still and play the damsel in distress, and everything would have been fine."

"I don't understand."

"Of course you don't." He huffed. "You never have. First, I thought it was because you'd known me as a kid and needed to see that I'd grown up and was ready to settle down, so I got a girlfriend and hoped that would do the trick. But you were still blind about what was right in front of you, and the bitch wasn't as dumb as I'd hoped. She knew I wanted you, and she did everything she could to keep me away from you. I had to end it before she said anything to make you suspicious."

"You broke up?" I asked, hoping he meant that and not that he'd hurt the poor girl.

"Yeah." He caught my eye. "That's when I knew I needed to step up my game."

"So, you started stalking me?" What happened to asking someone out? Not that I'd have said yes, of course, and perhaps he knew that.

He leaned forward, his gaze cold. "I figured it would go one of two ways. Either you'd like the attention, or you'd be freaked out and need comfort, which I'd be right there to provide. I didn't expect you to get on a plane and fly halfway around the fucking world."

I felt sick. All this time, I'd thought my problems could be attributed to some crazy fan, but it turned out the culprit had been much closer to home. I'd trusted him. Welcomed him into our lives. Let him fool me.

Tyler sat on the edge of the bed, never taking his eyes off me. "Now, thanks to you, I'm going to have to find another way to play this." He bit his lip, and for a second, he looked like the boy I'd known years ago. A bit lost. In over his head. "I don't want to hurt you. All I've ever wanted is to love you, but you just wouldn't love me back." He punctuated the statement by thumping a fist onto the bare mattress. "I've taken care of you. I'd have given you everything you ever wanted, but you never loved me."

Thoughts flew through my mind, one on top of the other. Jumbled. Desperate.

But it all came back to a single, unavoidable truth:

Tyler was obsessed with me. He didn't want to hurt me, he just wanted to have me to himself. I was an actress. I could make him believe his dream might come true. My life depended on it.

"I do love you," I said quickly, my voice raspy because of the dryness in my throat. "I've loved you for a long time, I just wasn't sure if you felt the same way, and when you got a girlfriend, I assumed you didn't."

"I don't believe you." His tone was flat. "I looked for any hint you might have feelings for me a thousand times. I analyzed every word and action. But I never saw anything. Besides." He dropped his trump card. "If you supposedly love me so much, why would you fly ten thousand miles to reunite with an asshole who doesn't deserve you?"

I thought quickly. "Because I hoped if I said I was moving away, you'd step up and make a play for me. But you didn't." I stuck my lower lip out in an exaggerated pout. I felt ridiculous, but he seemed to be considering my lie, so I'd take that as a small win. I glanced around the room, hoping to see something I could use against him, but nothing stood out as an obvious choice. "Do you not care about me enough to take a chance?"

He glowered. I might have pushed too far with that comment, but my thinking was sluggish, and I was having a difficult time gaging his mood.

"What do you call this, then?" he demanded.

"Good point," I said, cringing a little. Despite the screwup, he didn't come any closer and seemed to have lost some of the tension he'd been carrying a few minutes ago. I needed to keep him talking.

"This whole thing has been so clever of you." I rubbed my lips together, trying to moisten them.

"How so?" He sounded skeptical but interested.

"I never had any idea who you were." A complete

truth. "How did you make that phone call after the accident without Blair knowing?"

He rolled his eyes. "It was hardly a challenge. All I had to do was prerecord a message and pay someone I found on online to send it through when I gave them the signal."

Now that he mentioned it, I recalled that the voice on the phone had made a simple statement and then the call had ended. They hadn't engaged in conversation, nor had they even seemed to react to Liam's outburst.

"And keying my car?" I asked. "You weren't even in the country when that happened."

He shrugged. "I knew that greedy paparazzo was nearby because of the photographs he posted online, so I paid him to do it. He was only too happy to help out. It would have been great publicity for him if your people hadn't squashed the story. Delivering the Christmas gift was easy too. Everyone wants to make a quick buck these days, especially at that time of year. I hired some clueless idiot and promised a bonus if he made sure no one saw him. I told him it was a surprise for my girlfriend." He shook his head. "Moron."

I felt a chill. I'd never guessed that Blair's sweet friend was so calculating. I bit my lip—hard—and tasted blood. "I had no idea."

"I know." His grin froze my insides. "And that brings us to where we are. Unfortunately, I have to decide what to do with you next."

Chapter Forty-Eight

LIAM

I know you probably won't see this, but I need you to be okay. — text message from Liam to Kennedy, sent Monday 16 January

Time seemed to crawl while Nate and his fellow officers came up with a plan. I knew they had people out looking for Kennedy, and that thanks to Mum's communication skills, most of Destiny Falls had closed shop for the day to help with the search, but it didn't feel like enough. I'd briefly joined in but had returned to the police station when I couldn't still my frantic mind. I needed to be in the center of the action and up-to-date with any developments, which meant I was better off here. Based on the looks some of the cops had given me, I was lucky they'd allowed me to stay, so I tried to make myself unobtrusive, hovering in a corner and using an online group chat to help coordinate the community search.

We'd heard from the hospital that Blair had been drugged with ketamine. I'd instantly gone down a rabbit hole on the internet to find out what that meant. Apparently ketamine was an animal tranquilizer, often used as an anesthetic, but some people took it recreationally, which must have been how the stalker got his hands on it.

The phone company had confirmed that Kennedy's phone was within the vicinity of Destiny Falls, but due to the patchy coverage up here, they couldn't pin down a precise location. According to Nate, they thought she was most likely in the area between the township and the ski resort.

"Sergeant Braddock," Officer Mehrtens called as she strode into the room with a phone in her hand. "I think I've got something."

Nate cocked a brow. "What is it?"

"I've called all adventure activity providers within fifty kilometers, and none of them have any record of Tyler Johnson participating in a tour today. He isn't answering his phone and, if you'll recall, Miss Carter mentioned she thought Johnson previously had a romantic interest in her. What if he's the stalker?"

"You might be onto something," Nate replied.

I strained to make sure I didn't miss any of their conversation, my coordination role temporarily forgotten.

"That would explain how the perp knew the alarm code," he continued. "Johnson would have had plenty of opportunity to find it out. But he and Blair were together when the stalker called Kennedy while she was in our interview room."

"Calls can be faked," Mehrtens said.

"It's possible." Nate clapped loudly, drawing the attention of the other officers in the room. "We have a potential suspect. Tyler Johnson. Male, blond, midtwenties. Constable Mehrtens will circulate his personal details to you shortly." He nodded at Mehrtens, who leapt into action. "I want you to dig up any information you can about him and any connections he might have to sites within the area indicated by Kennedy Carter's mobile service provider." Nate pointed at the man with the wispy mustache. "You. Contact Blair Carter and get Johnson's phone number. There's a chance we'll be able to determine whether he and Kennedy are in the same location." He turned to another uniformed officer. "Patton, find out Johnson's movements from the moment he arrived in the country. I want to know exactly when he landed, everywhere he's been, and what he's spent money on."

"Yes, sir."

Nate paused for a moment to think. "We'll issue a public BOLO alert for Johnson and the rental vehicle he and Carter share. Carter should be able to provide the license plate and other details. It's possible Johnson has a secondary mode of transportation and somewhere to lie low, so it may be worth asking any locals if they've had dealings with him." He gestured at a tall female officer. "Anderson, I want you on that as a priority."

"Yes, Sarge."

My stomach knotted. I'd never liked Tyler Johnson, but I'd put my dislike down to jealousy over the fact he'd gotten to be part of Kennedy's life in L.A. when I'd never had that chance. Maybe I shouldn't have ignored the niggle telling me not to trust him. If I'd said something, Kennedy might still be safe.

"How are you holding up?" Nate asked quietly.

"Managing," I said, returning my attention to the phone in my hand and the search party's group chat because that was easier to deal with than the sympathy in my brother's eyes.

"Keep it up." He clapped me on the shoulder and got back to work.

Another hour crawled by. The community searchers cleared the buildings on the edge of the township nearest the ski resort. The rangers could find no sign of Kennedy or Tyler on the trails close to that edge of the township and were now venturing further afield.

Then Constable Anderson straightened and shouted for Nate. Finding herself the center of attention, her cheeks colored and she stammered, loud enough for everyone to hear, "Th-there's a farm cabin rented under Johnson's father's name. It's accessible by one of the private gravel accesses that comes off the road to Destiny Peak within the perimeter of the area flagged by the cell phone company. According to the property manager, Johnson has been renting it for several weeks."

A shiver of discomfort ran through me at the thought that he'd been quietly planning this while living right next door to Kennedy.

"Assemble a tactical team to storm the cabin." Nate's tone was authoritative. "We need armed officers in full protective gear. I'm trained in hostage negotiation, but hopefully those skills won't be needed."

My fists clenched at the thought that Tyler might be holding Kennedy hostage. Who knew what he'd do if cornered?

"I'm coming," I said.

Nate shook his head. "We can't have civilians getting in the way. It's too risky."

Anger flashed through me. I wanted to get in his face and yell at him. Remind him of how he'd feel if it was Tess or Grace who'd been taken. But before I could, my phone buzzed with an incoming message. When I glanced down, it was from him.

Nate: *We can't stop a civilian if he happens to follow us at a distance. But don't interfere.*

My heart lifted, and I watched as Nate assembled a

team, determined to follow as soon as they left. Kennedy needed me, and I wouldn't let her down.

Chapter Forty-Nine

KENNEDY

As TIME WORE ON, TYLER GREW INCREASINGLY AGITATED. At first, he'd spoken calmly, but now he couldn't seem to decide what to do, and it was causing him to spiral. With how long he'd been gone from town, he feared somebody would notice he was missing and make the connection. He said he couldn't let me go because I'd be able to identify him, but he hadn't been able to convince himself to take any other course of action.

According to his ramblings as he paced the length of the cabin, killing me would be the safest option, provided he could figure out how to dispose of my body. I was glad for his reluctance, but it seemed to be waning. He'd debated drugging me and hoping my memory would be fuzzy, but he didn't want to take the risk. He'd considered beating me until I wasn't capable of communicating anymore, but he didn't seem to have a taste for hands-on violence.

The way he muttered to himself turned me cold. With

every passing minute, he seemed to be becoming more erratic. I couldn't be sure how long his unwillingness to harm me would continue.

"Perhaps I could dose you and move you far from Destiny Falls," he said more to himself than to me. "They can't search the whole country, and my father has connections at the port in Wellington. If I could get you there, I might be able to ship you back to L.A."

"And then what?" I asked, unsure whether I wanted to know the answer.

He looked at me as if I was stupid. "Then I'd find somewhere to keep you."

An invisible band tightened around my chest. "K-keep me?" I stared at him. "Like a pet?"

"Like a beautiful bird." He sounded unhinged, the cracks showing through his usual facade.

I wanted to scream at him, but I held back. If the other option was death, I could handle being his caged bird. At least there was a chance I could break free or that somebody might find me.

"Okay," I said. "So do that."

"But where would we go? We have to get out of here." He kicked the edge of the bunk in frustration. "I'd charter a helicopter, but the pilot might not keep his mouth shut." He shook his head, dismissing that idea. "I need to get you to the car, but I can't trust you to go without a fuss."

"I'll behave." My stomach flipped at the possibility of getting outside the cabin. If my legs were freed and we were out in the open, I might be able to run. "I promise."

He hummed in thought. "We'd need to move soon. They could be looking for the car. If we get to Queenstown, I can swap it for another." He glanced at me. "I'm going to cut the rope around your ankles, but if you try to run, I'll be forced to shoot you." His expression was hesitant. "I don't want to do that."

Then don't, I almost retorted.

"I won't run." I opened my eyes wide, hoping I looked sincere. It would be best if he underestimated me. I allowed my lower lip to wobble. It didn't take much. "I don't like pain. Please, let's do it this way. I promise not to try anything silly." *Like staying with you for one second longer than necessary.*

"You'd better not," he warned. "Remember what I said earlier. I'm a good shot."

I nodded, hoping he didn't have much experience shooting at moving targets. I knew Blair disapproved of hunting, so hopefully Tyler—his friend—shared that sentiment, and there must be a difference between shooting at a target versus a person, right?

He reached into his pocket and extracted a Swiss army knife, which he used to sever first the zip ties and then the coarse rope. Blood flow returned to my feet. They prickled and burned, the sensation verging on painful. He returned the knife to his pocket and offered me a hand.

"Just remember, if you run, I'll shoot. And don't bother screaming. No one will hear you."

Dread curdled in my stomach.

Just where were we? I'd imagined us not far from Destiny Falls, but if he'd taken me somewhere remote, any attempt to run might prove pointless. He had the ATV, after all. Even if he missed the shot, he'd be able to come after me faster than I could run away.

Reluctantly, I took his hand. He pulled me to my feet. They throbbed uncomfortably beneath me, and when we took a few steps toward the exit, I had the strangest sensation that my limbs were separate from the rest of my body. They didn't seem to be going where I thought they should, and I felt dissociated from them. I wondered if it was an aftereffect of the drug or if it was because of the poor circulation to my feet for the past however many hours.

As we approached the window, a flicker of movement outside caught my attention. I glanced at Tyler, but he didn't seem to have noticed. I looked again, squinting to make out the details. The motion had stopped, but I could swear there were darker patches among the tussock that hadn't been there earlier. Perhaps it was a trick of the fading light, but I didn't think so.

My heartbeat picked up, and I felt as though the organ might race right out of my chest. I stared at one of the dark patches, noticing it had a faintly human shape. Had the police finally tracked me down? Were Tyler and I walking into an ambush? More importantly, were they as trigger happy as he was, or would they try to separate us before they started shooting?

A bead of sweat trickled down my spine. I hoped they wouldn't shoot immediately, but if they didn't, it would give Tyler the chance to use me as a shield, and then who knew what would happen? I couldn't risk it. I shivered, and Tyler noticed. He paused, shrugging out of his sweater and offering it to me.

"No, thanks," I said, aware that if someone was out there, the sweater might cause them to mistake me for him.

"Put it on." The way the gun twitched in his clasp made it clear I shouldn't argue. I did as he said. Once, I might have found it romantic if a man offered me his jacket, but now, I wished I didn't have to touch something that had been against his skin.

The sweater on, we continued to the door. I held my breath as he opened it, trying to make myself small in case bullets started flying.

None came.

I sought out one of the dark patches from before to see if I'd been mistaken, but I was almost certain it was a person. Tyler guided me to the edge of the small wooden porch where the four-wheeler motorcycle waited.

"I'll drive. You get on behind and hold my waist," he said. "If you run, I'll shoot."

"Okay." I felt a burst of hope mingled with fear. This was it. My moment.

As we started down the steps, I lurched to the side and shoved Tyler with as much force as I could muster. Then I ran from him as fast as my numb feet could carry me. I heard a shout. Figures rose from the tussock, weapons drawn.

There was a shot. A sharp burning pain tore through my shoulder. My feet stopped working.

Another shot.

I hit the ground.

Noise surrounded me. Murmured voices. A vicelike grip clamped on my good shoulder and rolled me over. Above me, the sky was an endless gray. A bank of cloud that seemed to go on forever. I stared up at it, unable to blink. My vision swam. Then a face appeared. A beloved pair of blue eyes awash with concern. Somebody was saying my name.

My vision flickered.

Liam's lips were moving, but all I could hear was the pulse banging in my ears and the sound of my own thoughts.

Black tinged the edge of my vision, slowly easing inward, swallowing Liam's golden face into the darkness.

Nothing.

Jostling. More shoulder pain. A blur of movement.

Blackness.

A stiff bed beneath me. White roof overhead. The wail of a siren.

Nothing.

Chapter Fifty

LIAM

Please, God, if you exist, save this woman. She means everything to me. I'll do anything. Quit swearing. Donate every penny of my savings to charity. Go to church every Sunday for the rest of my life. Just please don't let her die. - A silent prayer from Liam to the universe

Shot.

The word rattled around my brain.

The love of my life had been shot.

I'd seen it happen as if in slow motion through the video camera attached to Nate's vest. She'd broken away from Tyler and made a run for it. For an elated second, I'd thought she was free and that everyone would go home in one piece, but then she'd dropped like a puppet with the strings cut. I had to watch through the live video feed as the armed rescue team took Tyler down and rushed to Kennedy's side. At that point, I hadn't been able to wait any longer. I'd left the car and sprinted to them.

Now, I stared at her pale face as Asher tried to stem the bleeding. We were in the back of an ambulance, hurtling toward the Destiny Falls Medical Center at high speed.

"I can't lose her," I said. "Not again."

"You won't." Asher spoke as he worked, not stopping for a second. "It's a shoulder wound. She's bleeding a lot but should be all right as long as we get her to hospital soon."

The nearest full-service hospital was hours away. I may not know much about bullet wounds, but I doubted she had hours.

"Hold tight," the driver called.

Asher stabilized Kennedy, and I held onto a handle on the side of the vehicle as we swung around a corner. Although I couldn't see where we were going, I assumed that was the turn from the ski road onto the main highway to Destiny Falls. We weren't far now.

"She's so white." I reached for Kennedy's hand. "Is there anything I can do?"

"Just let me do my job." Asher's words had no temper behind them. They were brusque. Businesslike. If I didn't know him better, I might think this was no different from any other callout, but I could read the tension in his body. The intensity of his focus.

A few minutes later, we slowed and came to a stop. The rear doors opened, and Max leaped inside. He had a bag of medical supplies and placed it on the floor as he asked Asher to run him through Kennedy's condition.

"There's a chopper on the way," Max said. "I've cleared the landing pad behind the clinic. ETA is ten minutes."

Asher nodded. Max stepped up beside Kennedy, and I shuffled aside as he and Asher worked seamlessly. They had years of experience together, and it showed as they did what they could for Kennedy with few words spoken between them. The paramedic who'd been driving joined them, ushering me out of the ambulance.

A few minutes later, they carried her on a stretcher around the end of the building. I followed, listening to the roar of an approaching chopper. It was easy to spot in the darkening sky. Slowly, it descended. A door opened and Max and Asher loaded Kennedy inside. Asher jumped in, and Max glanced over his shoulder at me.

"It's going to be a tight fit," he yelled. "You want to ride with us or meet us there?"

In answer, I pulled myself into the chopper and claimed the only free seat. We rose into the air. I couldn't see Kennedy from my position, so I distracted myself from the agonizing worry by messaging the group chat to say we had her, were on route to the hospital, and that the searchers could go home. A moment later, I received a private message from Mum, asking which hospital we were going to so they'd be able to meet us there. Emotion swelled in my chest, and I blinked rapidly, rubbing at the spot over my heart. I tapped out a response and checked the time. What if we were too slow? I couldn't handle the thought.

The journey seemed to last forever.

As soon as we arrived in Christchurch, Kennedy was whisked away to surgery. I slumped onto a chair in a waiting room, and a few minutes later, Asher joined me. They'd wanted Max in the operating room. Time passed in a weird vacuum. We drank terrible coffee, bought a bag of peanuts from the vending machine, and Asher ate them while I stared into space. Sometime in the late hours of the night—or early hours of the morning—Max emerged and told us Kennedy was out of surgery and seemed to be stable but was still unconscious.

"Can I visit her?" I asked, desperate to see with my own eyes that she was okay.

"Not yet," Max said apologetically. "She's still under observation. They'll let us know as soon as you can."

Damn.

More coffee.

I choked down a protein bar.

As the light of dawn was breaking, the door to the waiting room opened, and my family spilled in. Mum and Dad, both travel weary and exhausted. Summer and Toby, with matching expressions of concern. Connor, still clad in his park ranger uniform and scowling at his surroundings as though they offended him. And lastly, Grace, with her arm around a deathly pale Blair. The only one absent was Nate, who must be dealing with Tyler and the paperwork associated with the arrest.

I stood up, and Mum enfolded me into a hug. The others gathered around, expressing sympathy and asking for an update.

"She's stable," Max said, and I was glad for it because I wasn't sure I could talk. I just soaked in the comfort of their presence. "We haven't been able to visit with her yet."

"We got here as soon as we could," Mum said. "But we thought we'd better pick Blair up on the way so he could see his sister."

"Not that I deserve to," Blair grumbled. "I can't believe I didn't realize it was Tyler all along. He is—*was*—one of my best friends. We were staying together. I should have picked up on something. If not that, then I should have at least put up a fight when he drugged me. Kennedy needed me, and I let her down."

"No, you didn't," I said, touching his arm. "You did the best you could. He caught you by surprise. You trusted him. There's no shame in that. I was the one who left her there. I should have insisted on taking a shift off."

Blair shook his head. "You left her with me. She should have been safe."

"Boys," Grace interrupted. "Stop with the self-blame. You can't change what happened, and Kennedy wouldn't want either of you beating yourselves up about it."

I opened my mouth. Then shut it. She was right. Blair met my eyes and gave me a slight nod.

"Family of Kennedy Carter," a voice called from behind us.

"That's us," Summer exclaimed, waving a hand in the air.

The nurse's eyes widened a fraction. "She's unconscious but able to receive visitors. I'd ask that no more than two of you enter at once. She needs her rest."

"Let's go." I tugged Blair. "We'll see her first," I said. "I'm her partner, and this is her brother."

"Okay. Come this way."

She led us down a corridor and into a small private room. I wondered if they'd isolated her from other patients so there wouldn't be anyone trying to sell photographs to the press. I forgot sometimes what a big star she was, but if anyone leaked what had happened—as they were bound to —the media would be buzzing for weeks.

Any questions or concerns about the media fallout faded as my gaze landed on Kennedy. She lay motionless against a sea of white, her body covered by blankets, the surgical nightgown she wore hiding her gunshot wound. She looked as though she were simply asleep and might wake at any minute. Blair went to her other side, and we each took a hand. I watched the soft rise and fall of her chest, relief filtering through my veins. She really was alive.

After a while, we left and let the others sit with her. When everybody had taken a turn, Dad offered to book a hotel room so we could catch up on much-needed sleep. I didn't want to leave Kennedy alone, and neither did Blair, so we waved the others off and both settled in the lumpy hospital chairs. At first, I couldn't look away from Kennedy, but after a while, the rhythmic beeping and whirring of the equipment around her lulled me to sleep.

When I woke, I lurched upright, desperate to reassure myself everything was fine.

I jolted in shock. Kennedy's eyes were open, slits of blue peeking between her eyelashes. Her lips moved, forming my name. My heart gave a painful thump.

Chapter Fifty-One

KENNEDY

EVERYTHING HURT.

My body felt lethargic, as if my limbs didn't want to work, and there was a dull throbbing in my shoulder. But none of that mattered when Liam's gorgeous face filled my vision, his eyes glued to me, his forehead crinkled with concern.

"Liam?" I didn't know what I was asking. Perhaps where we were. It clearly wasn't the tussock-covered hills outside the cabin Tyler had taken me to.

"You're okay, sweetheart." He kissed my forehead. I closed my eyes, soaking up the small gesture of affection. Whatever had happened, it seemed like all was right with the world again. I was here. Liam was here. And wherever "here" was, it appeared to be safe. "I love you, and everything is okay."

"W-what happened?" I croaked, my throat dry and a little painful.

Liam grabbed a water bottle from a cabinet nearby and held it to my lips. "Drink."

The cool fluid trickled into my mouth, providing welcome relief.

"Thanks," I said when I'd had enough. "Where are we?"

His Adam's apple bobbed as he swallowed. "You were shot in the shoulder, but you're safe now. We're in Christchurch Hospital."

"Christchurch?" Just how much had I missed? It was a good five- or six-hour drive from Queenstown to Christchurch.

"We flew here," he explained, as if reading my mind. "They wanted you to have the best possible medical care, and the smaller hospitals wouldn't have been as well equipped."

I started to nod, but my head ached. "Tyler?"

"Hopefully he'll be thrown in prison." The voice came from my other side. With difficulty, I turned my head and saw Blair sitting in an identical chair. Relief filled my chest.

"I'm so glad you're okay," I told him. "I wasn't sure what he'd done to you."

"Apparently he hid in the bathroom and waited for me to come in, then drugged me," Blair said. His tone was dull, his expression tortured. "I was fine when I woke. A bit woozy, a bit nauseous, but that's all." His lips pressed into a grim line. "I'm so sorry, Kenz. I was supposed to protect you, and I failed completely."

I reached for his hand but couldn't stretch far enough. Fortunately, he noticed and scooted closer. "It's not your fault. He was clever."

"I should have known there was a monster hiding beneath that nice-guy exterior," Blair insisted.

My heart clenched. I hated that he was beating himself up over this.

"I didn't see it either," I reminded him. "He was good at disguising himself. I never would have guessed he was the one behind everything."

Blair grimaced. "There were signs."

"You blaming yourself doesn't change what happened," I said as sternly as I could—which was, in fact, quite weakly. "So do me a favor and cut it out."

One side of his mouth hitched up. "Good to see that getting shot didn't make you less of a mom."

"Nothing could do that." I was pleased when his lips curled into a slight smile. I turned back to Liam, wincing at the pounding in my head. Was it the drugs that had done that? Getting shot? Or had I simply hit the ground a little too hard when I fell? I had a vague memory of going face-first into the dirt. "You got the letter?" I reached for Liam's hand.

"I did." His smile was gentle. "That was clever of you. We were able to narrow the search based on your phone's location."

"Good." I'd never been sure if I'd successfully activated the tracker or not. "So, what happened after Tyler drugged me?"

Blair and Liam exchanged a glance.

"We'll tell you the whole story soon," Liam said. "Meanwhile, my family are on their way over from the hotel, and they'd love to see you. Do you feel up for that?"

My heart stuttered. "They're here?"

"All except Nate. He's dealing with the shit storm Tyler created."

I felt wetness on my cheeks and realized I was crying. "Sorry," I sniffled. "I just can't believe they're here."

"You're one of us." Liam squeezed my hand. "They'll always be here for you."

"Okay." I swallowed hard and tried to get myself under control. "I'll see them."

Liam extracted his hand from mine and left. Blair and I sat together in comfortable silence, both of us mentally processing the betrayal we'd experienced and our relief that it was over until Liam returned a few minutes later with a crowd of familiar faces. My heart swelled as they clustered around me, smothering me with hugs and affection.

In moments like this, I missed my own family, but I counted myself lucky to have been adopted into this big-hearted group of Kiwis. But that triggered another thought. Had my siblings heard what happened?

"Blair, have you talked to Mina or either of the twins?"

He winced. "Yeah, I called all of them on the way here. I didn't want them to find out when a reporter approached them for comment."

"Thanks." At least that was one unpleasant job I didn't have to do.

"Don't thank me yet. They're on their way."

My mouth fell open. "What? All three of them?"

"Yeah." He grinned.

"But they have college."

Blair rolled his eyes. "They're students. Missing a few days won't be the end of their career."

The warmth blossoming inside me grew. Yeah, I was pretty damn lucky.

Chapter Fifty-Two

KENNEDY

"WE ALL HAVE TO SQUEEZE INTO *THAT*?" MINA ASKED, staring at the helicopter dubiously. She was probably running through collections of data on helicopter crashes in her head.

"Come on, Meens." Jamie slung an arm around her shoulders and squashed her to his side. "It's safer to fly than drive."

Her face scrunched and she eyeballed him like she wished he'd let go, but I knew she secretly loved her little brothers giving her a hard time. "How do you even know that?"

"You said so," he replied. "Must be true."

Her jaw dropped. "You actually listen to me?"

Joel poked her rib cage playfully. "You were muttering it to yourself the whole time we were on the plane. After that long, it got through even our thick skulls."

"You're not thick," she protested, shoving him. He made a big show of falling away, clutching his chest as if wounded, and his blond hair flopped into his eyes. I hid a smile. Sometimes my brothers reminded me of goofy golden retrievers. Silly and obsessed with food, but very loyal.

"This is going to be a long two hours," Blair said quietly.

Liam nodded in agreement.

It was Friday—four days after the kidnapping—and we'd chartered a helicopter back to Destiny Falls. The Braddocks had returned a couple of days earlier, taking their vehicle with them. We could have gotten a rental car, but I could afford to charter a private helicopter, and it would make for a smoother and quicker ride, so why not?

Still grumbling, Mina climbed aboard. Blair sat beside her, and the twins took the front row. I crossed my fingers and hoped they wouldn't try to lean out the door to get a better look at the view. They'd already announced they wanted to go skydiving in Queenstown while they were here, and who knew what other brilliant ideas they'd have. Liam and I sat in the back. He took my hand and clasped it tight.

"I love you," I whispered.

He raised my knuckles to his mouth and kissed them. "Love you too."

"Get a room!" Joel called, having glanced over just in time to see our intimate moment.

The pilot ran through a spiel about safety, giving the boys in the front row a particularly stern look. He closed everything up, settled in, and we rose into the air.

This helicopter trip was far more memorable than the other—although since I'd been shot, I thought I could be forgiven for not remembering much of the previous one. Sweeping green paddocks passed beneath us, gradually giving way to mountain ranges and turning green again as we traveled further south.

Eventually, we came down on the landing pad behind Destiny Falls Medical Center and clambered out. Despite the fact that the boys were in front, Mina was the first one through the door, collapsing to the ground with relief. Max hurried to Mina's side to check on her, but straightened after she'd explained about her travel-induced anxiety and general preference for being on *terra firma*. When everyone else had cleared out, Liam helped me down the steps.

Max greeted me with a smile. "I'm so glad to see you looking well."

"Thank you for everything. I hear you and Asher are responsible for making sure I was taken such good care of."

Max laughed. "It was a team effort. Everyone did their part—including, from what I'm told, you. Nate said they wouldn't have been able to take down Tyler so easily if you hadn't broken away from him. Apparently the kid was so shaken from shooting you that he went meekly as a lamb, although he lawyered up as soon as he was in custody."

"Of course he did." His parents would make sure he had the best legal representation money could buy. I'd be surprised if they weren't already in the country, throwing their weight around.

"Are you the doc?" Jamie asked, joining us.

"This is Max," I said quickly. "He's the local doctor and also Liam's brother. Max, this is Jamie."

Jamie grabbed Max by the shoulders and hauled him into a crushing embrace. "Thanks, man. Kenz is like a mom to me. It means the world to know you were there when she needed you."

Emotion prickled at the back of my throat. *Aww.* Maybe I'd done something right in raising my hellions.

"Any time," Max replied, then frowned. "Hold on, you know what? I'd rather this didn't happen again. But I'll be here if it does."

"Thanks." I kissed his cheek and then turned to Liam. "Are we going back to the cottage?"

"Actually...." Liam drew the word out. "I was wondering how you'd feel about staying at my place? Mum organized a cleaning spree while we were gone, so everything should be back to normal. I thought it might be easier for you to stay there since you were kidnapped from the cottage." He watched my face carefully, waiting to see my reaction. "I didn't want to bring back any bad memories when you're already vulnerable."

I blinked rapidly. *Do not cry.* "That's really sweet. Let's do that." I glanced at my siblings. "Uh, will we all fit?"

"We can make it work." Liam kissed my forehead, and I closed my eyes and breathed in his comforting scent.

"If not, we can always book a hotel," Blair said. "I don't want to go back to the cottages either."

"We'll figure it out," I said. "For now, let's just get over there. I need to sit down."

The helicopter pilot waved and ducked into the cockpit. I took Liam's hand and we walked around the Medical Center together. Out front, standing beside a car, was Asher. He nodded as we approached.

"I'm glad you're okay," he said, opening the passenger door for me.

Impulsively, I wrapped my good arm around him. "Thanks, Ash."

Somehow, I knew we'd moved past any hostility between us. He'd quietly accepted me back into the fold, and since he was Liam's closest friend, that meant something. I wanted him to know I appreciated it.

He returned the hug awkwardly. "Just doing my job."

Liam and Blair got into the car with us, while Joel, Jamie, and Mina piled into Max's vehicle. The drive to Liam's place didn't take long, and I was surprised to see several other cars parked outside. When we entered, a cheer went up.

I smiled so widely, my face hurt. They hadn't just tidied Liam's place—they'd also replaced his ruined furniture. Eugene and Heather were seated on the sofa, Summer was on an armchair, and Toby leaned against the wall, his legs crossed at the ankles. Even Nate and Grace were there, with Grace serving hot drinks and Nate acting as her assistant. My gaze lingered on them for a moment, noticing the way Grace seemed hyperaware of Nate's movements and noting the fact he seemed to know exactly what she needed and when. I wondered at their friendship once again. Eleven years ago, I'd thought they'd be married one day, and I still wasn't convinced they wouldn't.

Heather guided me onto an armchair, fussing and making sure I had a blanket in case I got cold—never mind that it was midsummer and the temperature reflected that. I thanked her and happily accepted her maternal bustling. It was nice to be on the receiving end.

"I can't believe you all took time away from work to be here," I said, when introductions had been made and everyone had gotten comfortable.

"Of course we did," Summer replied dismissively. "That's what family does."

Family.

I liked the sound of that. Especially when almost everyone I most cared about was in this room.

"So, what's it like to be shot?" Toby asked, earning glares from Summer and Heather. "You must have a badass scar."

Joel nodded approvingly and held his hand up for a high five. Meanwhile, Mina looked at the ceiling as if to ask the universe why men were such children. Their responses made me smile.

"I wouldn't recommend it," I told Toby. "I've got weeks of rehab ahead, and it hurts like hell."

"True." He inclined his head.

A knock on the door interrupted the conversation. I looked around, curious who it could be.

"I'll get it," Jamie said, already on his way to the foyer. His voice carried through. "Who are you?"

"Aiden. I'm here to see Kennedy." The familiar timbre sent a shiver down my spine—and not a pleasant one. Even though I knew now that Aiden hadn't been stalking me, I still didn't like the way he made me feel.

"Kenz? Are you open to visitors?" Jamie called.

I didn't really want to see Aiden, but since I was surrounded by people like this, it was probably the best time for it.

"Sure, but not for long. I'm tired."

"You heard the lady," Jamie said. "Make it quick."

Perhaps my baby brother had a future as a bouncer if the NHL career fell through.

To my surprise, Aiden shuffled in with a sheepish expression.

"Hi," he said, his gaze raking over me. "I heard about what happened, and I'm really sorry you went through that."

"Thanks." I didn't know what else to say, so I let the silence stretch. Everyone around us seemed to be watching with anticipation except Liam, whose face was screwed up as though he'd smelled something bad.

"Anyway." Aiden's feet scuffed the carpet. "It sounds like you've been dealing with this stalking situation for a while, and it occurred to me that I might have come on a bit strong." He flashed me a hesitant smile. "I'm sorry if I contributed to your distress at all. I can be quite forward when I want something, and I'm not good at hearing no."

I studied him. At least he had the self-awareness to recognize his issues. "You should probably work on that."

"I will." He scanned the occupants of the room, visibly nervous. "I'm heading back to the U.S. in two days, and my regular scheduled visit with the therapist is next week, so it'll be a good thing for us to cover." He took a couple of steps backward. "That's it. I wanted to apologize and let you know I'm leaving."

"I appreciate you dropping by." I raised a hand and waggled my fingers. "I hope your flight back goes smoothly."

"I'm sure it will." A little of his cocksure attitude returned. "I paid enough for it. Anyway, see you around. Or maybe not."

He strode out, closing the door behind him. Almost immediately, Joel got up and locked it.

"Well, he seemed like a dick," Joel said.

Everyone laughed, and the tension dissipated. I smiled. Finally, I was back where I belonged.

Chapter Fifty-Three

LIAM

I love you, and I'm going to tell you so every day until you beg me to stop. — text message sent from Liam to Kennedy, Saturday 21 January

THE NEXT MORNING, THE HOUSE WAS BLISSFULLY EMPTY. My family members had cleared out the day before, and Kennedy's siblings had risen early to drive to Queenstown and were due back in the evening. I loved having family around, but it was nice when it was just us two.

I cooked brunch—eggs, toast, and bacon—and made an excellent brew so we could banish the taste of awful hospital coffee from our memories. We were eating at the round wooden dining table that had turned up from somewhere when somebody knocked on the door.

I looked at Kennedy. "Are you expecting anyone?"

"No. Maybe it's your mom or Grace. They both said they might come by."

I sighed. "I wish they had better timing. You stay here. I'll be back in a moment."

I got up and went to the foyer to see who it was. I opened the door and found a pair of strangers on the doorstep. The man, who had messy brown hair and light brown eyes, seemed to be sweating like crazy. His companion, a petite brunette, stuck out a hand.

"Hi, you must be Liam," she said. "I'm Mikayla, and this is Gray."

"Um, hello." I remembered Kennedy mentioning her friend Gray, but I hadn't expected to meet him like this.

"Gray?" Kennedy appeared behind me, grinning widely. She walked up to the man and kissed his cheek. "I can't believe you're here!"

"Neither can I." He gave a weak laugh. "Mind if we come in?"

"Of course." She grabbed my hand and tugged me inside, making room for the couple to enter. "Liam, this is Gray, a very good friend of mine, and his girlfriend, Mikayla."

"Wait." A bolt of recognition struck as I stared at the other man. "That's where I remember you from. You were in a movie together." I couldn't believe I hadn't put that together sooner.

They exchanged a look. "More than one," Kennedy said wryly. "We've collaborated a lot over the years."

"Don't worry," Mikayla said, apparently picking up on where my mind was going. "The tabloids might say they dated, but it's not true. They've only ever been friends."

I grimaced. "Am I that easy to read?"

She laughed. "Only for someone who's been there. The idea of competing with a celebrity is intimidating."

"We came as soon as we could," Gray said gruffly. "Mikayla couldn't get away from work sooner, and I couldn't handle the thought of traveling on my own." His cheeks flushed, and I knew there must be a story there. "You should have told us things were so bad. I wish I'd been able to help."

Kennedy guided Gray to the sofa and touched the backs of her fingers to his forehead when he sat, perhaps checking his temperature. "There wasn't really anything you could have done," she told him. "Sorry if this has brought old issues to the surface for you."

"Gray had a stalker of his own a while back," Mikayla murmured to me by way of explanation.

"Don't be ridiculous," Gray groused. "I'm more concerned about you. Did you really get shot?"

"Yeah," she admitted. "But it didn't hit anything important."

"Thank God."

"Can I get either of you a coffee?" I asked, finally remembering the manners Mum had drilled into me.

"Yes, please," Mikayla said. "Maybe just for me though. I don't think Gray needs any extra stimulation, do you, sweetheart?"

"No, thanks." Gray flopped his head back against the armchair cushion.

I frowned, wondering what his deal was, but decided not to ask. I headed for the kitchen, surprised when Kennedy joined me a moment later.

"He has bad anxiety," she said softly. "It manifests in agoraphobia if he tries to leave his home. He's come a long way in the past few months. It's incredible that he's here at all. A year ago, he wouldn't leave his house."

"Wow." I couldn't imagine that. "Thanks for telling me. I thought he might be going through withdrawals or something."

"I figured." She cocked her head. "Need a hand?"

"Nah. I've got it covered. You go and be with them."

"Thanks." She smiled and returned to the living room.

I finished making coffee, poured it into mugs, loaded them onto a tray, and took them through to share.

Mikayla's eyes lit up. "That smells amazing."

"Liam does the best coffee," Kennedy said, a hint of pride in her voice. My chest puffed up.

"So," Mikayla said expectantly when we were all seated with drinks. "We want to hear the full story. No leaving anything out."

Kennedy launched into a retelling. I stayed quiet beside her, basking in her presence. Once she'd finished talking, Gray and Mikayla offered sympathy and to seek revenge against Tyler. I was pretty sure they were joking, but Mikayla's intensity made me wonder.

At lunch, I went to Taste of Destiny to pick up food for everyone. Mum and Summer both dropped by later in the day, and the group of us talked until late enough that I invited Gray and Mikayla to stay. It was obvious Kennedy needed her friends, and I was in a mood to give her whatever she wanted.

Chapter Fifty-Four

LIAM

*T*IME *PASSES DIFFERENTLY WHEN I*'M *WITH YOU.* — TEXT *message from Liam to Kennedy, sent during one of his work shifts.*

OVER THE NEXT MONTH, OUR LIVES GRADUALLY WENT BACK to normal. Gray and Mikayla returned to their hometown. Blair, Mina, Joel, and Jamie flew back to Los Angeles. Tyler was remanded in custody until his trial. And Kennedy slowly healed from her ordeal. I suspected the mental and emotional trauma would stay with her, but her shoulder had improved a lot, and she'd been speaking twice weekly with Gray's therapist.

I'd joined in on one of those sessions and reluctantly bared my soul about the panic I'd experienced when she vanished, then discussed ways we could help each other recover and move forward. It hadn't been a pleasant experience, but I was glad we'd done it because it helped me see what headspace she was operating from and know that she understood my perspective too.

On a Saturday in late February, as summer was coming to a close, I prepared a picnic and packed it into a backpack. I'd checked with Max, and he'd given Kennedy the all clear for the hike I had planned today. My stomach was a tangle of nerves and butterflies. I couldn't decide if I was more excited or terrified.

"Are you going to tell me where we're going?" Kennedy asked as she came into the living room.

I'd left her in our bedroom with instructions to dress for a walk in the forest, and she'd done as I asked, wearing a tank top and shorts that displayed her gorgeous legs to full advantage. Her hair was tied back, almost entirely brown now. She'd let Bailey cut it shorter, getting rid of the remnants of blonde dye. Summer's friend, who considered herself a budding social media influencer and lifestyle blogger, had been over the moon and had plastered photos all over her accounts. Once, that might have bothered me, but neither Kennedy nor I had minded.

After Tyler was arrested, Kennedy's name and picture were flashed throughout the media. We'd agreed they probably wouldn't leave us alone until we gave them the whole story, so we'd given an exclusive interview to a reporter Gray had recommended, Aria Simons. She'd been friendly, professional, and made sure the story came out the way we wanted. I'd wondered if Kennedy's fans might be angry she'd decided to give up acting in part because of me, but her adoring public seemed to love our unlikely reunion. Now, the excitement had more or less died down. People were no longer visiting Destiny Falls in droves for a peek of movie star Kennedy Cox, although the stream of tourists attracted by the town's romantic reputation remained steady.

"No, I'm not telling you," I said, slinging the backpack

over one shoulder. "You'll figure it out soon, but I want it to be a surprise for as long as possible."

She huffed. "You're no fun."

"You're impatient."

She grinned but didn't deny it. She kissed my cheek and leaned against me for a moment, sighing happily. Another perk of the past month was that we'd gotten to know more about each other again and had grown more familiar with the people we were now. At our core, we were still that young couple who'd fallen madly in love, but we'd developed and matured, and things were different in subtle and intriguing ways.

"Let's go." She bounced toward the door. She'd been eager to go hiking for a couple of weeks now, but I didn't want to encourage her until we were sure it wouldn't cause any issues with her injury.

Once outside, we got into her Subaru Outback. I'd decided to finally say goodbye to my beloved Ute. The damage caused by the crash—and Tyler tampering with the brakes—would have cost more than it was worth to fix. I'd get another vehicle soon—I had my eye on one in Queenstown—but in the meantime, Kennedy's Subaru could get us anywhere further than we wanted to walk.

She handed me the keys, and I drove us to the parking area at the base of the trails that went to Destiny Falls and Destiny Tarn.

Kennedy turned to me, her eyes alight with excitement. "We're going to the falls, aren't we?"

"Yeah," I admitted.

She beamed. "Did you know this will only be my second time going there? I didn't want to go again without you."

My heart melted. Kaput. I didn't know how I'd ever resisted this woman, even for a couple of weeks. She was so sweet. So perfect.

"I'm glad." I cleared my throat, my voice huskier than I'd have liked.

I got out and donned the backpack. I insisted on being the one to carry supplies, since she was still healing. Logically, I knew it probably wouldn't do her any harm, but my instinct was still to protect her in whatever way I could.

We started up the trail. When Kennedy spotted something she wanted to photograph, I handed her camera over. We made slow progress, but it was more enjoyable that way, even if it did give me plenty of time to stew over what was coming.

When we arrived at the falls, they were as stunning as ever. On the tail end of summer, the pool of bluish water at the base of the waterfall was smaller than it was during wetter seasons, but it was no less beautiful. Water cascaded down the mossy rock face, with tiered steps at the top seemingly cut by God.

Kennedy released a slow breath. "I forgot how much this place took my breath away."

"It's pretty impressive."

I wiped my sweaty palms on my shirt, laid the backpack on the ground, then sank to one knee in front of her.

"Liam?" Her eyes widened, glowing even bluer than usual. The falls and the sky had nothing on her eyes.

I reached into my pocket and withdrew the box I'd been carrying with me all day. I popped the lid open to reveal a simple diamond ring that glittered in the sunlight filtering through the trees.

"Kennedy Carter." My voice shook with emotion, and I drew a deep breath, giving myself a mental pep talk so I could continue. "You are the love of my life. I know we haven't been back together for long, but it feels like we've been waiting forever for our happily ever after. I don't want to waste any more time. Will you marry me and be with me for the rest of my life?"

Kennedy's eyes sparkled with tears. Good ones, I hoped.

"Yes, Liam." Her smile wobbled. She seemed as overcome as I was. "You're right. Let's not waste any time. I want to get married and be your wife. I want to have the children we always talked about, and have a life full of love and color."

I rose to my feet and took her hand, gently sliding the ring onto her finger. "I will cherish you," I promised. "Every single day."

Her lips curved and she looked at me as if I were something special. I really was the luckiest bastard on the planet.

Chapter Fifty-Five

KENNEDY

"I LOVE YOU SO MUCH," I WHISPERED, STRETCHING UP onto my toes to kiss him before standing back to admire the way the ring glittered in the light. "It's beautiful."

He smiled tenderly. "Then it suits you."

I shivered. I didn't think I'd ever get used to him saying things like that. I hoped I never did because I never wanted to take him and what we had together for granted.

"I don't want a big wedding," I told him. "Nothing fancy. All I want is to be married to you, and soon."

He grinned. "How does next month sound?"

"Perfect." Perhaps it would freak people out. I knew there was a lot to organize. But I also knew that our family would be happy to help. The wedding was only one day. Our marriage would be forever. I glanced around, noting that the clearing around the falls was empty, and we hadn't passed anyone on the way there either. The summer tourist season was winding down, and autumn would be quieter before things picked up again in time for skiing to begin. "We should celebrate properly," I suggested saucily.

He raised a brow. "What did you have in mind?"

"You packed a blanket, right?"

He nodded slowly.

"Well, there's a nice mossy clearing through the trees over there. We should get naked."

His lips twisted in a smirk. "Are you suggesting we have a quickie in the woods?"

"Maybe." I winked. "There's no one else around, and we'd be able to hear somebody approaching."

He gave me a wry look. "You're giving us a bit too much credit, I think. When I'm inside you, there's nothing else I see or hear. But if you're game for it, I am. And if anyone comes along, you can explain to my mother how you corrupted me."

I grinned. "Deal."

We made our way over to the mossy spot I'd singled out, and Liam took a fleece blanket from his backpack and spread it over the ground. Standing over it, I whipped my shirt off and dropped my shorts, leaving me in panties and a sports bra. I reached behind myself to unclip the bra, but Liam batted my hand away and did it himself. When the scrap of fabric fell away, he dipped his head and kissed the raised skin above and to the right of my left breast where the bullet had exited my chest. His body buzzed with energy, and I smoothed a hand down the back of his head.

"I'm still here," I murmured.

"I know." He straightened and drew me close, his clothes rasping deliciously against my bare skin. "But I came so close to losing you."

"Don't think about it." I pulled him in for a kiss, parting my lips so he could deepen it. We kissed until I ran out of breath, and I pressed closer, loving the feel of him and the sexy contrast of his fully clothed body and my nearly nude one. If I'd been in L.A., I might have worried about paparazzi catching me during a moment like this, but in Destiny Falls, I no longer had to worry.

We sank to our knees, still kissing, and I grabbed the hem of his shirt. He yanked it off, obliging me. The roughness of his chest hair against my breasts made my toes curl. I worked his shorts open and tugged them over his firm butt, then slipped my hand inside his underwear and palmed him. He was hard and hot. His pupils dilated as he held my gaze while I wrapped my hand around him and teased him with touches that weren't quite enough.

But then his palm grazed over my belly and he dipped his fingers into my panties, skimming over my clit, returning the favor. He kept the contact light, and every time I leaned into him, he pulled away.

"How do you want to do this?" he asked, casting a nervous glance at my scarred shoulder.

"Sit down," I said, loving the way he followed the instruction. "Underwear off."

He peeled them off, and I straddled him, settling above his straining erection. The lighter blue flecks in his irises flared. Placing my hands on his shoulders, I worked my hips, sliding along his length, tempting him to grab me and sink deeper. His head fell back, and he groaned. The low, sexy sound made me even wetter.

"You feel so good," he panted. "Stop teasing me. Take it all. I know you can."

I undulated against him like a cat, rubbing my body against his from groin to chest, loving the way desire darkened his eyes and flared his nostrils.

"Fuck, you're incredible." He leaned forward and claimed my mouth. Our tongues tangled, and I continued to tweak my hips back and forward, giving both of us a little of what we wanted but not enough of it. "Get on my cock," Liam growled, his eyes wild, face twisted in a snarl. He'd reached the end of his tether.

I lifted up and positioned the head of his cock beneath me. We'd been going without condoms for a while, since we were both safe and I was on birth control. Although I suspected I might go off it in the future. Slowly, I took him into my body, feeling him stretch me and heat me from the inside out. When I was fully seated, I rocked my hips, whimpering at the sensations that rocketed through me. He was so deep, and in this position, I had wonderful pressure against all the best places.

"Ride me," he urged, gripping my hips and guiding me into the rhythm he wanted.

I moved above him, falling into a rhythm of give and take. He met me with his thrusts, hitting spots inside me that no other man ever had. My breaths came shorter. He gasped and grunted, the sounds driving me wild. I tossed my head back, staring up at the sky as I was wound tighter and tighter. Liam slid a hand between us and pressed my clit. The world fractured, and I shuddered as my release tore through me, relentless in its intensity. Beneath me, Liam stiffened and jerked, finding bliss as I clenched around him.

I fell against his chest, breathing heavily. His hand smoothed down my back and over the curve of my ass. We lay together, surrounded by trees and birdsong. I smiled, knowing I probably looked a little goofy. Liam smiled back. In that moment, my body sated and my heart so full it might burst, I realized I could no longer say that the last time I'd been truly content was eleven years ago, because at this very minute, I knew beyond a shadow of a doubt that I'd never been happier.

As I rolled off Liam and we started gathering our

clothes, I glanced at the waterfall and remembered the black-and-white photograph of the first couple to be married here. Whoever they were, I wondered if they'd felt as free and perfectly at peace as I did in this same place. I hoped so.

Chapter Fifty-Six

KENNEDY

Hi Liam,

I love you, and I can't wait to marry you today. I wanted to share something special with you on our wedding day. Something that will let you know you were with me every moment of every day we were apart.

Attached to this email, you'll find a dated log of over two hundred emails I typed to you over the years. They've been sitting in my inbox, acting as a kind of journal. I never thought I'd actually be brave enough to send them, but here you go. Read them or not; it's your choice, but please understand that I've never cared for anyone the way I do you. You're my best friend, my first love, and hopefully, my last.

I'll see you at the falls.

K xx

MY DRESS WAS SIMPLE. FULL LENGTH AND STRAPLESS. Classically elegant. And in no time at all, it was going to be dirty beyond repair. The bridesmaids—Mina, Summer, and Grace—were hovering nearby, waiting for the rest of our transportation to arrive. Somewhere, a phone rang. Mina hurried over, pulling it from her purse and offering it to me. I frowned. Who would be calling fifteen minutes before our wedding ceremony was due to begin?

"Hello?" I said.

"Hi, Kennedy." It was Jeff. "I finally managed to track down some information you wanted."

"Oh?"

"Yes, the names of the people in the photograph you sent through."

My eyes widened, and I ushered Grace over, putting him on speaker. "Who are they?"

"The woman, identified in the note as Jewel, was otherwise known as Pearl McIntyre. The man is Mr. Charles Smith, nicknamed Rocky because of his work in the mines. That's all I've got at the moment, but I wanted to let you know as an early wedding gift."

"Thanks, Jeff."

"Now, go get married."

Smiling, I ended the call.

"Pearl and Charles," I mused. "They sound like a romance novel waiting to happen."

Grace smirked. "I might have something in the works."

"No! Really?" I wasn't sure why that delighted me, but it did.

Grace put a finger to her lips. "I don't like to talk about my books until the first draft is written. I'll tell you then. But I have a lot of research to do first."

The roar of a motor sounded nearby, and a four-wheel motorcycle came into view with another three trailing behind. Connor lifted the visor on his helmet and nodded for me to get on. Biting my lip, knowing that my designer dress was going to be absolutely trashed—but not really caring—I straddled the motorcycle and wrapped my arms around his waist. The bridesmaids climbed onto their rides, and we all headed for the trail up to Destiny Falls. Connor had been working all week to widen the trail enough for the four-wheelers to get through, and it took a surprisingly short amount of time for us to arrive in the clearing beside Destiny Falls waterfall.

Liam stood near the water, the falls forming a perfect backdrop behind him. He was smiling, his eyes crinkled at the corners, and looked mouthwatering in a black tuxedo. Asher stood beside him. Liam had asked Eugene and Blair to be the other groomsmen, so he hadn't had to choose between his brothers. Blair's smile stretched the full width of his face, and it made me happy to know he was on board with our wedding.

Connor helped me off the motorcycle, and Gray approached, looking dapper with only a slight sheen of sweat on his forehead. He looped his arm through mine and escorted me the short distance to Liam, then kissed me on the cheek as we separated.

"Be happy," he murmured.

"I will." I gave into impulse and hugged him. Outside of my family, he'd been the most important person in my life for years, and I was so glad we'd settled in the same beautiful country.

I joined Liam and took his hands. We gazed into each other's eyes as we recited our vows. We hadn't gone for anything flashy or unique. All that mattered was the promise we were making to be together for as long as we lived. He slid a band onto my finger, nestling it beside my diamond engagement ring, and I put one onto his, smiling at the knowledge that now every woman who saw him would know he was unavailable.

At the end of the ceremony, the officiant delivered the line I'd been most anticipating, and butterflies stormed my stomach as Liam swept me into a panty-melting kiss.

Somebody hooted. Others cheered. I felt Liam's lips curve against mine.

"Let's continue this in private later," he suggested.

The officiant announced us husband and wife, and we turned to face our assembled friends and family. It was a small group, since we hadn't wanted to cause any damage to this den of natural beauty, but all the important people were here. Our closest friends. My family, and Liam's. United.

I turned to Liam. "I love you," I said. "Now, tomorrow, and every day after."

He curled his arm around me, drawing me to his side. He pressed a kiss to my temple. "Thank you for coming back to me."

"I'll never leave again."

Together, we joined our people, a long afternoon of love and merriment ahead.

A long *lifetime* of joy.

THE END

"Your first love isn't the first person you give your heart to—it's the first one who breaks it."
~ Lang Leav

GRACE - 16 YEARS AGO

I stood on Nate Braddock's doorstep, a bag of lemon drops in one hand and my heart in the other. I knocked, my breathing shallow. I couldn't believe I was going to do this. Two years after my out-of-control crush on my best friend started, I would finally tell him how I felt.

When no one answered, I cracked the door open and peered through the gap. A light was on in the living room, and I could hear the TV. I pushed the door open further, took my shoes off, and padded in. Max, Liam, and Connor—three of Nate's brothers—were sprawled on the couch and armchairs, watching an action movie. Liam greeted me with a smile, Connor with a slight tip of his head, but Max, Nate's twin, seemed to pale.

"Hi," I said. "Is Nate around?"

"He's in his room." Connor sounded bored. "Or maybe the shower."

"Um." Max wet his lips. "You might want to wait for him to come out."

I frowned. "Why?"

Nate and I shared everything with each other. Max had never suggested I shouldn't just go in to see him before.

He hesitated, visibly lost for words. Before he could say anything, a little girl skipped into the room, nearly tripping over the ends of her flannel pajamas.

"Toby won't let me into the toilet," she whined. "Max, tell him to hurry up. I'm tired, and he's been in there for ages."

Max sighed, and I took advantage of his distraction to slip past them and down the hall. I'd come to ask Nate to be my date to the senior dance, and I wouldn't be distracted from my mission. It had taken me weeks to work up the courage, and once I had, I'd wanted it to be perfect, so I'd bought a bag of his favorite candy and waited for a night when I knew his parents would be out. If I didn't ask soon, I might explode.

I knocked briefly on Nate's bedroom door, then pushed it open.

I stopped short.

There, lying on his bed, wearing nothing but one of Nate's rugby T-shirts, was Maddy McLaren from school. My heart sank and my stomach rolled nauseatingly. Maddy raised an eyebrow at the sight of me and made a show of tidying her tousled blonde hair. I bit my lower lip, unsure of what to say. Maddy was everything I wasn't. Confident, outgoing, flirtatious. I'd had no idea Nate might be interested in her, but my eyes didn't deceive me. Whatever I'd walked in on wasn't innocent.

Maddy swung her legs off the edge of the bed and sashayed toward me with a sexiness I'd never be capable of.

She reached out, and I thought for a moment she was trying to take my hand, but then she snatched the bag of lemon drops from me and smirked.

"Thanks." Her voice was husky and self-assured, as if she was found half-naked in guys' bedrooms every day. "It was so sweet of you to bring these over for us. I know how much Nate loves them." She winked. "I'll make sure he gets them."

I didn't move. I couldn't. I was so shocked.

Maddy McLaren was here in Nate's bedroom. In his shirt. On his bed. Had they…?

Oh god. I didn't want to think about it.

My heart felt like it was battering against the inside of my ribcage, and I struggled for air. I was too late. I'd missed my chance. Nate was with someone else.

Maddy seemed to take my hesitation as a refusal to leave, because she narrowed her eyes and leaned close. "Look," she hissed. "I know you and Nate have some weird BFF thing going on, but he's mine now. I've been with him in a way you haven't, and if I were you, I'd leave before he gets out of the shower. If you stay, you'll only embarrass yourself more."

My eyes burned. A choked sob rose up my throat, and I clapped my hand to my mouth and backed away. I wished I had something snarky to say back—a way to put her in her place—but I'd always been better with words on paper than in person. Besides, she was right. She had Nate and I didn't.

I turned away and noticed Max standing in the hall. I hung my head and refused to meet his eyes. As if this couldn't get any worse. He must have known what I was about to walk in on, and he'd tried to warn me, but I hadn't paid attention.

I backed out of the room and began to brush past him, but he wrapped an arm around my shoulders and guided me to the room next door. His bedroom. I entered, barely noting the organized desk and rows of academic awards on his shelves. It was all I could do to hold myself together.

Max pulled me into his arms, and I buried my face in the crook of his neck. All of the Braddock boys were tall, but I was unusually tall for a girl, so we fit well.

"I'm sorry," he murmured. "He's an idiot."

I sniffled, self-conscious about getting snot and tears on him. "I'm the idiot. I should have said something sooner, or just realized I didn't have a chance." I huffed. "If he was actually interested, he'd have already done something about it."

Max didn't deny my claim, which only made me feel worse. He hugged me close, and for a brief second, I wished with all my heart that *he* was the Braddock I wanted. Max was smart, kind, and he and Nate were supposedly identical—although with their different haircuts and clothing styles, it wasn't difficult to tell them apart.

Why couldn't it be him?

My heart gave a pathetic squeeze. Oh, yeah. Because Max wasn't my best friend. He wasn't the guy who'd threatened a bully when they'd been making fun of my height. He wasn't the boy who'd listened as I confessed that I sometimes hated my parents for leaving me here, even though they'd done so in order to help communities living in extreme poverty in Sudan. You weren't supposed to hate people who devoted their lives to others like that, but Nate understood my bitterness. He sympathized. I wasn't sure Max would do the same.

"I'm sorry," Max said again. He pulled back and swiped tears from my cheeks.

"What am I going to do now?" I asked hopelessly. "When Maddy tells him—"

"She won't," he interrupted. "Their thing is new.

You're his best friend. She won't say anything in case she loses him."

I pressed my lips together. Even if Maddy stayed quiet, I wasn't sure I could go on being Nate's best friend while seeing him with her. It would hurt too much. But then, I couldn't give him up either.

"Look." He scanned my face, waiting to make sure I was listening. "It's up to you what you want to do next, but if you keep acting like things are normal, Maddy will stay quiet. At least, for now." He sucked in a breath, held it for a moment, then released it slowly. "If you come to the dance with me, she'll probably forget about it altogether."

"Go… with you?" I patted my pocket, where the two tickets I'd purchased sat ready for use. "Like, as a date?"

He shook his head. "Just so we both have someone to go with. We'll have fun together, won't we?"

I thought about it. He was offering to help me save face. Even if no one else had witnessed what happened tonight, I knew I'd be obvious if I turned up to the dance solo and sent longing gazes at Nate all night. If I was good at anything, it was making the best of a situation.

I straightened my spine and nodded. "Okay, let's do this."

A Place to Belong

Acknowledgments

The start of a new series is always a massive undertaking. There have been so many people involved in bringing the first Destiny Falls stories to life, and I can't thank them enough. My friends, family, and the author community are so supportive and make it less intimidating to dive into a new project.

Thank you to Lindee Robinson for the photographs used for this cover and the Stay With You cover. They are gorgeous and I'm blown away by the designs Shannon made with them. Absolutely stunning.

Thank you to Kate with your help fine tuning the story, and to McKinley for being an awesome cheerleader.

Thank you to all the readers who told me what they wanted to see from me next. Hopefully you've enjoyed it!

And thank you to all new readers. Whether this is the first book of mine you've read or you've binged my entire catalogue, I'm so grateful to you.

About the Author

Alexa Rivers writes about genuine characters living messy, imperfect lives and earning hard-won happily ever afters. Most of her books are set in small towns, and she lives in one of these herself. She shares a house with a neurotic dog and a husband who thinks he's hilarious. When she's not writing, Alexa enjoys travelling, baking cakes, eating said cakes, cuddling fluffy animals, drinking copious amounts of tea, and absorbing herself in fictional worlds.

www.ingramcontent.com/pod-product-compliance
Lightning Source LLC
Chambersburg PA
CBHW051126190726
48290CB00006B/1713